blackwater moon

A note from the publisher

Dear Reader,

At *Pantera Press* we're passionate about what we call
good books doing good things™.

A big part is our joy in discovering and nurturing talented home-grown
writers such as B. Michael Radburn.

We are also focused on promoting literacy, quality writing, the joys of
reading and fostering debate.

CAN YOU READ THIS?

Sure you can, but 60% in our community can't. Shocking, isn't it? That's
why *Pantera Press* is helping to close the literacy gap, by nurturing the
next generation of readers as well as our writers. We're thrilled to support
Let's Read. A wonderful program already helping over 100,000 pre-
schoolers across Australia to develop the building blocks for literacy and
learning, as well as a love for books.

We're excited that *Let's Read* operates right across Australia,
in metropolitan, regional and also remote communities,
including Indigenous communities in Far North Queensland, Cape
York, and Torres Strait. *Let's Read* was developed by the *Centre for
Community Child Health* and is being implemented in partnership with
The Smith Family.

Simply by enjoying our books, you will be contributing to our unique
approach and helping these kids. So thank you.

If you want to do more, please visit www.PanteraPress.com/Donate where
you can personally donate to help *The Smith Family* expand *Let's Read*, and
find out more about the great programs *Pantera Press* supports.

Please enjoy *Blackwater Moon*.

For news about our other books, sample chapters, author interviews and
much more, please visit our website: www.PanteraPress.com

Happy reading,

Alison Green

blackwater moon

B. MICHAEL RADBURN

PanteraPress
good books doing good things™

First published in 2012 by Pantera Press Pty Limited
www.PanteraPress.com

Please send all permission queries to:
Pantera Press, P.O. Box 1989 Neutral Bay, NSW Australia 2089 or info@PanteraPress.com

A Cataloguing-in-Publication entry for this book is available from the National Library of Australia.

ISBN 978-1-921997-09-9 (Paperback)
ISBN 978-1-921997-13-6 (Ebook)

Cover and Internal Design: Luke Causby, Blue Cork
Cover Image © Gunnar Larsson/Nordicphotos/Corbis
Edited by: Kylie Mason
Proofread by: Desanka Vukelich
Author Photo: Courtesy of the author
Typesetting by Kirby Jones
Printed and bound in Australia by McPhersons Printing Group

Pantera Press policy is to use papers that are natural, renewable and recyclable products made from wood grown in sustainable forests. The logging and manufacturing processes are expected to conform to the environmental regulations of the country of origin

Also by B. Michael Radburn

The Crossing

For Mel,
my safe harbour

It's the oar in the water that counts

Prologue

All my life I've wondered about the bad things men do; about the many faces evil can present. Why it is that good people can do bad things, and bad people can find it in their hearts to do good. Is evil inherent? The darkness within? I don't know. I gave it a name when I was a kid; when I first recognised it staring back at me through my father's eyes. I called it the badshit.

I'm not sure where to start this journal, so I'll commence with the day I smelt honeysuckle on the wind for the first time since I was a child; the summer of '83.

TWO silver-blue rings encircled the afternoon sun as if it were the unblinking eye of the gods. A layer of ice crystals drifting where the air was too thin for man, the sun's light refracting its own image. Andy couldn't remember seeing anything like it. He smiled, the memory reminding him of an old friend, a ghost from his youth, and turned his attention back to the Ford.

Screwdriver clenched between his teeth, he bent awkwardly over the engine bay of the faded blue utility. Pulling at the frayed accelerator cable, he noticed the few greying hairs on his arm for the first time, not surprised after the salt and pepper began creeping in at his temples last year. He listened to the timing of the old V8. There, he thought with a wry smile, sweet as. The engine sang its highway song, not as well as it used to, but then who would at its age?

Dropping the screwdriver into the toolbox at his feet, he spat the taste of its oily steel from his mouth. He limped around to the open driver's side window where he bumped the side mirror as he reached inside to turn off the ignition. The motor died with a stammer as he pulled a rag from his overalls' pocket and wiped his hands, catching his reflection in the upturned mirror. His eyes were dark now, having lost the soft hazel of his youth, and the peppering of grey in his short cropped hair was prominent. His cheekbones sat high on his face, void now of the freckles that once bridged his nose as a boy. Andy hadn't put on much weight on since leaving the army. Stepping around to the front of the Ford, he leant against the grille, taking the opportunity to massage the dull ache in his bad leg.

A lawnmower droned in the distance, the smell of freshly cut grass drifting like a lazy dog's dream in the sun. It was the scent of memories, of summers gone. He brushed sweat from his brow, tasted the salt residue in the corners of his mouth. Glancing down at his watch he saw two p.m. tick over.

It was early February 1983, as hot and humid as any southern summer can get. All things considered, life was good, but at thirty-five, and with all he'd been through the past twenty years, he also knew how suddenly life can change, some days feeling as if tragedy was only ever a moment away, shimmering on the air like a distant mirage.

'*Aaaandy!*'

Searching for the source of the cry, he stared down the pitted road that ran past his home, the narrow lane winding through a corridor of she-oaks toward the dead end beyond. Although Riverchase Lane was in the forgotten part of town, the old suburb nearer to the river bends, most days its obscurity and isolation suited Andy. Breathing in time with the wind gusts, he listened beyond the song of the oaks, their haunting whistle hypnotic as he began wondering whether he'd imagined the cry.

'*Aaaaaandy!*'

His stomach tightened. *Nathan?*

Wrestling with the thick balloon vines and lantana that strangled the trees there, a dark-haired boy of twelve fell from the shadows into the roadway. Not Nathan, but Mike, his friend. Andy's belly tightened another notch. So where was Nathan? For a moment it appeared as if the barrier of vines would never release him, but the boy broke free, staring wide-eyed and desperate through the dust kicked up where he landed. Although fifty metres away, Andy could make out the terror on the boy's face, and for a brief instant shared it.

Where was Nathan?

It was then he heard the siren wail from the prison farm upriver, faint like an intimate whisper, the wind carrying it far from its Cyclone-wire fences. The sound heralded something unwelcome. Andy swallowed, his attention returning to the silver-blue rings in the sky.

Dear God, he mouthed as the boy ran toward him, remembering what he'd been told all those years ago. '*The real monsters in this world are right out there in the daylight.*' It made him think of wolves; then he smelt the honeysuckle on the wind, and he was back there.

Passage

1

There comes a time in life when the past becomes elusive and it's difficult to fathom whether we call upon our memories, or whether they call upon us. Either way, the things recalled must be lived with for better or for worse. One of my earliest recollections is of summer 1959. I was looking for Sputnik. Not Sputnik 1, that tin ball burnt up in the atmosphere a year before, but the big one, Sputnik 2, with the little dog on board.

WEARING blue jeans and a tattered white singlet, eleven-year-old Andrew Walker lay spreadeagled across a red tartan blanket in the twilight surroundings of his backyard. Andy needed a haircut, his stringy brown fringe constantly falling across his eyes. Annoyed, he brushed it back. Round-faced, hazel-eyed and lightly tanned, a line of fading freckles ran across the bridge of his nose from one cheek to the other.

The warm November night was an hour old as the honeysuckle and jasmine hung in the air. Andy searched the darkness for the bright dot that was Sputnik 2 gliding across the stars, but it wouldn't be easy with the full moon rising. Blackwater moon, his father called it; when the full moon touched its own reflection on the river. Some evenings the satellite showed itself above the continent's east coast, but most nights it was hard to find gliding around the Earth to see fourteen days and nights to Andy's one. On board was the lifeless body of Laika the dog, the first living creature sent into space. Andy had read that she lasted six days before her air had run out; often imagining her sightless eyes gazing forever upon the Earth.

He came well-equipped for the evening, his chest covered with the crumpled star chart cut from *The Greater Western* newspaper; this month's constellation was Orion. Shield and club in hand, Orion the Hunter came around every summer, the jewel in his sword, the great Orion nebula, easily discernible through the battered pair of his father's World War II army issue binoculars.

The smell of honeysuckle was so strong he could almost taste it. He put down the binoculars and closed his eyes. The Walker family's white weatherboard house stood tired and worn among the other homes of Blackwater. Summer nights grew busy around dusk, with nearly every window and door in town open in expectation of a cool southern breeze. Andy knew the southerly would explore the streets when it arrived, stealing the town's sounds and secrets, public property for anyone who cared to listen. And he always cared to listen.

Babies wept while mothers sang nursery rhymes in soft voices. Televisions echoed canned laughter while radios played everything from Johnny O'Keefe's rock-n-roll to static-filled serials. A newsflash here, a dropped dish there. Cats cried in mournful wails and dogs barked as a solitary black bird serenaded the impending night. Andy swiped at a mosquito buzzing around his ear as delicate glass wind chimes and the rustle of his star chart announced the southerly. Lifting his face to the breeze, he let it caress his freckled skin, brushing his fringe back over his eyes.

He turned his attention to his own home, listening to his mother and older sister, Ellenor, talking over the tinkle of dinner plates while they washed up. Ellie spoke of boys like she'd just invented them, while their mother attempted to appear interested, knowing they'd been contrived years ago, with little change to the model since.

Their conversation moved to the big news in town, the thalidomide baby two doors down. Born without arms or legs, the Murphy baby had not been seen by a soul since coming home from hospital. There were more and more of these children being born around the world, Andy often seeing them in newspapers and on TV.

His eyes glassy from staring, Andy blinked, catching sight of a long-tailed shooting star streaking across the eastern sky. Burning yellow and white, the celestial visitor broke into three pieces before the night swallowed it.

'Wow!' cried Andy.

There was a shuffle of curtains back from the kitchen window. 'Did you find your satellite, Andy?' his mother Mary called out.

When he looked up he saw her face, the hard years softened by the light from behind. She always looked to Andy like she was fighting a smile. Why would a person do that? Ellie held the curtain back as his mother wiped her hands on a tea towel. Her hands always seemed younger to Andy, smooth skin and short nails often ready to pinch his nose or pat his cheek. With every passing year, Ellie was more like her. Yet although they shared the same straight dark brown hair and light complexion, Ellie had the only blue eyes in the family, eyes that Andy swore could see right into his soul.

'Shooting star!' he told them. 'Everyone make a wish.'

Andy's wish was simple: for his father to come home sober without the darkness inside him, the moods that came over him from time to time – and not always when he'd been drinking. His mother said he'd caught it in the war. There was no proper name for it, just a tension that came and went. Anyone from outside would say he was angry, but it was more than that; Andy came to call it the badshit.

What upset him most was that the badshit was reserved for the family, an event never exercised outside these walls. Although his father could hide it from the rest of the world, he could never conceal that look dwelling behind his eyes from Andy.

The rusted spring return of the front door screeched like a tortured animal. 'That'll be Frank,' he heard his mother say to Ellie. It was more like a warning than an announcement. 'Try to be nice to your father, Ellie. Sometimes that's all it takes.'

'I will if he will,' Ellie replied. Andy recognised her tone: it was acid; a challenge.

Heavy footsteps along the hallway followed and Frank Walker's lunchbox fell to the kitchen floor with a cluttered thump. He was here, and everything changed, like charged electricity in the air before a storm. Andy heard the dining room chair dragged out from under the table without so much as a hello. Brushing away another mosquito, he pictured his father's wiry frame at the kitchen table. His short curly hair, greying against his seasoned face, would still have the fine quarry dust through it, his faded uniform smelling of cigarette smoke and the truck's diesel fumes. Andy touched his own face, exploring the features, glad to have more of his mother's blood in his veins.

'You're home early tonight, Frank,' said Mary. The charged air grew strained in everyone's chest. 'Let me get your dinner off the stove.'

There was the light-footed shuffle of her shoes on the lino, a brief 'Oh!' as she realised the plate was too hot to pick up without oven mitts, then the sound of a dinner plate being placed on the Laminex table-top.

'Here,' she said, 'lamb chops and three veg.' Her voice faltered. Andy imagined her face now, drawing on her long suppressed smile as best she could.

Everyone waited to hear his reply. Waited to see whether the badshit had got under his skin that day. The unease expanded, bristling at the edges and pushing at the walls, everything hingeing on his mood or how many beers he'd had at the Quarryman Hotel on the way home.

There was the slightest tinkle of cutlery. The grating sound of a knife cutting through to the plate. Then …

'Ah … Jesus bloody Christ, woman!' The heavy plate skidded across the tabletop. 'It's too bloody hot to eat!'

Andy lay motionless, detached in the backyard, the invisible boy, his breath turning into a sigh in its release. He heard Ellie storm down the hall shouting, 'Well, you could think about being here when the rest of us eat instead of pissing our money away each night!' The screen door screeched open, then slammed shut. Ellie was gone again.

'Ellie, please …' their mother pleaded, her footsteps following her daughter down the hall, her voice trailing off with each step. But it was too late.

'Let her go,' spat Frank. 'She's nothing but a –'

Andy covered his ears; covered them so tight the only sound left was the pumping of his heart. His eyes squeezed shut, tears forming in the corners. When he opened them again, those tears distorted the image of a little white dot sailing across the sea of stars, and suddenly he felt as one with Laika up there, drifting alone, a silent witness.

2

I recall 1960 rolling in like a storm, the new decade bringing with it a fresh insight into the world – not the world as a whole, but the small corner I found myself in. It was the year I realised how little I knew of my own family; my own history. As if the cocoon of my childhood was no longer guarding me from life's truths, from the things that shaped my very being yet often went unnoticed.

AS far as Andy knew, the badshit was in everyone's family and the ignorant bliss of childhood made it true. When it wasn't blatantly present in his father, Frank Walker would merely appear indifferent. Andy knew he'd fought in World War II, in a place called Borneo. It wasn't as if his father ever sat him down and told him the stories. The information was drip fed, overheard in conversations with other veterans, or comments spilt out during Mum and Dad's fights. It wasn't so much a secret, but a chapter of his father's life that Andy wasn't worthy of knowing about, a chasm that couldn't be crossed between them.

He also knew Frank had gone to Japan after the war with the Commonwealth Occupational Forces. He kept black and white photographs of Hiroshima in a dusty shoebox above their wardrobe, photos that rarely saw the light of day. 'That's where they dropped the big one,' he would drunkenly announce whenever he took those memories out, momentarily forgetting the distance he placed between him and his son. Andy remembered the time he took the box from its hiding place, riffling through the photos to find his favourite, the solitary dome left standing in the sea of destruction. He'd got a clip around the ear for that stunt.

Andy never knew what his dad had seen over there in those streets of ash, but whatever it was made him what he is today. Not all of it good; not all of it bad; but Andy suspected that's where the badshit took hold. Where they dropped the big one; where so many perished in a single extraordinary flash; where only blast shadows on walls recorded the presence of people.

Somewhere amid his father's misery, his mother began drinking too. Yet she was a shadow drinker, keeping enough of the grocery money to buy the bottles of vermouth Andy knew she hid around the house. Then there were the tablets she called Prince Valium, and days spent in bed, before racing around in the afternoon to cook dinner and tidy the house before anyone came home. These were the things he noticed on school holidays or when he was sick at home, and it was these times he wished for his big brother. His name had been Albert, named after their grandfather. Albert was born between Ellie and Andy, sometime after their father came home from Japan.

Andy found out about Albert after the Haywood Agricultural Fair. While Ellie and their father lined up for food, Mary gave in to

Andy's badgering to see the freak show on the carnie strip. She paid sixpence and they stepped into the striped tent. Inside it smelt of damp canvas and diesel, the fumes drifting in from the generator burbling outside. They were greeted by the bearded lady, a big soul with a small, mousy voice who let Andy touch her long thin whiskers. Then came the half man, half woman who wore a strange tuxedo and evening dress combo and smelt of a sickly perfume. Andy lingered at the baby calf with a withered fifth leg hanging off its back, feeding it handfuls of chaff off the pen floor out of pity.

They followed the exhibits to the back, where a canvas wall divided the tent, one tattered corner folded away for access. Inside were dusty wooden shelves of liquid-filled jars holding the most amazing things, the shelves backlit with fluorescent lights that dimmed every time the generator faltered. Andy led his mother through the corridors, eager to take in the collection of oddities. Coiled snakes – one with two heads – and a cane toad the size of a football. There was even a large glass container with a Tasmanian tiger floating in it. Andy kept a tight hold of his mother's hand, passing one exhibit after another until Mary suddenly stopped. He tugged once, twice, but she wouldn't move. Looking up, he noticed she was crying, and knew this was more than the quiet tears shed when she thought no one was around to see.

Shaking off his hand, she reached out, gently stroking the jar before her. Andy stepped back to see what she was looking at, then recognised it from the drawings in his school science books. Floating in a cradle of tan formaldehyde, eyes shut as if sleeping, was the form of a well-developed foetus. A boy. Mary was crying hard and loud, tears flowing freely, her nose running, streaking her powdered face.

'Oh, my baby,' she whimpered.

Andy stepped away, confused and afraid.

'Oh, my sweet, precious baby.'

He didn't know where she was at that moment, but it wasn't here, and it wasn't a good place.

∗

They drove home in silence, Andy tearful, feeling isolated in the back seat with Ellie until she reached across and held his hand. Their mother rested her head against the window, staring out at the passing night, the road droning beneath them, the smell of sawdust lingering on their shoes. It was strange, being so close to Ellie, for until then he had never felt much like a brother to her, more like a witness to her life, no different to watching *I Love Lucy* on TV. When they pulled into the driveway, Frank guided his wife into the house, the bedroom door soon closing behind them while the two invisible children stood watching. It was strange to see such tenderness in his father after so much anger, but there you had it, love in its many forms, and the badshit nowhere to be seen.

Ellie walked with Andy through to the backyard where they sat on the steps outside the kitchen and for a moment listened to a blackbird.

'How are you feeling, kiddo?' she asked him.

Andy's eyes remained red from crying. He sniffed back his running nose, wiping the excess on his sleeve. 'I don't understand,' he said. 'What happened back there? Why was Mum so sad?'

'It was the baby in the bottle.'

'So what,' he said. 'I bet the dumb thing wasn't even real.'

'It was real to Mum.'

'I don't get it.'

'Andy,' she said, 'what happened tonight should have happened years ago.' She hesitated. 'Mum miscarried a child before you were born and … Well, I think that's why she's so unhappy sometimes. I think that's when it all began to go wrong for her.'

'What's … mist-carriage?' Andy asked, stumbling over the word.

'Miscarried,' Ellie corrected him. 'It's when a baby dies before it's born.'

Andy looked confused. 'What happens to it?'

'That's the thing,' she answered. 'As best I know they just took it away. I only hear little things about it from time to time, but I've heard enough over the years to put together what happened.'

He turned to her. 'Took it away? That's not right.'

They sat in silence for a moment.

'Boy or girl?' Andy asked.

'A boy.'

Andy considered the situation. 'So I could have had a big brother?'

'Yep,' she said. 'His name was Albert I think.' Ellie laid her arm across Andy's shoulders and kissed him on the temple, the first and last time she would ever do so. 'I think I'll check on Mum,' she said, disappearing inside. 'Look after yourself, kiddo.'

He sat and listened to the sounds of Blackwater. He heard a baby cry somewhere and wondered what life would have been like with a big brother around. 'Albert Walker,' he whispered to the cosmos, wondering if his brother could hear his name spoken out there.

＊

As time passed, Andy noticed Ellie becoming increasingly independent, and by sixteen she was spending more time away from home. He felt abandoned and unsettled.

Ellie kept the camphor-wood glory box locked at the foot of her bed with a brass padlock, the scent of mothballs filling the room whenever it was opened. Andy often watched Ellie taking things out, carefully folding them and returning each item as she'd found them.

Not long after her seventeenth birthday, Andy was lying on Ellie's bed, watching as she conducted her ritual of the camphor box one more time. A familiar event, but this time he realised the meaning behind the routine and didn't like it. The box held a collection of dreams, a sneak preview of life without the badshit around … without *him* around.

'Ellie?' His voice was a whisper.

Most of the box's contents were still on the floor.

'Ellie?' he repeated a little louder.

'Uh huh,' she answered lazily, folding a tablecloth.

'Don't go.'

She paused. 'Go?' she said. 'Go where?'

'What am I going to do with Mum and Dad if you ever leave?'

'I'm not going anywhere, Andy.'

'Then what's all this stuff for?'

'It's a glory box. Stuff … That's all it is. Stuff for when I get married.'

'Are you going to marry your boyfriend someday?'

'None of your business.'

Reluctantly, Andy let his sister finish repacking in silence, sitting on the edge of her bed.

'Promise me,' Andy said finally.

She pushed the box back into its place and sat next to him. 'Promise you what?'

'Promise you'll never leave me here with this mess.'

They stared at each other for a moment, the plea hanging fragile in the air between them.

'I can't promise that, kiddo.'

No, deep down he knew she couldn't.

∗

Returning home from a day's fishing, the first thing Andy heard was his father's temper. Andy reached the gate as Frank Walker stormed out of the house, nearly taking the screen door off its hinges. Andy stepped out of his way, the body language more than enough to go to ground on. Next, he heard his mother crying. Dropping his fishing gear, he followed the sound through the house to Ellie's room, where his mother sat alone on the edge of his sister's bed, her head cradled in her hands. It reminded him of the incident at the fair, and a twinge of fear trembled through his body.

The camphor box was missing. 'No,' he whispered, running over to Ellie's chest of drawers, sliding each open until he was convinced of the inevitable. 'No! No! No! No!'

Ellie was gone, leaving him alone with the badshit to clean up after the fights.

3

Most towns seem to embrace change over time, but not Blackwater. Not even the fire of 1930, which razed almost every building on Main Street, could change the town for long. Like the phoenix, the town rose from the ashes, not anew, but just the way she'd perished, rebuilt brick by brick into a monument to its former Art Deco glory.

'Like being an actor stuck in some old-time movie,' my mother once said.

And so it remains to this day, the council by-laws insisting that all new buildings on Main Street maintain the old façade in honour of the dead of 1930. Seventeen perished the night of the firestorm, their names later etched in bronze on the monument at the Queens Bridge Junction, the first thing you see coming into town, the last thing you see leaving.

ANDY sat on the bench outside the Palace Picture Theatre wishing he had money for a ticket as he watched Lonesome, the police dog, do his rounds without the town's sergeant in tow. It was common to see Sergeant Red Adams and his long-haired Alsatian going in and out of the Main Street shops, talking to the owners and often sharing a Cornish pasty from the bakery. But on the occasions when Adams was called out, his dog would do the rounds without him.

'Hey, Lonesome,' Andy said as the dog meandered past, his coat dusty, in need of a bath.

The dog stopped to look him over, yawned, then walked on. *No threat here … Everything okay.*

Lonesome was one of the things Andy liked about Blackwater: the familiarity. Everything had a local name, names not found on any store-bought map. Like Two Rivers, where the smaller Hawksnest River merged with the Salesbury that ran wide through town, its waters so clear you could see the riverbed at its deepest. The nearby Shallows, and the Pond. The abandoned picnic grounds at Two Rivers, and the ruined sandstone cottage by the Pond, no roof or floor anymore, just thick sun-bleached stone walls and a chimney stack. Behind the ruins was a rickety wooden jetty where some of the best fishing could be found using flour dough rubbed with the fennel growing wild on the riverbanks as bait.

This was where he often sat watching the Blackwater rowing crews go through their paces. There was something peaceful about the sport, something ordered and structured, qualities missing from Andy's own life. It was a picture, a painting of light, movement and energy upon a natural canvas, oars plying the water in idyllic unison like Viking longboats in search of world's end. There was something about the boats and the water, a connection held deep in his soul that he couldn't quite place. The rowing club had a boathouse north of Queens Bridge in town. There, the river's dark water ran widest and deepest along its steep banks, flowing dead straight for three miles before snaking east toward the coast.

*

The river brought things to Blackwater. Strange things at times. A sack of kittens, just one of six alive by the time Andy fished it out. Stark white in colour and barely alive, it nevertheless bounded from the hessian sack, peering over its soggy shoulder before disappearing into the fennel stems by the bank. That cat proved to be a survivor, growing big and feral over time, and mean. His mother once told him that most white, blue-eyed cats were deaf, but this one did okay for itself. He frequently saw it roaming the shadows down there, its white coat matted with burrs, dry blood caked black around her mouth from the last kill.

Not all gifts the river brought to Blackwater were wanted. Some mornings they were found drifting in the shallows or caught on the bank, and sometimes Andy was there to see them arrive with his best friend, Eddie Dugan.

Eddie hated his name, reinventing himself as Butch after a cartoon character when he was five years old. His mouse-brown hair was always trimmed to a flat-top crew cut, and Butch carried a little weight, a condition his mother called 'big boned'.

While fishing from the jetty over the Pond, the two boys spotted a yellow VW Beetle floating toward them from over the rise of the

Shallows. It teetered in the water, inching nearer to the rapids before cascading through the white water and surfacing in front of them. Still swaying, the car drifted past and they could see no one was inside. Then, maintaining its grace, it slowly lifted its exhaust pipe to the sky and sank, the sun flashing farewell on the ripple it created.

Andy turned to Butch, and there was a knowing silence between them. No debate about why this happened, or where the car came from. Maybe that was the beauty of being best friends. Not everything requires comment.

The river brought Bartholomew in the floods that same year. It took two weeks for the floodwaters to subside, silt and mud left high on the lower banks downriver where many of the bigger trees had been ripped from the banks. Although devastating parts of the riverlands each time they came, the floods occurred often enough to be a part of life here, the town's steep riverbanks sparing it each time until the water burst its banks at the sand quarries downstream. For weeks after the floods, a stench of death grew down by the Two Rivers picnic grounds. But as much as Andy and Butch searched, its source eluded them.

At the end of an afternoon's swim, both boys were lazing in the shade of a tall grey gum. It was late summer, the air hot, but the water already had a cool autumn bite. Andy opened his eyes to gaze into the tree canopy above … and there it was. Wedged halfway up the tree – the carcass of a black and white Friesian cow.

'Wow,' said Andy, sitting up.

Stirred, Butch drew a quick breath at the sight above them. 'Jeez,' he said.

They stared, disappointed that the mystery was solved. Now reduced to a sagging bag of bones, the carcass's eyeless head tilted slightly to one side appearing every bit as curious about the boys as they were of it.

'What are you looking at, Bartholomew?' said Butch, throwing a rock at the remains. The stone hit its haunches with a dull and dusty thud, an explosion of flies bursting off their prize before landing again.

'That's a boy's name,' Andy reminded him.

'So?' Butch threw another stone. *Thud.*

'Cows are girls, ya dickhead.'

'She doesn't care what we call her.' Another stone. This one missed, landing in the river. 'Anyway, man,' said Butch, 'she looks like a Bartholomew.'

They continued staring.

'I guess,' said Andy.

Bartholomew slowly fell apart over the course of that year, but the boys always said hello as they passed, and Butch always threw a stone her way.

*

For Andy, the worst thing the river brought them came in May, a month before the Queen's Birthday weekend. The river was wearing its winter clothes, the banks stripped of greenery except for its pockets of she-oaks and balloon vines, and the canvas backpack that markedly stood out in the water.

Andy and Butch were hanging out in the ruined cottage, choking on cigarettes Butch had stolen from his father's bedside table. Andy tried to look cool, but spat into the fireplace a lot instead, the taste something he could not get used to. While trying to memorise the Abbot and Costello routine, *Who's on First?* Butch suddenly exclaimed, 'Hey, what's that?'

'What's what?' Andy replied coughing, brushing his fringe from his eyes.

'Out there.' Butch stood by the window frame, his cheeks red from too much sun, and pointed to the end of the jetty. 'See? In the water,' he said. 'I think it's a bag. Maybe a backpack.'

Andy spotted it. 'Race you,' he said, running out through the doorway, pushing Butch off balance as he passed, laughing as his friend stumbled.

But Butch caught up, a mere pace behind as Andy made it to the end of the jetty first. The water was still murky from the floods, but drawing closer, they noticed that the pack seemed to be full. This excited the boys, the prospect of finding camping gear inside spurring them on – knives, compasses, who knew what?

While attempting to pull the waterlogged backpack onto the jetty, the body, hidden beneath the pack rolled over; a putrid stench released as it broke the surface. It was a teenager, and as his bruised and swollen face stared up through lifeless eyes, the two boys cried out as one.

'Oh, shit, man!' cried Butch, still wheezing from the run. '*Oh, shit! Oh, shit! Oh, shit!*'

'*It's a kid!*' shouted Andy, his heart racing, the smell gagging.

'*He's dead, man. Oh, shit, Andy, he's dead,*' Butch spat, standing, pushing, shoving, anything to get away from it. In his haste, he knocked Andy into the water on top of the body.

Fear and repulsion stabbing at his senses, Andy thought he could feel the arms shifting around him, instinctively pushing himself away before losing his footing on the smooth stones of the riverbed. On his first attempt to resurface, he came up beneath the boy, dead arms again exploring the waters around him. His breath almost spent, Andy tried again, this time breaking the surface. The teenager was floating on his side, Andy no more than an inch from his grey face. He attempted to scream, but swallowed water instead. Coughing, he kicked away beneath the jetty to the other side, where he clawed his way up onto the boardwalk. Shaken and cold, Andy lay staring at the body where the current had lodged it between two piers.

'You okay?' Butch wheezed.

Andy rolled onto his side, looking Butch in the eyes. 'No thanks to you.'

Butch shrugged, the closest thing to an apology Andy was going to get. 'You touched it, man,' he said with a shiver.

'No shit,' said Andy.

The Greater Western newspaper ran its story on the front page with a picture of Andy and Butch by the jetty. There was also a photo supplied by the boy's family, smiling; his name was Colin Delroy. It was difficult to relate the smile to the bloated body imprinted on Andy's memory. But he thought about Colin Delroy a lot after that. At times he could close his eyes and see the boy's face in the muddy waters again, like a dream he couldn't quite shake. Butch made a memorial to the incident by carving a simple statement in one of the soft sandstone bricks of the ruined homestead.

Butch & Andy
Legends
1960

4

The Queen's Birthday weekend proclaimed winter's arrival, the night so full of stars I thought you could reach up and brush stardust from their bellies. I remember rockets hissing into the night, exploding in a shower-storm of colour.

The bonfire was built in a vacant lot opposite my house, the neighbourhood pitching in weeks before, depositing any junk that would burn, and was so hot it could singe hair within ten feet. And still burning days after was the car tyre on top, a crown placed on the night with all the pomp and ceremony of a royal coronation.

ALMOST every block on Blackwater burnt its own beacon in the crisp winter air, laughter echoing like hovering moths in the light. Andy watched as children scrawled their names in the air with silver-hot sparklers that burned down to little fingers. Tin buckets were full of Tom Thumbs that exploded like machine-gun fire, and the air was thick with the scent. Catherine wheels nailed to grey weathered fences whizzed in bright circles as more rockets were launched from the necks of empty beer bottles, filling the night sky in windswept curtains of colour. Then, *Boom!* – a thunder cracker splintered someone's mailbox and a group of teenagers ran hooting into the night.

'I see you, Jim Donovan,' cried an old man. 'I see you runnin', and I'm tellin' your parents what you and those hoods have done.'

Most of the younger kids were in their beds by eleven, yet many of the adults remained by the dwindling fire drinking beer and cheap wine, the men singing out of tune to a scratchy Hank Williams record. Andy remembered his father telling him how Hank died of a broken heart alone in the back seat of his Cadillac one night. How his driver pushed along the desert highway to Hank's next venue without knowing his boss was dead.

Andy sat on the front steps of his house, watching the fireworks in the distance slow, and by midnight falling silent like the cease-fire of a war zone. Fighting sleep, he watched his mother and father across at the bonfire, praying they could stay happy tonight. And he thought they might. After all, he could sense when the badshit was around, and tonight it was somewhere else, tonight it had found some other host.

Turning toward the stars, Andy hoped to glimpse Laika before sleep took hold, but instead remembered the kid in the river. He felt strangely closer to the dead boy than to his own parents.

The sound of an engine drew his attention to a car driving slowly down the street, dipping in and out from under the streetlights. A cherry-red Holden with whitewall tyres, its interior pitch-black except for the glow of a cigarette tip as the driver dragged on his smoke. The car slowed even more, stopping briefly in front of Andy's house. He shivered, and felt a strange presence lingering between himself and the driver. What it was he couldn't explain, yet the connection remained in the night air until the car drove on, its engine growling like an animal searching for prey.

That's when he felt it, like cold silk brushing the back of his neck. The badshit had returned, somewhere close, maybe in that car, maybe behind the burning tip of that cigarette.

The Privilege System

5

My life took a turn that winter because of something simple: packing my mother's groceries at the supermarket. If I'd known, I would never have set foot in that place.

WINTER hung over Blackwater like a grey cloud, having dissolved autumn's colours. Yet as dawn's light peeled away at the enduring sheets of morning mist, a white frost blanketed the lawns, leaving cream frozen in milk bottles on door steps, and the milkman's footprints pressed in the icy grass.

Although Greenways was a small supermarket, it was the biggest of the two in town, its curved Art Deco façade typical of the Main Street buildings, pretending to be something it was not.

In his thirties and reeking of aftershave, Kyle Tucker held himself straight and square-shouldered, compensating for his height – only five foot four – as if reaching for a few extra inches. His complexion pale, his black hair thinning and parted low on the left in the beginnings of a comb-over, he paced the aisles of Greenways whistling tunes from *Bandstand*. Wearing black pants and an over-starched white shirt, a row of coloured pens lined his breast pocket like a soldier's campaign ribbons. His trademark bowtie was neatly in place; a different colour for every day of the week. Blue today, he'd decided. Blue like daybreak.

Kyle had woken that morning from a nightmare. The same one, about the wolf, about the Game going wrong. A bachelor, he rose alone before daybreak, every light in the house burning until the sun had melted the rim of frost from the windows, the natural light washing the residue of fear from his eyes. The warmth through the glass felt calming. He'd looked at his boat in the drive with pride, her sleek timber bow protruding from beneath her canvas cover.

At Greenways, people only ever saw the face Kyle wanted to show them; what he called his everyday face. He grinned. His hands rose to his tie, checking it for the air of neatness he wished to portray, drawing people's attention toward his smile, his eyes, his everyday face.

'Hello there, Mrs Walker,' he said approaching the checkout. 'How's Frank?'

Kyle made it his business to know everyone. Good, bad or indifferent, he liked to think he held the key to all their closets; liked to think he knew where all the Blackwater bodies were buried, where the secrets were kept. Because secrets, he knew, were like weapons.

Mary shrugged. 'Frank's just fine, thank you.'

As there were no grocery boys on their aisle, Andy Walker was packing his mother's bags.

'And how are you, Master Andy?' Kyle leant against the end of the checkout, his arms folded as he watched the boy pack the last bag. It wasn't rocket science: hard items on the bottom, soft on top. Dairy and frozen goods together in a double bag to keep them cool, and never mix soap or detergents with food. The kid got it. Not all of them did.

'Fine thanks, Mr Tucker.'

'Come on now, Andy. Call me Kyle.' He winked over Andy's shoulder toward his mother. 'No airs and graces here, son. Everyone in town calls me Kyle. Mr Tucker is my father's name, and, quite frankly, he's welcome to it.'

'Thanks, Kyle,' said Andy, a sense of reluctance in his voice.

Kyle slapped Andy's back. Not a pat on the head for little kids, not gently on the shoulder like something small and frail, but on the back, firmly, like a man.

Andy placed the last bag on the floor as the cashier said, 'Five pounds six, please, Mrs Walker.'

Mary reddened as she drew her handbag closer to her face, her free hand rummaging inside. 'Oh, dear,' she said. 'I seem to be a little short.' She glanced back at those queued behind her. 'I'm sorry,' she said again before turning back. 'Please, dear, I'll have to take a few things out.'

Kyle placed one hand on Mary's arm while closing her handbag with the other. 'Now, now,' he said to the cashier. 'Mrs Walker has been a customer for as long as I can remember.' He guided her through the register. 'Ring up the till and we'll work the rest out later.' He spoke quietly so no one else in the queue could hear.

With an indifferent flick of her hair, the cashier did as she was told.

'I'm sorry, Kyle,' Mary said, noticeably embarrassed. 'It's just that things are so expensive these days and I –'

'Mrs Walker, please,' said Kyle. 'Think nothing of it.' He picked up two of the four grocery bags while Andy took the others. 'I'm not going to worry over a few shillings so why should you.' He added, 'Go home and forget about it.'

He walked Mary and Andy to the front doors with the gold *Air Conditioned* sign.

'Well,' said Mary. 'Thank you again.'

Kyle handed her the two bags. 'You're most welcome,' he said as the doors slid open. 'Goodbye, Andy,' he added with that same slap on the back. 'Oh, and Andy?'

'Yes, Mr … er … Kyle,' Andy stammered.

'If it's okay with your mother, I may have a position opening up for the afternoons. Could lead to some weekend work as well.' Kyle looked at Mary. 'What do you think, Mrs Walker?'

'Can I, Mum?' Andy asked. 'I could save for that telescope I want.'

'I can't see a problem. We'll ask your father tonight. I'm sure it'll be okay.'

'It'd be a shame to let those packing skills of yours go to waste,' Kyle added with a smile. 'Come in Saturday morning at nine for an interview.' His expression sobered. 'No promises, now.

There'll be other boys applying, too, and the job will go to the best candidate.'

'Okay, Mr … er … Kyle.'

*

Andy began the walk home with his mother. They stopped at the Quarryman Hotel where she told him to wait on the footpath. The sound of a radio playing a horse race drifted out, carried by the smell of cigarette smoke and beer.

While Andy waited, his attention was caught by a squeaking wheel on the pavement. It was their neighbour, Mrs Murphy, pushing a pram that had seen better days. He nodded hello as she passed, wondering if the cheesecloth covering was to keep the sun off her child, or hide the thalidomide damage from the world.

When his mother returned a few minutes later, he noticed the bottle-shaped brown parcel pushed deep into one of the bags. In view of what had happened at Greenways, he knew she often held a little grocery money back for booze. Being young didn't make him stupid.

6

It rained the morning of the interview, the day arriving with a wicked southern cold front. I listened to the weather against my bedroom window while I dressed in the grey suit mum had bought me for my sister's confirmation two years before. But two years is a long time for an adolescent, and the damn thing didn't fit.

ANDY stood in front of the mirror and sighed. 'It looks dumb,' he told his mother.

'The suit looks fine,' Mary said, although Andy heard some doubt in her voice.

'I can see my socks.' Andy pushed the trousers down to cover them and sighed again. As his belt drifted lower his shirt-tail fell out. 'It's too small, Mum!'

'Nonsense!' But again, she was a little doubtful. 'Change your socks to black ones and give me those pants.'

Andy did as he was told, and his mother unpicked the stitching from his trousers' hem. He didn't know why he couldn't wear jeans and a shirt. If anyone from school saw him in the suit he'd be mincemeat.

Sitting on the edge of his bed, he felt goose bumps forming on his exposed legs. 'I'm gonna look stupid for the interview.'

The wind rattled the window.

'You won't look stupid,' she countered, throwing the trousers back at him. 'Try them now.'

Andy slipped them on and tucked in his shirt. There was still an inch of sock showing but the black wasn't nearly as noticeable.

'Look at my arms.' Andy held them by his side, three inches of white cuff protruding beyond the coat sleeves. 'You're signing my death warrant if anyone sees me like this.'

Mary bit her bottom lip, having just about had enough. 'It's not the kids at school you'll have to worry about if you keep this up.' She stood back to consider the problem. 'Well, take the coat off and fold it over your arm at least. No son of mine is showing up for a job interview in anything less than a suit and tie.'

He peeled off the tight-fitting coat and walked past his mother toward the door. 'I look like a clown.'

Mary gave him a gentle clip behind the ear. 'Hurry up or you'll be late, bozo.'

*

A gust of cold wind turned his umbrella inside out in front of the Murphy house. As he struggled to turn the umbrella back, he heard a baby's cry through one of the windows. He peered through the window trying to glimpse the baby. Just as he forced the umbrella right, the window slammed closed, and the crying stopped.

Andy arrived at the supermarket drenched. He stood across the road beneath a shop's awning, Greenways staring back at him through its glass-brick window eyes as the rain ran down its curved façade.

Like being an actor stuck in some old-time movie, he thought.

At a break in the traffic, Andy crossed the road, entering the store with ten minutes to spare, his clothes clinging to his body, his hair flat against his scalp. No shoppers yet, just four boys his own age wearing blue aprons. One stood at the end of each checkout aisle, chatting to the teenage girls at the registers. The girl who served his mother recognised him, rolling her eyes at his wet clothes, while the fourth boy pushed a broom across his shoes. *Welcome to Greenways*, he thought.

The boy with the broom stopped and turned, leaning on the handle. 'Sorry,' he said, 'but we open at nine.' His nametag read *Toby*. He looked vaguely familiar, no surprise in a small town, though given they were the same age, Andy thought he really should know him from school.

'I'm here for the job interview,' Andy said.

'That so?' the boy said, scratching his scalp through tan-coloured hair. He looked him up and down, his eyes finally settling on the puddle growing at Andy's feet.

'I got caught in the rain.'

'You sure did.' Toby nearly smiled.

Andy sensed he was unaccustomed to smiling.

'Follow me, new kid,' said Toby. 'Kyle does the interviews in his office out the back.'

7

People can be in your life forever, but contribute nothing to it. And others can drift briefly through and leave so much – that was Toby.

GUIDING Andy through a set of swinging plastic doors into the storeroom, Toby zigzagged through a maze of stacked boxes to Kyle's office, a fibro-clad windowless room built off the back wall.

He gestured to the row of plastic chairs outside the door. 'Wait here until nine,' he said. 'Kyle's a stickler for timing.'

Toby paused, waiting for the new kid to sit. He rarely asked their names; after all, few made it through the interviews. It was easier this way, he reminded himself, then turned back toward the supermarket aisles.

'Thanks, Toby,' the new kid said.

Toby kept walking, his right hand drifting to his nametag. 'Don't mention it.' Weaving through his shortcut, a wave of anxiety caught him off guard. That kid … He turned back, wanting to know what it was about him that triggered this flood of emotion. Just another kid, he told himself. Just another one for Kyle.

Toby squeezed between a row of crates by the cool room where he could see the kid sitting outside Kyle's office. There was little chance of him being seen, the light was dim. He watched, resting his chin on his arms across the lip of a crate, his brow furrowed, his eyes searching the new kid's own. He watched the clumsy attempts to straighten wet clothes, pulling at pants legs, flattening the jacket over an arm and wiping shoes dry with a handkerchief. Toby smiled.

'You really want this job, huh?' he whispered.

The smile felt good, but the usual feelings of guilt wiped it from his face; he had no right to be happy. Then he saw what he was looking for in the kid's eyes. *That was me once.*

He watched the kid stand, compose himself, and approach Kyle's door, arm paused ready to knock.

'Don't,' Toby whispered, looking at his watch. It was right on nine.

8

*Privilege. It was a word that evoked something special
to me back then. An honour. A benefit. Soon, it had a
whole new meaning.*

KYLE heard the knock on the door, looking up from the stack of invoices on his desk. He checked his watch.

'Come in,' he called, his hands instinctively straightening his bowtie. Red today. Deep red, for the dawn sky. A shudder ran through his body, recalling the dream. He shook it off, and stood up behind his desk with a smile, pleased the Walker boy's eyes were drawn to the tie.

'Andy,' Kyle said. 'Good to see you.' He stepped past the boy to close the door. 'Please,' he said, 'sit down.' He gestured to the wooden chair in front of the desk as he returned to his own high-backed leather one. He watched in mild amusement as Andy sat, his wet pants sounding like a fart when he slid into the chair.

Kyle noticed the boy's red face. 'You really got caught in that rain, huh?'

'I sure did,' Andy said, his eyes scanning the room and falling on Kyle's steamer chest in the corner.

'Well, it tells me one thing,' said Kyle, drawing Andy's attention away from the chest. 'You're punctual. Too many of my boys would roll over and go back to sleep rather than face that weather. Shows a lot of good, honest character.'

'Oh, a little rain doesn't bother me, Mr Tucker.'

Kyle could see that Andy was uncomfortable, first interview jitters perhaps. Nothing he hadn't seen before in kids his age.

'That's good, Andy. That's really good.'

Kyle jotted notes onto a pad behind the silver cigarette box, noticing how Andy raised his chin to see what he was writing. He saw the boy's eyes widen, distracted once more and realised the beast had shown itself – his shirt sleeve had ridden up to reveal the wolf's head tattoo.

He took a cigarette from the box and lit it with his Zippo before settling back into his chair, taking a moment to study the boy's expression. 'Something wrong, Andy?'

'No,' he replied. 'It's just –' He pointed at Kyle's arm. 'You don't look like the type of man who has one of those.'

Kyle rolled his sleeve up, exposing the whole image, considering it himself as if for the first time. The wolf was snarling, eyes wide, jowls moist in anticipation of a kill. He remembered the pain behind each needle prick, the commitment. 'A moment of weakness,' he said before rolling down his sleeve. Drawing on his cigarette, he smiled. 'Tell me, did your mother make you wear that suit?'

Andy's face flushed. 'Uh huh,' he said, embarrassment seeping back into his expression.

'Listen, I can see you're uncomfortable, but don't be. I've been conducting interviews here for a lot of years, and after a while you learn to form an opinion long before a person opens their mouth.' Kyle drew on his cigarette again. 'And do you know what I see in you, Andrew Walker?'

Andy shrugged, wincing as a wisp of cigarette smoke drifted into his eyes.

'The thing I saw when you walked in all soaking wet and wearing a suit two sizes too small was *character*. That storm couldn't stop you. There's determination. And you wore that suit out of respect for your mother. Well, let me tell you, respect is getting hard to find these days.'

Kyle stubbed out his cigarette in the ashtray. 'You risked embarrassment out of respect for your mother, and that, young Andrew Walker, means you have integrity. So what do I have rolled up in that soggy package? I have punctuality, determination, respect and integrity. Those things can open a lot of doors for you.'

'Thanks, Mr Tucker, I really would like a shot at this job.'

Kyle's hands drifted to his tie, making small adjustments. 'What do your parents think about it?'

'Mum's fine, and Dad's all for it too. He says I've got to help out with the housekeeping bills.'

'Well, I can't say you've got the job for sure, but I *can* say you stand a really good chance.' Kyle contemplated Andy for a moment. 'I'm not talking into the wind with all that stuff I said. I meant every word. I also know you pack a good grocery bag because I watched you. But I owe it to the other candidates to consider it properly. Any questions?'

'No questions, Mr Tucker. I just want to say that if you decide to give me this job, well, I won't let you down.'

'I'm sure you won't, Andy.' He tapped his fingers on his desk. 'You know, son,' Kyle continued, 'I do things a little differently around here. I work on a …' he paused, '*privilege* system. Do you know what I mean by that, Andy?'

'Not exactly,' he confessed.

'Well, it's probably the simplest reward system there is. You work hard, do as you're told, and you can earn certain privileges around here. You know, lighter duties, staff discounts and even a little extra money in your pocket. It's a good way to keep things honest, I find.'

'I won't let you down,' Andy repeated.

'No,' Kyle said. 'I don't think you will.'

*

Despite the lighting, it was dim in the storeroom, the stacks of crates and boxes casting shadows across the corridors, the lack of windows denying any natural light. Andy felt disoriented once the door of Kyle's office closed behind him. The faint sound of piped music seeped in from the shopping aisles beyond the maze. He glanced left, then right, and decided to follow the music.

'You're going the wrong way, new kid.'

Andy gasped, embarrassed.

'Sorry. Didn't mean to scare you.' Toby stepped out from between a row of boxes marked *Tomato Soup*. 'Follow me.'

Andy stayed a pace behind, realising this wasn't the way they'd come before. Toby opened a fire exit to the rear car park, and Andy breathed a sigh of mild relief with the fresh air. The rain had stopped and beaded water glistened off car roofs as the sun tried to break through.

'How did the interview go?' Toby asked.

'I'm not sure,' Andy said. 'But Mr Tucker kept talking like I had the job.'

Toby sat on the steps by the loading dock, his peach-fuzz chin stubble catching the morning light. 'What's your name, new kid?' he asked.

'Andy. Andy Walker.'

Toby pulled out a crumpled pack of Camel cigarettes from his apron pocket and lit one with confidence. 'Smoke?' He offered the packet to Andy, blowing three perfect rings.

'No, thanks.'

Andy suddenly placed the boy's face, and his story. He remembered his mum and dad talking about it. He was Toby Broughton, who'd dropped out of school a year earlier to look after his mother, who had contracted cancer and couldn't work. His father had died when he was a baby, so it was just the two of them. But this wasn't the Toby he remembered. This Toby, at thirteen, had what Andy's father called the thousand-yard stare.

Andy studied the boy's face as he looked across the car park, his features as worn as an old man's.

'Are you allowed to smoke here?' Andy asked.

'Did you get the privileges speech in there?'

'Yeah.'

Toby slipped the packet into his apron. 'Half price after hours. One of my privileges for being a hard worker.'

Toby was beginning to make Andy feel uncomfortable. 'Well, I'd better go', he said.

Toby looked him up and down. 'You know,' he said, 'if you get this job, you'll need someone to show you the ropes.' He took a final draw on his cigarette and crushed it out on the step. 'If you make it I'll look out for you, okay?' He added, 'You know, keep the wolves at bay.'

9

I commenced work at Greenways the following Monday afternoon. Kyle wore a yellow bowtie. It occurred to me how rare those ties were – the only place I'd seen them before was in old movies. Some days I can still see every stitch and fold in that yellow bowtie. It's the little things that stay in your mind that mark your crossroads.

TWO weeks on, Andy stood in the office to request extra hours. This time he noticed the detail in the room, the rear wall plush with leatherbound books, the windowless decor that was more shadow than light. The room's raked ceiling and ornate furniture made it appear like a cluttered dusty attic. He noticed the old steamer chest in the corner with its locks – and, he supposed, its secrets.

'So,' Kyle murmured, rubbing his chin, 'you're looking for extra work, huh?'

'If it's available,' answered Andy.

'You saving for something special, or have you got yourself a girlfriend?'

Andy blushed. 'I'm saving for a telescope.'

'Oh, the noble science of astronomy. Is that what you want to be, Andy? An astronomer? Or maybe an astronaut or … or – what do the Russians call them? Cos-mo-nauts.' He smiled. 'You want to be some kinda stargazer or something?'

As much as Andy felt Kyle was trying to be funny, it struck him that he had no idea what he wanted to be when he left school. All he knew was he didn't want to drive trucks like his dad.

He considered his answer. 'For now I suppose it's just a hobby.'

Kyle laughed. He took out a cigarette from the box on his desk and lit it with his Zippo. 'Well, I suppose we could roster you on Saturday mornings and see how you go. You've certainly picked things up okay.' He paused, his thumb repeatedly flicking the lighter's cover. 'This telescope,' he queried, 'how much will it cost?'

'I'm not sure. I don't even know where to buy one. I see them advertised in the back of my comic books all the time, but they're from America.'

Kyle turned to him. 'I tell you what we'll do, Stargazer. Commencing this weekend, I'll start you packing groceries on the checkouts. That'll top your pay up nicely. We'll record half of that on your pay envelope and the rest will be cash, that way your parents won't go raising your board money or …' he turned his attention to the Zippo, placing it by the ashtray, ' … or your father won't drink it.'

Andy flushed. The drinking. The fighting. It all happened at home, and he believed that's where it would stay. But no, everything gets out.

'That would be great,' Andy said softly, his head bowed.

Kyle stepped around the desk, gently lifting Andy's chin to meet his eyes. 'Listen here, Stargazer,' he said. 'You're not responsible for your parents' actions, okay?' He smiled. 'Just promise me something.'

'Sure.'

'Promise me I'll get a look through that telescope. I've always wanted a glimpse of heaven.'

*

A week after Andy's first Saturday, Kyle called him to the office, handing him a book entitled *The Beginners' Guide to Astronomy.*

'Oh, my,' was all Andy could say, delighting in its weight, savouring the smell of ink and paper, the promise of something wonderful before even turning a page.

'I was in the city yesterday. Saw this in a bookshop window and thought of you.'

Andy thumbed through the pages. The city. It was a two-hour drive from Blackwater, but it may as well be a place of myth. He had only ever been there once, on the train with his mother, *a day in the city*. Sydney, the Emerald City, its bright lights reflecting off clouds to the east of Blackwater at night to mark its place.

'I don't know what to say,' Andy said. 'How much do I owe you for the book?'

'Not a thing, Stargazer,' said Kyle. 'Let's just say I'm pleased with your work. Let's just call it the first of your privileges.'

*

A few weeks on, around six, the staff began filing out of the store to head home, one or two remaining behind. Andy hadn't stayed late yet, so he couldn't say what went on or how long the others hung around. Most of the boys had a street-smart look about them, an attitude Andy envied. He hoped a little might rub off on him. Perhaps that's why he stayed so close to Toby and his thousand-yard stare; it made him believe Toby was unbreakable. Until the Saturday that myth was shattered.

At first, Andy thought he'd heard someone laughing among the boxes in the storeroom. It was late in the afternoon; apron and nametag stowed in his locker, he was ready to go home. Intrigued, he searched between the rows and under the steel shelving, eventually leading him to the plastic chairs outside Kyle's office where he found Toby.

He was sitting alone, his face cradled in his hands as he rocked on the chair. But Toby wasn't laughing. 'Stupid game,' he muttered to himself, sniffing snot back into his nose. 'Stupid, shitful game.'

Andy noticed a dull gleam beneath the door to Kyle's office, unsure if anyone was inside until a shadow darkened the thin band of light. He considered approaching Toby to see if he was okay, but decided against it. He slipped away.

10

*My friendship with Toby seemed unavoidable, leaving
me wondering who needed the relationship more. For me,
I guess he was the brother I never had, but I wouldn't
learn his true motivation until it was too late.*

EVEN though they were under age, the two boys tried to get into
the morning session of Hitchcock's *Psycho*. Toby stood in line,
cigarette hanging from the corner of his mouth to look as old as
possible. 'Two for *Psycho* thanks, love,' he said in his deepest voice.

'Come back when you can shave,' said the girl in the ticket
booth.

Accepting defeat, they decided to return for the matinee,
The Time Machine. Meanwhile, the boys bought hamburgers
and waited beneath the jacarandas by the riverbank beside the
Blackwater Rowing Club. Unwrapping his burger, Andy heard a
distant siren sounding like an air raid in the war movies.

'What *is* that?' he asked Toby. 'I've heard it before.'

Toby listened. 'That's the siren from the Goodridge prison
farm over at Burnley,' he said, his lips red from beetroot. 'It backs
onto the Hawksnest, maybe five miles upriver.' He paused. 'You
can't always hear it. My mum says it has something to do with

wind direction and the sound bouncing off the mountains.' He laughed. 'Sounds like one might have gotten away.'

'Do you think so?' Andy asked.

Toby shrugged.

The two boys sat in the park until noon, their stomachs full, the taste of greasy burgers still on their lips. Later, as they watched *The Time Machine*, a sense of pride filled Andy because Rod Taylor, an Australian, played the lead role. Andy had read H.G. Wells' book a year ago, and also had the Classic Comic version in his collection, but he still jumped when the Morlock creatures first appeared.

When the boys emerged from the cinema, the mountain's shadow was already reaching across the flood plains.

'That's better,' said Andy rubbing his eyes to adjust to the light. 'No Morlocks out here.'

'Wanna bet?' Toby said dryly.

'Huh?'

'Monsters,' said Toby. 'They're everywhere.' Toby stopped in the street and turned to Andy. 'Tell me what a monster looks like?' he said.

Andy saw the intent in Toby's eyes, glazed and unblinking, and realised this was meant to be a serious topic, although he couldn't see how. 'Relax,' said Andy. 'I know there's no such thing as monsters.'

Toby laughed harshly, leaving Andy feeling uncomfortable. He'd never seen him like this.

'You don't get it, Andy, and you *need* to.' Toby began raising his voice. 'You really need to. You see they *are* out there … all around us. The real monsters in this world are right out there in the daylight. They don't wear horrific faces. No gnashing fangs or tearing claws. No lumbering gait. No single eye in the middle of their bloody forehead, or slimy, scaly skin to give them away. I mean, that would be great! If that was the case then we could run a mile whenever we saw them coming, maybe even track them down and kill 'em before they could do any harm. No, Andy! The real monsters out there look like anyone and everyone.'

Toby fell silent, his eyes glistening. Andy didn't know what to say or think, but his friend was hurting, and he remembered the time he discovered him crying in the storeroom.

'I … I'm sorry … I should go,' Toby said.

He ran back along Main Street, disappearing through the new line of patrons that had formed in front of the theatre.

Andy walked home confused. He stared at the people passing, but all he could see were the same old faces. *They look like anyone and everyone.*

A car's horn sounded. Andy looked over in time to glimpse Kyle driving past in his cherry-red Holden. He gave Andy a wave and smiled.

Through the Wolf's Eyes

11

*There are days of my youth I remember with clarity …
The river's jacarandas were bare in the winter sun. I
remember sitting beneath their scattered shade watching
the rowing crews head upriver. The fluid motion of
the boats mesmerised me, and the longer I watched, the
stronger I was drawn to the sport. A long day of school had
just ended, with yet another two hours of supermarket
work ahead of me. I was tired, and considered calling in
sick, but then remembered Kyle's privileges speech, and
the weight of the astronomy book in my hands. So I did
the right thing.*

THE cool air enveloped Andy as he walked through the sliding
doors and into the familiar smells of country produce. Bundy
card *click-clack*, apron due its end-of-week wash, and his nametag
too crooked for Kyle's liking. He slipped off his wristwatch, the
one left to him by Grandpa Walker, and stored it in his locker.
Just another Friday until Kyle closed the doors behind the last
customer at six p.m. Near the end of his shift, Andy was sweeping
the floor between the checkouts, aware of his apathy in each stroke,
listening to the muzak, when Kyle approached him.

'Hey there, Stargazer,' he said, 'you doing anything tonight?'

Andy kept sweeping. 'Nope,' he said lazily.

'I was thinking maybe you'd like to stay back. You know, with the other guys.'

Andy's sweeping slowed to a halt as he realised the privilege in the invitation.

'If your parents are expecting you home I'll understand,' Kyle said. 'I could even call them if you'd like.'

'No,' Andy replied. 'That's fine. They won't be home for a while yet anyway.' Some Friday nights they wouldn't get home until midnight or later. There was a time when it upset him, made him sick with worry – funny how things change. Funny how living with the badshit for years hardens the spirit.

'Great. Come around back when you're done.'

Andy resumed his sweeping with a sense of urgency as Kyle walked away, suddenly feeling a little less weary.

'Well,' came a familiar voice from behind him. Andy turned to see Toby standing in aisle two, bucket in one hand and a dripping mop in the other. 'Haven't *we* scaled the social ladder?'

Andy could smell the ammonia in Toby's bucket. It was difficult to read his mood. Half of the store's lights were turned off, the shelves casting shadows in the aisle. Andy stopped sweeping. 'It was nice to be asked after all this time,' he said.

Toby stepped into the light as the muzak was switched off. He seemed nervous, glancing around to see who was in earshot.

'Andy,' he said quietly, 'now, more than ever, you've got to listen to me.' His mood was decidedly serious. 'You've got to –'

'Still sweeping, Andy?' Kyle came from nowhere. 'Sorry,' he said, staring at Toby, 'did I interrupt something here?'

Toby avoided eye contact, staring down at his bucket instead. 'No,' was all he said.

Kyle stood waiting for something more from Toby, and Andy noticed his expression became suddenly cold. Then, as if waking from a daydream, the familiar smile returned as he turned his attention to Andy. 'Well, good,' he said. 'How about you both leave that and come around back. I've got some beers going.' He tapped the side of his nose. 'Our secret.'

The two boys followed Kyle through to the storeroom, the plastic doors swinging open to the sounds of boys' voices, some laughing while another sang along with an Elvis song on the radio. Andy and Toby were greeted with the smoky haze of cigarettes and the sound of beer cans cracking open.

Andy breathed it in. *So this is what happens back here.*

*

Around eight, Kyle left the boys and unlocked the office. He went to the desk drawer with the carton of chewing gum inside. No one leaves without it. No one goes home stinking of tobacco or beer. Routine was important. He paused, sitting back in the chair, listening to the laughter from the storeroom. A feeling of remorse came over him, his face turning sullen. *Was I ever like them?* Subconsciously he reached for the wolf tattoo on his arm and rubbed it. He swung his chair around, his back to the boys' voices, facing the steamer chest. Sometimes, their laughter was all it took to send him back to where it all began. He felt his hands trembling, clutching them together to gain control. *Control is everything.* He stared at the chest for a moment, the memories returning, taking him to the Game.

The hands, he thought, rolling them over from palm to back. Capable of … control. His mind wandered, drifting through time, no longer knowing if the hands before him were his own or his father's.

There was a knock at the door, and Kyle drew a deep breath like a drowning man breaking the surface. He wiped his hands down the front of his shirt. He took a moment, swivelling the chair toward the door, his everyday face back in place, his hands toying with his bowtie. 'I'll be right out,' he said, grabbing a fist full of gum packets from the drawer.

✳

The others began drifting away for home as Kyle handed them packs of gum. 'You know the drill, boys. If your parents smell anything untoward on your breath or clothes we'll all be swimming in it.'

By nine o'clock, only Andy and Toby remained while the crackling transistor radio counted down the Friday Top 10. They moved to the fresh air on the back dock, Kyle looking up at the clear night sky.

Andy had had two cans of beer, and they left a fog in his mind that he had never felt before. He burped, the taste bubbling back up his throat.

'You okay?' Toby asked.

'Fine,' Andy said, grinning.

'So tell me the name of that star right there, Stargazer?' asked Kyle, pointing to the western horizon. 'The yellow one above the mountains?'

Andy followed Kyle's finger with difficulty. 'Antares,' he said. 'I think … See there,' he added pointing a little to the left. 'That's the tail of Scorpius the scorpion. There's his curled stinger, his body, his two nippers.'

The Milky Way shone across the dark sky, and Andy, still grinning, wondered where Laika might be tonight.

'It sure is beautiful,' Kyle said softly.

They all stared at the bright yellow heart star, Andy feeling a sense of pride at his knowledge of the cosmos.

Toby threw back the last of his beer. Andy tried doing the same but the three attempts it took to drain the can left him bloated. He wanted to belch again, but nothing shifted. His stomach gurgled and his head swam.

'You know what I feel like doing, boys?' Kyle said to the night. 'I feel like going fishing.'

'It's a little late for that,' Toby offered.

Andy sensed a tension beneath the quiet words and wondered what was going on between the two.

Kyle swung around to face the boys, his expression cloaked in darkness. 'Of course it's too late *now*, Toby,' he said harshly. His voice returned to normal. 'No, I was thinking of Sunday. What do you say, Andy? You like fishing?'

'Sure,' Andy said, having to sit on the step. 'I fish a lot at the Pond.'

Kyle waved the suggestion away. 'Ah, the Pond,' he said dismissively. 'That place is full of mullet and eel. No, I'm talking about going upriver in my boat. Up where old man bass lives. Past the Narrows.'

'Sounds great,' Andy said slurring his words slightly. He turned to Toby. 'You coming?'

But before Toby could reply, Kyle answered for him.

'Uh, actually, I was hoping you could work at the store on Sunday, Toby. You know, end-of-month stocktake.' The two stared at each other. 'You *know* you could use the money.' There was a pause. 'How *is* your mother anyway?'

Andy belched, long and loud, eyes wide in surprise as the beer gas finally shifted. 'Sorry,' he said, covering his mouth, giggling.

Toby stood abruptly and ran down the stairs two at a time. 'I've got to go,' was all he said. But the friction between Toby and Kyle remained in the air, an uncomfortable silence in Toby's wake. Andy noticed how Kyle switched off for that moment, staring at his hands.

'Well,' Andy said, 'I'd better get going too.' He stood and faltered. 'My parents will be home soon.'

Kyle's hands dropped to his side. 'Sure,' he said, still a little distracted, wiping his hands on his pants.

'What time?' Andy asked.

'What?' said Kyle.

'Fishing, Sunday – What time?'

'Oh, yeah, um, I suppose I could pick you up around eight,' Kyle said. 'Make sure you tell your parents about it tonight, okay?'

'Sure.'

'Oh, and here.' Kyle pulled out a pack of Wrigley's Spearmint. 'Chew some of this on your way home.' Kyle watched him stagger away. 'You sure you're okay?'

Andy raised his hand. 'Fine. Just fine.'

12

Greenways had become my escape from the badshit at home, its lure stronger than anything my instincts were telling me. By the time I realised that a wolf prowled Blackwater, it was too late. Yet where there were wolves, there were often hunters.

TAPPING the spent pipe on his boot heel, Sergeant Red Adams sat on the bench outside the police station in the cool of the evening, the taste of port-wine tobacco lingering in his mouth as he rummaged in his pants pocket for his cleaning pick. The nickname 'Red' had stuck since he was a kid, yet he preferred it to his christened name, Hadrian. Lonesome, his Alsatian, lay sleeping at his feet, his leg twitching against Red's boot. *What do you dream of*, he wondered, *chasing cars? Rabbits?* He smiled at his old friend as he found the pick and began cleaning the chamber of his pipe, suddenly getting a whiff of Lonesome's coat. 'You're overdue a bath, boy.'

He placed his cap beside him on the bench and brushed the hair back off his forehead, reminding himself he was in need of a haircut. Cupping the ivory bowl in his free hand, he placed the pipe in his top pocket and saw a few strands of hair caught between his fingers. He was only forty, but noticed more hairs on the comb every day, his once rusty hair already getting a few browns and silvers.

Change was coming, in more than his appearance, and he sensed he needed it.

The routine at Blackwater the past ten years had made him a little complacent. He was gaining weight and growing lazy. A year ago he had three constables under him. Now, it was trimmed down to Burrows, just two months out of the academy. In another year, the Blackwater station would be closed, the town falling under a wider jurisdiction as part of the commissioner's rural consolidation.

Lonesome stirred at his feet and stretched with a mild groan. He opened his eyes to check if Red was still on the bench, relaxing when they made eye contact.

Red leant forward and stroked the dog's side. 'You okay there?'

Lonesome whimpered, appearing keen to get back to his dream.

'This is it, boy,' said Red, swiping at a mosquito by his ear. 'Our last year on the river.' Red drew a deep breath, listening as the final bus for the evening turned in the cul-de-sac and headed back toward the Queens Bridge turn-off. 'New posting. New challenges.' Red was aware that his new job may not tolerate a dog hanging around the station, but he would have to wait and see. Not everyone loved dogs. His ex-wife claimed Lonesome stank of wet socks and old boot leather, but Red never smelt it. She got the house and he got the dog. He smiled at the memory, long over the hurt. 'Wouldn't have it any other way, boy,' he said to Lonesome. Sitting back, he returned his cap to his head and rested both arms along the bench's backrest.

Red saw Blackwater like the river: calm, slow and purposeful; beautiful. And like the river, it was the darkness that lay beneath Blackwater's surface that kept him guarded, causing him to ponder the file that left him sleepless on nights like this. The file of loose ends.

Red stood and stretched. Lonesome stirred too, standing with him, suddenly awake and alert, his ears raised, his eyes wide as he sniffed the air. Their attention was caught by the two boys talking outside Greenways. It was a little late to be out on the street at their age, but he couldn't be bothered moving them along.

'It's okay, boy,' he said, patting the dog's head. 'Time to go inside.'

Lonesome followed, trotting past Red as he locked the door of the police station behind them. Burrows had gone for the day, and Red decided he, too, would leave shortly. They walked around the counter to where the office and a small cell were located. Lonesome curled up on the blanket in the corner while Red hung his hat on the wall hook beside Burrows' desk, the ordered neatness and framed photo of the constable and his smiling fiancée a stark contrast to the clutter on his own. He picked up the frame, Burrows in uniform, cap under his arm, the boyish grin, neat dark hair and a look in his eyes Red had forgotten he'd once had too. Twisting the frame to the light, he caught sight of his reflection in the glass: his own eyes were weary, his expression blank. He placed the photograph back on his desk.

Loosening his top shirt button, Red sat at his desk and kicked off his boots. He packed a portion of tobacco in his pipe and lit it, drawing shallow puffs until it was alight. Reaching for his only photo, he brushed dust off the glass with the back of his hand. There he stood, not long out of the academy himself, his father's arm draped proudly over his shoulder, his free hand cupping the same pipe Red now used. 'I miss you, Pop,' he said, returning the frame to the only clean patch in the dust on his desk. As he pulled open his middle drawer, he scratched at the day-old stubble on his chin. Inside the drawer was a single unlabelled manila folder. Red clasped the lip of the pipe between his teeth as he flipped through the file's contents.

This was the ritual, to dust off the file on nights like this, when the loose ends got under his skin. A collection of things that didn't fit. The dead Delroy boy in the river a few years back. People moving away suddenly. Unexplained assaults, usually out-of-towners passing through. Runaways. Good kids going bad. All happening in Blackwater.

He shuffled the case details around on the desk in front of him, looking for that invisible thread linking them together. He drew on his pipe. *Loose ends*, he told himself. *Unfinished business*. A year away from transfer, he didn't want to spend the rest of his career scratching an itch he couldn't satisfy.

13

The badshit was never far away.

WHEN Andy stepped out of the alleyway on his way home, he wasn't surprised to find Toby waiting under the streetlights. Storming out on Kyle tonight had been odd.

'What's going on between you two?' Andy said abruptly.

Toby walked beside him. 'I can't say.'

The beer in Andy's system was taking hold, his stomach churning. 'Well, bloody hell Toby! I don't understand why you get so upset with the man. I know he's kind of weird sometimes, but he looks after us like no one I've ever known. I don't feel like a kid around him. None of us does! He pays us well, treats us like adults and … and – Well, look at the privileges, Toby. Look at tonight.'

'Oh, the *privileges*,' Toby's voice broke. 'Yeah, good ol' Kyle will suffocate his chosen ones in privileges … until it's time to pay up.'

Andy stopped. 'What? What do you mean, pay up?'

'Look, it's hard for me. With my mum sick with cancer, I need this job so bad.' He began crying. 'I've got to pay for her medication until … until she … until she dies!' He was bawling, mucus seeping from his nose. Toby slid down against the shopfront until he sat with his head bowed, arms curled around his knees. 'He's got me,

Andy. Until my mum dies, he's got me. I want to get away but I can't, not until she's gone … And I don't want her to die. She's all I've got.' Toby gasped for breath.

Andy slid down beside him. 'Maybe your mum will get better,' was all he could think to say. 'Then you can quit.'

'That's just it. I don't think she *will* get better. The doctors treat me like a kid and tell me nothing. It's like I'm invisible at the hospital. Mum's the same, because she doesn't want to upset me. But I've grown up a lot in a year. I've had to.'

'What about getting another job?' Beads of perspiration were forming on Andy's top lip. He didn't feel well.

'Do you have any idea what a thirteen-year-old gets paid in the real world, Andy?' Toby didn't wait for an answer, wiping his nose with his shirt sleeve. 'Kyle pays me above the basic wages. I can't get that anywhere else. One of my *privileges*.'

'Then why are you so hard on him?'

'Because … Because –' Toby stood up and began walking. 'Look, Andy, don't let him dig you in too deep like he did with me! You've got to be careful. You've got – You've got to call in sick on Sunday. You've got to cancel that fishing trip.' He shook his head nervously. 'Don't tell Kyle I told you that, okay? Just call it off. Rethink the privileges. Do your work, take your pay and just go home each day. Do that, and you'll be okay.'

'But why?' asked Andy, struggling to keep up.

They stopped by Queens Bridge. Toby turned, took Andy by the shoulders and looked him in the eye. 'Just be careful,' he said.

Pausing, he saw the colour drain from Andy's face. 'Are you sure you're okay? I think you had too much to drink.'

'Nah, I'm fine,' said Andy, before unleashing a stream of vomit that missed Toby by inches.

*

Andy walked home chewing his gum and thinking about Sunday, his head clearer for purging at the bridge. He suddenly realised he'd left his wristwatch back in his locker, and for a moment considered going back. But Kyle had probably left for the night. The watch was his grandpa's, left to him in his will, entrusted to him. It tore him up inside, but he would have to wait. Maybe Kyle could let him in on Sunday.

He continued home, thinking about Toby's words. But rounding the last corner, he heard the familiar sounds ahead. *Not tonight, please …*

The badshit had come home.

He recognised the yelling from the front gate and could see the neighbour's curtains peeled back. He sat on the top step of the house where he and Ellie used to huddle, a wave of exhaustion rolling over him. He missed her, but every day that passed made him understand why she left. But what about *him*? How could she have left him with this? Andy cupped his hands over his ears to smother their arguing, rocking backward and forward with the rhythm of his gum chewing. *What would Ellie do if she were here?*

But as hard as he pressed his hands to his ears, he could still hear their voices.

How could you … Where were you when I … Bastard … Bitch … You don't know what it's like to … You're wrong … Look at what you've done …

Andy felt, rather than heard, the crash from inside. Something thrown, broken. He jumped up and ran into the house, the screen door squealing shut behind him. Something clenched tighter as he ran toward the kitchen, a spring winding taut with each step, waiting to release.

'Jesus,' cried his father, 'you bloody nearly killed me, you bitch!'

Frank Walker lay propped clumsily against one of the kitchen chairs, probing his head for damage. Blood streamed down his face. Andy's mother stood over him, frying pan raised in warning. *This was the badshit at its worst.* Andy's jaw clenched, the image burning into his memory. The pathetic sight of his father on the floor. His mother, standing like a Titan, stronger than he had ever seen her before. The mess. Their tidy Friday-night clothes ripped and smeared with Frank Walker's blood.

Andy could feel the thing growing inside him, his senses suddenly sober and clear. Felt it leach out from every pore, his body no longer able to contain it. The thing was pure, and strong, frightening and reassuring at the same time, its strength carrying him forward. And when it was out, Andy knew it instantly. It had a name.

The very essence of the badshit … *Rage …*

Andy kicked the chair supporting his father out from under him and Frank Walker collapsed to the cold lino. '*What are you doing?*' Andy shouted, spit forming at the corner of his mouth. 'Look at you! Look at both of you!' His mother reeled back, almost tripping, her glazed eyes confused at her boy's outburst. She lowered the frying pan and Andy tore it from her hands. He smashed it repeatedly on the kitchen table until the Laminex top began to splinter. 'You see,' he spat. 'You see how dumb it looks?'

He flung the pan as hard as he could at the kitchen window, ripping the curtains and shattering the glass. He stood before them in silence, his chest heaving as he stepped back toward the hallway feeling strangely liberated. Stopping to assess the damage, he stared with a newfound clarity into the stunned faces of his parents. 'You must stop,' he said. 'Don't you see? You're killing each other!'

He clenched his eyes shut and waited. The silence remained and in time the rage subsided, receding inside his body. Tired and confused, he shuffled outside to the front step. So familiar, he thought, sitting there alone. Cupping his hands to his face he felt his body quivering, realising what stopped them fighting was his rage. He wondered whether the badshit that cursed his family was finally inside him as well. And like a cold, hard slap in the face, Andy realised he was now his parents' guardian.

Exhausted, he let himself fall back onto the veranda's boards and stared into the Milky Way. And like an old friend, there was Sputnik, gliding across the heavens, its light cutting across the tail of Scorpius before fading into the northeast.

14

It was the first time I recognised the rage, but it left me feeling confused. Was it a strength? A weakness? Was it something I developed in Ellie's absence – a shield? Or worse, was it living in me all along? I remember the fear, a burning question. Was the badshit genetic, no different to brown eyes and dark hair? Was it unavoidable?

IT was eight-thirty in the morning, the taste of breakfast's French toast in his mouth, his head still nursing the lingering remnants of his first hangover. Friday night had cast its shadow over the whole weekend, so when Sunday arrived, fragments of rage remained in Andy like the silence in the house. It left him considering Toby's warnings, but none of it made sense. Why should *he* turn his back on the privileges just because Toby said so?

Sitting on the front steps, he fidgeted with the laces of his canvas gym boots, fingernails dirty from digging for worms, his cane fishing basket and bamboo rod lying at his feet. His neck itched from the woollen jumper he'd slipped on over his T-shirt. *So where is he?* Kyle was half an hour late.

Last night he had dreamt that the cat he'd saved from the river years ago stood before a fresh kill by the water, thanking him for saving its life, and telling him the debt would be repaid. Andy shook his head. *Crazy dream*, he decided. By nine o'clock, he thought Kyle wasn't coming.

Today, of all days, he needed to get away.

The guilty silence inside the house was more stressful than the fighting, like a bomb quietly ticking. Andy turned to carry his gear back to his room when a car horn sounded. Looking over his shoulder, he saw Kyle pulling up with a speedboat in tow. The name painted on the boat's polished timber bow read *Night-Mare*, its white letters written across the silhouette of a sprinting horse.

Nightmare, Andy mouthed.

Kyle stepped out of the car and began walking up the path. 'Hey there, Stargazer. Sorry I'm late,' he said. 'Had to run past the shop first and check on the stocktake.' He was wearing dark blue swimming shorts and a burnt-orange windcheater. Andy thought it strange – without his trademark bowtie he didn't seem like Kyle at all.

Andy met him halfway. 'I was beginning to think you weren't coming.'

Kyle took Andy's basket and rod. 'Uh uh, no way,' he replied walking to the boat. 'There's a mighty bass upriver with my name on it.' Kyle tied the gear down beside an Esky that rattled with bottles when he bumped it. Andy examined the boat. It was a timber clinker-built inboard, its chromed air filter exposed above the engine cover. He imagined the sound when that baby fired up.

As Andy sat in the car, he remembered bonfire night when Kyle drove past his house. He touched the dashboard and breathed in the smells of leather and car polish. It was so clean inside. Kyle stared in at him through the open window. 'Aren't you going to say goodbye to your folks?'

'No,' he said, 'it's okay.'

'Rough night?' Kyle asked.

'Same shit, different night.'

Kyle sat behind the wheel and turned over the engine. 'Okay,' he said, 'no goodbyes.'

The car pulled out as Andy noticed his mother standing behind the nylon curtains, not much more than a shadow. Their eyes briefly met, but Andy couldn't wave or smile. Instead he stared ahead, a surge of sadness rolling over him before he closed his eyes. *My parents' guardian*, he thought. *Surely this isn't how it's supposed to be.*

They drove along the Driftway's terraced marshlands to the southwest boat ramp above the Shallows, where Andy had to wind up his window against the smell of stagnant water. At the ramp, Kyle waited on two other boats before backing *Night-Mare* into the river. The car and trailer in the car park, Kyle pushed off and started the engine twenty feet from the bank. It coughed repeatedly, then, with a plume of blue smoke and the stink of burnt fuel, the V8 came to life. It roared uncertainly with every rev before settling into an arrogant don't-mess-with-me idle that promised power at the touch of the throttle.

Andy sat back in his seat as the boat's bow lifted out of the water with a surge. It cut through the Salesbury River, Andy's weight pressing into the leather as a wake of white water trailed behind. As they sped past the other two boats, Andy realised he'd never been this far upriver before. Orchards gave way to the grasslands at the foothills, and grazing meadows soon became empty, steep and rocky as they neared the gorge. He felt as if the mountains were about to swallow them. Then he saw the white cat, big and shabby, making her way along the ledges of the steepening banks, a litter of six tabbies following her, one just as white as her, perhaps heir to the throne. Andy smiled when she made eye contact with him, recalling last night's dream. *So you're still out there, old girl.*

Kyle pulled back on the throttle and *Night-Mare's* bow dipped into the water as they slowed.

'What's up?' Andy asked.

'The Narrows,' Kyle replied, standing to see over the windshield. The boat crawled, the hull vibrating.

Andy stood, resting his chin on the lip of the windshield. Here the river squeezed from its eighty-yard width through Blackwater to a swifter ten yards. A deep gorge opened to their right, its creek having deposited coarse sandbanks and river stones over generations to create this slender passage. Andy could smell the she-oaks that clung to the sandbanks as Kyle nudged the idle speed forward to keep *Night-Mare* steady against the increased current. The channel appeared dangerous, large rocks standing sentinel inches below the surface on the edges, leaving little more than three boats' width of clean water between them. *Are we really going through there?* he wondered, noticing that the two boats following remained cautiously behind.

'What now?' asked Andy.

Kyle craned his neck to see as far up the channel as he could. 'Not a problem,' he said. 'Done it a million times.'

Andy realised the river was actually falling through the Narrows, and that he was looking at the body of water backed up on the other side.

'How?' Andy asked, his eyes wide and cautious.

'Carefully,' said Kyle. '*Very* carefully.'

The sense of adventure wasn't lost on Andy.

'I'm going to go as slow as I can up the centre,' Kyle said, cutting a line in the air with his open hand to demonstrate. 'But I'll need you to be ready with that bargepole.' He nodded toward the wooden pole on his left. 'Just in case we drift toward the edge.'

Andy didn't have to think about it. 'Okay,' he said unhooking the pole from the portside gunwale.

'You'll have to be careful,' said Kyle. 'Although I'll be throttling up through here, we won't be going all that fast until we break through the clean water on the other side. You understand?'

'Got it.'

Andy clambered over the windshield and onto the forward deck, eventually straddling his legs each side of the bow before giving Kyle the thumbs up.

Gradually, *Night-Mare*'s engine began to roar as it cut into the Narrows current, murky shapes beneath the surface inching greedily toward its keel. Andy nudged the bow away from the rocks, the water rushing past, the boat reverberating with the illusion of tremendous speed.

The upward passage soon began to expand as the boulders and sandbanks subsided. Andy relaxed, feeling like an explorer cutting new ground as he rested the bargepole across his legs. Up here, the water had a gentler, glassy appearance and the mountain's rugged escarpment reflected on the river's surface. Dropping the revs, Kyle circled back to take a look at where they'd passed.

'Shit a brick,' said Andy, his heart racing.

'If you thought that was fun,' said Kyle, 'wait till the trip back down.' He placed a cigarette in his mouth, patting his shorts for his lighter. He took a box of matches from the dashboard when he couldn't find his Zippo.

They sat quietly for a moment, enjoying their victory over the river while watching the other boats turn back downstream. Andy noticed one of the skippers tip his hat to Kyle.

'The chicken shits are turning back,' said Andy, waving away a veil of Kyle's smoke.

'Yep, seems we have the place to ourselves.'

As they travelled upriver, Andy felt a sense of peace. But when he looked over at Kyle, he noticed that hollow expression he'd seen on Friday night. He watched Kyle stare at his hands on the wheel, his brow creasing as he raised one palm to his face, studying it closely.

'Kyle?' Andy's voice was measured, calm. 'Kyle? You okay?'

Kyle blinked, and slowly looked back over the windscreen at the river course ahead, both hands clutching the wheel again. 'What?' he said without expression, wiping his hands down his shirt. He looked over at Andy, meeting his stare. 'You say something, Stargazer?' He flicked his cigarette over the side unfinished as he pressed lightly on the throttle.

'I thought there was something wrong.'

'Nah,' Kyle said dismissively, his hand drifting to where his bowtie should be. 'I get a little distracted sometimes.' He smiled reassuringly. 'Now let's go get us that bass.'

15

I began to relate more to Toby, probably because he came into my life around the same time I found out about Albert, but it was also the way he looked out for me. I wish I'd known how much he was torn between looking after his mother and looking after me.

TOBY Broughton sat on the edge of the Greenways loading dock staring across the vacant car park. He watched as two boys rode their bikes around the parking bays, kicking at an empty cardboard carton each time they passed. Toby sighed heavily, trying to remember a time when his Sundays were like theirs. He looked at his hands: old man's hands; the faint residue of nicotine stains beginning to appear on the tips of his fingers, the taste of his last cigarette growing stale, the craving for another already growing. *God*, he thought, *what have I become?*

As the boys on their bikes began doing lazy figure-eights, Toby's thoughts turned to his mother. Her hair had all but fallen out now, a bright floral scarf wrapped around her head. Her skin was the colour of old parchment, and her eyes were glazed from the painkillers, her body frail, gaunt. Toby closed his eyes, attempting to remember when she was well, but it grew difficult, like a dream fading with every passing hour after waking. He couldn't remember her smile, dwindling like the dream itself, just a shadow on his mind.

It was late in the morning, nearly eleven he saw as he glanced at his watch face which distorted as he resisted tears with the only weapon he had left: anger. Toby felt a deep self-loathing. *They'd be way past the Narrows by now*, he decided. *Please, God. Just let him fish today*. His mind raced with mixed thoughts of friendship and betrayal; of the role Kyle had placed him in. The hunter's decoy; the pampered beast that leads the others to … to Kyle's stupid Game. But he couldn't do it any more.

The boys on their bikes progressed to tight circles around an abandoned shopping trolley, their laughter high and shrill.

'Be careful, Andy,' he whispered.

16

I remember looking for the badshit in my own eyes that morning before the fishing trip. I've never looked so deeply into the mirror, so carefully, searching for that glimmer. I also remember the sense of relief when I couldn't find it. Yet soon I would recognise it in someone other than my father, and I'd know the badshit was legion.

'BE careful there, Andy.' Kyle let him take the wheel at half speed. 'Keep her out of the weed.' He pointed to the shadowy patches along the banks. 'That stuff can hide all sorts of obstacles. Rocks, logs, you name it. Keep her just left of centre and we'll stay in the deep water.'

Andy adjusted his course.

'That a boy.' Kyle relaxed into the seat. 'How about you open her up a knot or two now.'

The V8 growled as Andy's hand nudged the throttle, the bow lifting an inch or two as the breeze brushed through his hair.

'You're doing fine,' Kyle said over the engine sound.

Andy felt strangely liberated, Friday night drifting away with every mile beyond the Narrows. The further they travelled into the mountain pass, the steeper the sides of the gorge became, rugged in its stone-hard climb to the wide expanse of sky. Weathered sandstone towered above the deep green of the river. Giant grey gums clung to the sides, their thick roots clenching to each crevice like desperate claws upon the refuge of fern-covered terraces. Every sound *Night-Mare* made echoed off the cliff face as its wake licked at the rocky edges through acres of weed.

Kyle shifted to sit up on the back of the seat. 'Okay,' he said, reaching for the wheel, 'I'll take it from here. We're coming to a great fishing spot to our right.' Kyle slid across behind Andy as they made the transfer, the boat dropping to an idle on approach.

The eastern wall had slipped years ago, leaving a yawning sandstone scar where a mound of rock and twisted deadfall collected at the gorge's base. A wide half-moon-shaped basin formed the opposite bank where a narrow gully opened into the river. A thin sandy beach marked the rim bathed in sunlight, and a mountain stream spilled beneath the border of lantana and ghost gums.

'That's Frenchmans Basin,' said Kyle. 'Nice, huh?'

'I've never seen anything like it,' Andy said.

Kyle edged the boat as close to the deadfall as he could. 'Take the grappling anchor from the forward sponson and drop it over the bow. Make sure you tie it to the nose-cleat first.'

Locating the three-pronged anchor, Andy tied it off before dropping it over the edge.

Kyle switched off the engine.

There was an awkward silence before the river sounds began creeping through the curtain of tranquillity. Water slapped at the boat's hull, the anchor rope creaking taut against the flow as a gentle breeze whispered past Andy's ears. He could even hear the wind in the escarpment like a gentle rustling in the heavens. An eagle cried out, Andy searching the sky to where the creature circled into the thermals. The sun was climbing too, breaching the top of the gorge where blue sky touched the grey-shaded stone.

'Break out the fishing gear, Stargazer, and I'll show you how to catch a bass or two.'

Andy shuffled over into the observer's seat where he handed Kyle the rods and fishing baskets. Moments later they sat on the engine cover preparing their tackle, Andy dipping into his tin of garden worms.

'Nope', Kyle said shaking his head. 'No bait.' He passed the boy a rusted Capstan Tobacco tin, its contents rattling. 'Here, trout lures. About the only way to catch bass up here. Go ahead, take a look.'

Opening the tin, Andy counted a dozen or so assorted lures. 'Which one should I use?' he asked. 'They're all different.'

Kyle considered the sun's position for a moment. 'We'll be in full sun in a little while. Why don't you try a chrome one.'

Andy copied everything Kyle did before taking up his place at the stern, their bare feet dangling in the water as the sun peeked over the edge of the gorge. 'Watch,' Kyle said, casting out behind the boat. The lure hit the surface ten feet from the boat with a plop, the line quickly extending as the current took up the slack. The lure danced within inches of the surface, the light reflected off its sides.

'The fish get in under the rocks and deadfall, see,' Kyle explained, slowly winding in past the rocks. 'You've got to tease them out with something they need; something they want. It's like life. When you know what something wants then you can generally lure it right where you want it. It's all about the lure, Andy. The bait.'

Andy watched the chrome shimmering.

'See,' said Kyle. 'See how it looks like a silver guppy swimming around out there. You can't see the hook, can't see the trap, just that silver belly swimming by. It's food to the bass. It's what he needs. And the bass is no different to you or me, Andy. It can't fight its instincts.'

Behind the flickering lure a foot or so of silver-grey shadow drifted out from under the rock fall. Teasing the line with his finger, Kyle slowly inched it in. *Can't deny what it needs.* The shadow drew closer, considering the bait, then struck.

'*Got ya!*' cried Kyle, letting the reel run. 'He'll want to take it in under the rocks,' he said winding it back a little. 'But we don't want that.' He stood, steadying himself while working the rod. 'Grab the net, Andy.' The strained line danced in all directions with the desperate efforts of the fish, Kyle winding until the creature's grey side flickered in the sun's rays. 'Okay, okay, sweep him up.'

Andy scooped up a portion of river water into a bucket, then took the catch net from the back seat to retrieve the fish, its weight bending the bamboo handle as he lifted it in over the boat's side. Kyle grasped the catch to pull out the hook, the fish wriggling in a desperate act to pull free from his grip before he let it slip into the bucket.

'There you go,' he said, slapping Andy on the shoulder, his breathing laboured. 'Now you try it, Stargazer.'

They fished for two hours, catching five bass between them.

*

By mid afternoon Kyle pulled up anchor, started the boat and steered toward Frenchmans Basin. *Night-Mare* parted the weed where its bow slipped onto the sand, gently stopping at the western end of the beach.

'I just love it up here,' Kyle said, surveying the area. He cut the engine, absorbing the calm.

Andy stared in silence.

They stepped out of the boat onto the beach and set a travel rug in the shade of a gum sapling where gnarled mistletoe overhung the beach high in the branches. The sun was warm and comforting for the time of year. Andy peeled off his jumper and threw it in the boat.

While Kyle unpacked the Esky, Andy ran across the shallow stream to explore the length of deserted beach, lantana forming an impenetrable wall at its perimeter. On his return, he found a piece of driftwood and threw it out into the basin, pausing a moment to watch it float. Although he couldn't say why, he began to feel uneasy, suddenly thinking of the big brother he never had, of Albert. And of Toby, whispering the words *be careful*.

Kyle called, waving a sandwich in the air.

Shaking the troubled feeling off, Andy ran back. Reaching Kyle, he found him sitting on the blanket with a bottle of beer in his hand, the Esky open beside him.

'Help yourself,' he said, chewing a mouthful of sandwich and flicking through the latest copy of *Post*. He paused a moment to swallow. 'Oh, and here. I opened a beer for you.'

'Thanks,' said Andy taking a sandwich and the bottle from him. *God bless Greenways*, he thought. He sat cross-legged on the blanket. Thirsty, he washed down the first mouthful of food with his beer. The taste recalled Friday night, reminding him of his limitations. Just the one today, he decided.

The afternoon lingered. The sun crept across the sky, slowly casting shadows from the eastern wall of rock. No one passed the basin in that time, not so much as a canoe, the solitude becoming isolating – uneasy.

Andy rolled over, his back to Kyle, who lay soaking up the last of the sun. As Andy glanced at the beach and its wall of lantana and cliffs beyond, he heard it again, somewhere far off like a memory: *be careful*. Andy closed his eyes for a moment, the beer making his head swim worse than it had on Friday night. He felt lost, far from home, even though getting away this morning was all he could think of. He didn't know why, but the place made him think of Kyle's tattoo. Maybe it was the beer … The world swam around him, a strange taste lingering in his mouth – he heard a voice call his name. Then the same voice saying, sorry, and suddenly he couldn't breathe.

17

*It was the first time I'd faced my mortality, too young,
my innocence stripped away in a single action. I'd never
been more afraid, suddenly remembering the Delroy
boy floating down to Blackwater, guided into my life,
into my arms, by the same river that had shepherded
me to Frenchmans Basin. Strange, but when I regained
consciousness that day, my first thought was of Toby.*

TOBY stood in Kyle's office, his eyes closed, listening to the muzak
piping through the empty store. His mind drifted, contemplating
his role in what was happening. *Find out about their home lives.
Give the information to Kyle. And ignore whatever happens next.*
His eyes jolted open with a start, his fist clenching the papers in
his hand. *I can't do it anymore!* He reached across to the panel
and turned off the sound. The only reason he'd turned it on that
morning was for company, a distraction. Placing the stocktake
sheets on the desk, he felt the hour pressing in, and he knew …
Knew Andy had played the Game by now. He couldn't feel sad any
more, a lifetime of sorrow used up in a few short years. But he still
had enough hate and anger left to burn.

   Yeah, burn … Burn, baby, burn …

Toby realised how well Kyle played the trust angle. He did it carefully, gently and patiently, until it came time to take what he needed. Then the wolf took over, and wolves knew nothing of tenderness. Trust is a tool, a weapon. Kyle knew about guilt too. Guilt and blame. He could play the Game with a kid and make him feel he was to blame for the whole thing, sending him away scared, fearful the world may find out and not understand.

Then there were those who never came back. The runaways, that's what the paper called them. That's what Kyle called them too. But – what if they hadn't run away? What if Kyle had something to do with their disappearances? That meant Toby did, too.

Composing himself with steady breaths, Toby straightened up the papers on Kyle's desk, his hands quivering, betraying the calm he tried to portray. He swallowed bile that burnt his stomach, clenching his jaw until it ached. The soft light gleamed off Kyle's Zippo on the desktop, catching his attention. Considering the potential in such a small flame, Toby held the lighter and flicked it to life, thinking how easy it would be to set fire to the building, the smell of burnt lighter fluid filling his nostrils. But could he stop there? Burn, baby, burn. Setting fire to every building on Main Street. Burn, baby, burn. Just like 1930, washing away each shadow, the flames flooding the darkness until there was only light. He closed his eyes again, imagining the sweet justice of it all, until the Zippo's heat became too much for his thumb, and he let the lighter slip through his fingers to the table.

The flame reminded him of his mother. For all the doctors did, she was still dying, her life flickering, waiting for death's breath to blow it out.

And the bills mounted.

And his own pain grew.

And … *and if she would just die, I wouldn't need this stinking job!*

18

Before I began these journals, I knew this would be the hardest thing to write about. That one moment, early in my life, that would shape the rest of it forever. Only when I realised what was happening, did Toby's scattered warnings make sense.

CONSCIOUSNESS trickled in with each laboured breath, nudging the heady dimness out, and his eyes opened slowly, cautiously. Andy's wrists cramped in painful spasms and he realised they were bound behind him. He tried to call out, but his throat felt dry and grating, each breath strained, as he slowly became aware of the loose cloth around his neck. Trying to focus, he was aware of the afternoon light, soft and filtered, void of detail. Then he made out the grey shape moving in front of him. *A face?* Fighting the pain in his wrists, he tried to compose himself, blinking to clear his vision before opening his eyes wide in an attempt to concentrate on the features before him. It took time, but the image became clear. It was Kyle.

A wave of panic rolled over him, and he tried to stand, failing, realising his legs were bound too at his ankles. He could feel his heart racing, each gasp hurting his throat more. *What has the bastard done to me?* he wondered. *What was in the beer?*

'Try not to move,' said Kyle, holding a cup of water to Andy's lips. 'Drink.'

Initially Andy wouldn't part his lips, but the sensation of cool water was too much to resist. He drank, sipping cautiously at first, then drawing deeply, easing the fire burning in his throat.

'Wha – What's going on?' Andy croaked.

'Relax,' he said. Andy recognised that distant expression, Kyle's face so close he could smell beer and tobacco on his breath. 'I know you're scared, but it's almost over.'

'What?' Andy said, his mind still groggy from the spiked beer, a headache forming behind his eyes. 'What's this all about?' He heard his own words slurred, the bitter taste of Kyle's poison still on his tongue.

Kyle's gaze was fixed on Andy's eyes. 'It's just a game,' he said. 'A game my father taught me.' He calmly straightened the cloth around Andy's neck like a scarf, brushing it flat against his throat where a thick knot was tied, then down across his chest like a father dressing his son for school. 'You ever hold your breath until you passed out?' he asked. 'You ever play that game with your friends, Andy? See who can hold their breath the longest?'

Andy shook his head, another surge of panic rushing up his spine.

'You ever watched a person's eyes as they pass out? It's like they're dying.' Kyle's hands fell back to each end of the cloth, clutching them firmly.

'Please don't,' whispered Andy, tears welling.

His bleak eyes peered into Andy's. 'Just one more time,' Kyle said, pulling the cloth tighter, the knotted piece pressing into Andy's throat, denying him air.

*

It was that moment when nothing else mattered, when the control of life and death lay in his hands – and his hands only. Kyle felt the usual fog engulf him in that moment, felt the cotton cloth press into his clenched fist. He saw the knot slide into the cavity of the boy's throat, heard the breath stop with the rush of blood flooding the boy's face. The eyes widened, white discs surrounding pin-prick pupils, staring back, pleading for air, for life. *Yes*, Kyle thought, *my choice.*

But the boy had little fight left in him, his pupils dilating quicker this time, filling with their blackness, the arch in his back not as pronounced as before. *It was better when they resisted.* Kyle maintained the same strain on the choker, knowing he still had time to save the boy's life. The knot was the key, all the pressure falling on one point, just enough to stop the flow of air without leaving any marks or bruising around the neck.

Then it happened, the moment of death taking hold, all expression gone, eyes deep pools of black oil, the body limp. *Live or die?* he wondered, then the fog lifted. The Game was over. It didn't always lift in time, but today it did, and he let the choker slip from his hands. He took a deep, controlled breath, as if for the boy, his eyes drawn from Andy's down to his own hands. The red mask lifted from Andy's face, and a gurgled gulp was drawn deep into starving lungs. The boy was alive, *his* choice, but the boy was alive.

'Stargazer,' he said, lightly slapping Andy's face. Kyle tried to summon his everyday face, but it was difficult. 'Hey, Stargazer.'

Reaching for the pocket knife he kept in the Esky, he pulled out the short blade and sliced the wide tape binding the boy's feet. Andy's eyelids flickered, and he began to weep as Kyle reached behind and cut the tape binding his wrists. With a sob, Andy fell to his side, his hands clutching his throat as he drew in precious air.

It's over, Kyle thought, abruptly wondering where his father ended and he began.

✳

Desperation filled his body, and Andy plunged back into consciousness, panting, a wave of pain surging through his brain, his eyes gripped by the light as he rolled onto his stomach, face in the sand, grit in his teeth. Lifting himself to his hands and knees, he instinctively backed away, crawling like a wounded animal toward the water, tear trails streaking his cheeks, his eyes fixed, yet unfocused, on the wolf tattoo. Oddly, Kyle appeared frail, the strength that held Andy captive now wilted and spent. His strained breath settling, Kyle sluggishly opened his eyes, watching Andy retreating toward the water.

'Where are you going?' Kyle asked, a bemused smirk forming.

Andy slid into the water unable to speak. It was cold, but cleansing. Inching in, his legs parted the riverweed as the dead man's fingers caressed his flesh. He paused neck deep, letting his face submerge to wash the sand from his eyes and hair, drawing a mouthful of water to spit out the grit from his teeth as he resurfaced.

All his life, Andy had sought refuge upon the river, and today was no exception. Almost too cold to stay in, it enveloped him like a mother's arms. Trembling, his skin drew around his muscles, but he couldn't leave. *So what happens now?* he wondered, the river seeming ten times wider, its cliffs a hundred times higher, and the tangled lantana a thousand times thicker. He was trapped, and realised the trap had closed the moment he boarded *Night-Mare*.

So what happens now? The question lingered like a stuck record. Surely Kyle couldn't take him home and forget about all this? Surely he knew Andy would tell his parents.

But Andy could only imagine one answer. *Kyle has to kill me!* A guttural moan escaped his throat, his heart racing as the picture formed. Kyle couldn't let him go home. Andy felt the weed brush his flesh, suddenly feeling as if the basin was full of dead boys. He felt like throwing up. There was no comfort to be found in the water any more, but Andy feared the beach. He imagined the bodies of the dead weighed down with river stones, reaching up, surrounding him, keen for another companion.

He found the strength to drag himself on shore, stumbling across the sand to find shelter in a cavity in the lantana. He watched Kyle lying on the sand and noticed the melon-sized river stone by the blanket, the thought suddenly clear, bringing with it a strange sense of comfort and empowerment.

Kill him! Before he kills you.

Andy watched as Kyle sat up; watched him take a cigarette from the pocket of his shirt and place it between his lips. His hands quivered as he shook his head in mild disgust before climbing onto the boat. Straddling the bow, he cupped his hands over either side of his face like a man adjusting a mask, before they fell back to his lap. 'Why don't you come out of there,' he said.

Andy shook his head.

'Come on out,' he repeated, 'it's over.'

'No,' spat Andy. 'You'll kill me!'

Kyle frowned as he lit his cigarette. 'Come on out, Stargazer. No one's going to hurt you.'

'Don't call me that!' Andy shouted, cringing at the pain in his throat, the hairs on the back of his neck standing tall, anger rising to the surface. 'Why, Kyle? Why did you do that to me, you bastard?' Fear was the only thing stifling the badshit, the rage, and the power that he needed from it.

Kyle stared, Andy recognising a strange hint of remorse emerging in his eyes before shaking it off. 'Because, sometimes …' he looked away momentarily, '… sometimes I have to.' He brushed a hand over his tattoo.

Andy's body began to tremble, mouthing words that escaped as a mere whisper.

Kyle jumped down to the sand. 'Think of it as a game. That's all. Now, dry yourself off. We're going.'

Andy didn't understand.

'Come on, I'm taking you home.'

To Andy's astonishment, Kyle kept his distance. He packed the gear while Andy dried himself down, even started to whistle like he did back at the store, as if nothing had happened. Whistling louder now, he untied the rope, pulled himself on board and started the engine.

'Push us off and jump in,' said Kyle, standing behind the wheel.

Andy looked at him with a defiance that came from deep down. 'You know I'll tell.' His stomach turned and tightened, the badshit making its way to the surface. His shield.

'No you won't,' Kyle said calmly. 'Now push us off.'

'*I will!*' he shouted, his fists clenched, kicking sand at the boat. 'I'll tell, Kyle! So *fucking* help me, I'll tell the world.' The badshit had arrived, his hands shovelling sand, throwing it at Kyle and the boat in a frenzy. His chest heaved in frustrated rage, his attention drawn to the river stone near his lantana refuge. He leapt at it, his face flushed, lifting it above his head as he paused over *Night-Mare*'s lacquered bow.

Kyle sighed heavily as he turned the engine off. There was something oppressive about the silence this time. He sat on the back of the seat, his calm feeding Andy's rage. He reached into the Esky to pull out a beer as Andy's arms began trembling with the weight of the stone.

'Go ahead, Andy, if it'll make you feel better.' He opened the bottle and drank deeply. 'But listen carefully … Everything is all right now.' He wiped his mouth. 'It's over, okay? I'm not going to hurt you. I told you, it was just …' he searched the air for the right words, 'a game.'

'There were other kids!' Andy said, no longer able to hold the stone, dropping it in the water as the surge of rage subsided. 'What happened to them, huh?'

Kyle took another swallow of beer and stared into Andy's eyes. 'They're okay,' he said. 'They decided not to come back to the store, that's all.' He shook his head. 'I didn't hurt them,' Kyle said slowly, before fixing his stare at the water. 'This aside,' he said quietly, gesturing around the basin, 'I did everything for them. You know that.'

'Everything? What the *fuck* is everything!' Andy cried, the words echoing off the canyon walls. 'The privileges? Half-price cigarettes? A few fucking dollars in the hand just so you can play some sick game?'

'You don't know what's going on up here,' Kyle said, tapping at his temple, blood rising to his face before calming himself with a few deep breaths. 'And with a bit of luck, you never will.' He composed himself. 'Now get in the boat or I'll leave you here to rot.' He started the engine again, throwing the bottle over the side. That's when Andy recognised it: Kyle had dealt with the badshit too, somewhere in his own dark past.

Andy looked away, peering around at Frenchmans Basin, realising he had no choice. He pushed the boat off the beach and clambered onto the bow, climbing into the front seat to sit as far from Kyle as he could.

'Go ahead. Tell the world, if that's what you want,' Kyle continued calmly. 'You know I'll go to prison – maybe.' He shrugged. 'Tell your parents when you get home, but – tell them what? I mean, I can divulge shit too, Andy. Shit you won't like. Shit you wouldn't want your friends knowing about.'

'It doesn't mean they'll believe you,' Andy said between clenched teeth.

Kyle steered the boat toward Blackwater. 'Oh, I know it and you know it, but I'm wondering about your friends once that seed is sown.' He inched the throttle forward. 'Kids can be cruel, you know.' He relaxed back into the leather seat and smiled, one arm resting over the side of the boat. 'And let's face it, Andy. Fear goes both ways.'

'What do you mean?'

'I mean just that. This thing is over, so what scares you more? Me getting away with it? Or your family and friends finding out some sick and twisted version of the truth? And I've seen enough of humanity's dark side to spin some pretty sick shit about what happened up here, Andy. Even if they believe your version of events, there'll always be an element of doubt.'

A tear ran down Andy's cheek, the breeze quickly drying it. What he wanted most was for his mother to hold him and tell him everything would be all right.

*

When they reached the boat ramp, the drugged beer had worn off and Andy's head was clear but aching, his mouth dry but still tasting of Kyle's poison. He reached for his fishing gear. 'I'll walk from here,' he mumbled.

Kyle held his wrist before he could lay a hand on his stuff. 'Now what would your parents think of me if I didn't take you home?' His grip was firm.

Andy felt he had no choice and went with him to the car so Kyle could tow *Night-Mare* out of the water. The way Kyle slipped back into his public persona made Andy mad, his knuckles turning bone-white on the chrome door handle. He wanted to jump from the car as they drove back down the Driftway, still angry enough to tell his parents despite what Kyle had told him. *I'll take my chances*, he thought. But the wave of bravado dissolved as soon as Kyle pulled up outside Andy's house. The driveway was empty, the house shut tight, his dad's car gone. *No one home.* Andy's heart sank.

19

Most mornings you wake and never know what kind of day you're going to have. But then there are those other days, when the feeling of trepidation makes you want to stay in bed.

ANOTHER day had passed, and despite the drawn blinds in his bedroom, Andy could feel daylight's presence waning into evening as he lay on his bed, his transistor radio playing softly from the bedside table. He had skipped school for the past week, remaining in his room most afternoons and evenings, self-exiled from the world outside. But he felt so alone, the secret so heavy. *Fear goes both ways*, kept echoing in his head, regardless of his attempts at distraction. He surrounded himself with comics, his astronomy books and Airfix plastic models of rockets and planes; familiar things from before the Game. But something was missing, small, old, quietly ticking away – Grandpa's watch.

Torn at first, his decision to remain silent grew easier to bear every day, deciding Mum and Dad couldn't cope with what had happened. Easier because it was over, yet the fear was still inside, coming to him in wakeful dreams of suffocating, of being trapped, of drowning, its union with the badshit evident in how easily his fear turned to rage.

He rolled onto his side, the dim light barely revealing the spot on the night table where he usually placed the watch. Groaning, he sat on the edge of his bed, accidently kicking over the pile of comics he kept within reach. Staring up at him was *The Hulk*, green face contorted in a picture of rage. 'You wouldn't like me when I'm angry,' the voice bubble proclaimed. Andy gave a painful laugh. Is that the face of the badshit? He switched on the nearby lamp and stepped over to the mirror, head raised, chin extended to check the bruising around his neck. It was gone. There'd been surprisingly little anyway, and when his mother had asked about the minor discolouring, he'd told her he'd walked into the rope tying the boat to the beach.

Although they knew something was wrong, Andy was aware they couldn't fathom its severity. All he wanted to do was leave Greenways and never return, hoping that would fix everything, but his father was pressuring him about the board money, and his grandpa's watch remained in the locker. Worse, Kyle had phoned Andy's mother through the week to check on his wellbeing. That's when he realised – *this bastard knows what he's doing!*

Returning to his bed, Andy let himself fall into the ruffled doona, his feet touching the three-day-old newspaper. He rolled off it, brushing it to the floor. Two items of news filtered into his bunker that week: President Kennedy committed the United States to landing a man on the moon before the end of the decade – he'd taped the clipping to the wall with all his other space-race articles; but also, he'd read in the obituaries that Toby's mother had passed away. He thought about Toby's pain, feeling closer to him, but unable to face him, his own anger wanting to blame Toby for what had happened. *Anger and fear make strange bedfellows*, he thought.

He had to end this. Stop the fear before it stopped him. *Tomorrow*, he thought. *Once and for all.* He looked again at where Grandpa's watch should be then turned off the lamp.

*

He stood outside Greenways staring at the glass doors in the mid-morning light; the words *Air Conditioned* parted each time someone walked through. Studying his reflection, he saw the pain in his eyes staring back, pleading. How can I go back in there? His stomach tightened, holding his breath as the doors opened yet again, expecting to see Kyle smiling like nothing had happened, his row of pens chattering to that damn bowtie. There he is. That's the boy who played the Game. He exhaled, nodding politely to a frail woman with blue-grey hair pulling a vinyl shopping cart. He was unsure about a lot of things, but not this. He needed to finish things up, needed to go in there and get Grandpa's watch; leave no reason to return.

'You gonna stand there cluttering up the footpath all day, young Walker?'

The voice startled him. Andy turned to see Sergeant Adams and Lonesome crossing the street toward him. He paused. His mouth was open, but no words came out. *Tell him!* the anger inside cried out. *No!* shouted the fear. *He won't believe you.*

'Well, Walker?'

Andy tore himself from the policeman's stare, his attention drawn to Lonesome, who sat beside his master with the same inquisitive look.

'I ... I'm going into the store,' was all he could say. The doors opened again, and once more Andy expected Kyle; his heart rate rising once more.

✳

Red watched the boy enter the building, looking down at Lonesome for confirmation of what he was thinking. There it was again. That spark gone from a boy's eyes. He took his notepad from his breast pocket, licking the tip of the short pencil he kept between the pages. *That same look,* he wrote beside Andy's name. Staring up at the sign over the door he added: *Greenways.*

Replacing the pad, he buttoned his pocket and whistled quietly over his tongue, the signal for Lonesome to follow him. *Unfinished business,* he thought. They began the walk back toward the station house when he saw Burrows driving the paddy wagon past, looking bored and restless behind the wheel. He felt sorry for the young constable. At that age, they all wanted to see action. But it was unlikely here. He felt the weight of the notepad in his pocket and remembered.

Some of the worst cases in his career were preceded by silence.

*

Andy made straight for his locker, his heart racing faster. Once he had the watch, Kyle could throw him out. It wouldn't matter. His stare fixed on the floor, avoiding eye contact, he ran into another boy rounding the corner to the loading dock.

'Shit!' he spat, looking up. Then, 'Toby?' His heart sank further.

Toby stared into Andy's eyes and recognised the pain. 'Andy. I'm – Look, I'm so sorry –'

'You should have told me,' Andy said, trying to walk around him.

Toby grabbed Andy's arm. 'I know, and I tried,' he said desperately. 'You have to believe me.' His eyes welled with tears. 'I tried but – My mother, you see. I needed the money. You know that, don't you?'

'I know,' Andy whispered, head bowed. 'And I read about your mother's … about her …'

'Death,' Toby finished. 'It was always gonna happen, Andy.' He let go of Andy's arm. 'I don't expect you to understand, but it's a relief. She's not in pain anymore.'

'I'm sorry, but it doesn't change anything. You should have told me about Kyle. About the Game.'

'Don't hate me,' Toby whispered. 'Look,' he said reaching into his shirt pocket. He pulled out a folded piece of paper. 'It's a letter,' he said, 'telling everything about Kyle and his bloody privilege system, his shitty Game. I spent all last night getting it right.'

'A letter? What are you going to do with it?'

'I've got a plan.' He glanced around to see who was in earshot, then guided Andy to the door of Kyle's office. 'I'm going to set something up. Something that'll expose Kyle and have him locked away forever.' Toby laughed, wiping away tears as he opened the office door and stepped inside. He pulled the long black phone cord from its socket shattering plaster from the wall. 'Go,' said Toby. 'Go get Kyle! He's out on the loading dock.'

Andy felt breathless. He couldn't face Kyle … Or could he? Yet if he was ever going to strike back, it was now. Suddenly he didn't feel so alone. He turned to run, briefly considering collecting his watch from the locker first, but Toby's sense of urgency was too great.

'Hey, Andy.'

He turned back. 'Yeah?' That's when he noticed something different in his friend's eyes. And it struck him. *Even after his mother's death, he was happy.*

'I just want to say thanks.' He smiled. 'You know, for being my friend.'

Andy prayed enough of Toby's bravado had rubbed off on him to go through with this. He found Kyle standing at the dock, his back to Andy as he signed off a delivery docket, the truck driver taking back his clipboard and tipping his cap before climbing back into his cab to drive away. Looking nervously at his feet, Andy reassured himself he'd be fine. Nothing could happen here.

Kyle turned, leaning against the pallet of canned soups as he checked the inventory list. He looked up, straightening his posture when he saw Andy. He looked every bit the store manager in his white shirt and black bowtie.

'Andy,' Kyle said, 'you're back. I didn't think –'

'Not for long, Mr Tucker.' He heard the tremor in his voice, wondering if Kyle could too.

'Please,' said Kyle, gesturing Andy to step closer. He glanced around to see who might be watching, Andy recognising a glimmer of the badshit surfacing for a moment. 'Come on over and we'll talk about this.'

Andy paused a moment, thinking of Toby. 'Sorry,' he said, recognising the opportunity. 'Not here. In private.'

Andy saw a spark of hope in Kyle's eyes. 'Sure,' he said. 'We'll talk in my office.'

Walking back, Andy's bravado faltered as they left the safety of the daylight on the open dock, a sudden wave of nausea weighing him down. But when they reached the office door, they stopped.

'That's odd,' Kyle said frowning. Hand paused on the handle, he watched as a shadow moved steadily back and forth along the gap under the door. Kyle stepped closer, listening for any footfalls on the other side, instincts bristling. Glancing at Andy, he appeared suddenly cautious, reluctant to open the door.

'That's probably Toby,' Andy finally said. 'He told me he wanted to talk to you about something.'

Kyle's expression turned to mistrust, his face taking on the expression of the predator, the badshit on the cusp of brimming over. 'Toby knows better than that,' he said. 'I don't like people in there when I'm not around.'

Andy shrugged. 'Sorry,' he said. 'I forgot to tell you.'

Kyle's lips pursed and Andy heard him mutter something under his breath. He threw open the door, where Andy could see inside. 'No! Oh … Nooooo!' Kyle howled, falling against the doorframe. '*No – no – no – no – fucking – nooooo!*'

The first thing Andy noticed was how gentle the movements were, yet the expression on Toby's face was the opposite – red and bloated, nothing gentle about it at all. Toby had hanged himself from an exposed roof beam, but Andy felt like *he* was the one suffocating, like in the Game. He fixed his eyes on his friend's swaying, twitching body, casting a shadow across the room.

Kyle's legs gave way. He crouched on the floor beating the doorframe with a clenched fist, 'You stupid, stupid kid,' he said.

Andy desperately shook Kyle's shoulders, adrenalin surging through his body, his instincts taking over. 'Shit, Kyle, help me,' he shouted. 'He might still be alive!'

Climbing onto Kyle's desk, Andy lifted his friend's limp body, a wheeze of escaping air coming from Toby's throat. '*Toby! Toby!*'

he yelled, but he didn't respond, his body a dead weight in Andy's arms.

Kyle stopped pounding the doorframe, his attention drawn to Andy's struggle.

'Kyle, please,' Andy shouted. 'You've got to help me!'

'Stupid boy,' Kyle whispered shaking his head.

'*Kyle!*' Andy screamed, kicking papers off the desk at him. He glared, watching as the colour drained from Kyle's face. Then, with a sudden burst of energy, Kyle stood and took Toby by the legs, lifting him.

'That's it,' said Andy reaching up to where the cord was tied. Toby's weight had pulled the knot too tight to undo with his fingers. 'Knife!' he yelled.

Straining to keep hold, Kyle reached into the desk drawer where he kept several box knives and handed one to Andy. It took heavy sawing to cut through the cord, Toby's body slipping over Kyle's shoulder. Struggling with the weight, Kyle gently placed Toby on the floor. Looking down, Andy noticed that the phone cord had nearly pierced Toby's flesh, and that his letter was protruding from his shirt pocket.

'Andy!' Kyle shouted, fumbling to loosen the cord. 'Checkout one – go out front and call an ambulance … Quickly!'

Andy ran through the storeroom to the light of the aisles, knocking a woman's trolley over. 'Hey!' she cried. He ignored her. Nudging the girl at the register aside – *Sally* her nametag read – he grabbed the phone's handset, his finger paused over the dial before realising he had no number to call. *How do you call an ambulance?* he wondered. It looked so easy on TV.

'What the hell are you doing?' Sally cried, snatching the handset from him. 'Are you crazy?'

'Ambulance!' he cried. 'Toby needs an ambulance.'

Sally's face grew pale. 'Oh, no,' she whispered, and dialled the emergency number.

When he knew she had gotten through, Andy ran back to where Kyle cradled Toby's body in the doorway, to tell him the ambulance was on its way – but realised it wouldn't help.

Kyle looked up into Andy's face, his eyes red, his cheeks wet. 'He's dead,' he said. He wiped his fallen tears from Toby's face. 'Stupid, stupid boy.'

Andy couldn't comprehend Kyle's remorse, not after seeing the worst he was capable of. How could those two personas share the same body? He wanted to tear Toby's body from Kyle's arms, but knew he couldn't. With the cord loosened from his throat, Toby appeared at peace. If it wasn't for the welt around his neck, he could have been sleeping. Then a note of alarm rose in Andy. *It's gone! The letter!* He scanned the floor. *Nothing!*

'There was a letter,' Andy said quietly, knowing it was a challenge.

'What?' asked Kyle, slowly peering up at him.

It was never far away, thought Andy. 'A letter,' he repeated, fighting to keep eye contact, 'in Toby's shirt pocket.'

Kyle's tears remained, but Andy recognised that they lingered within the eyes of the predator now. 'There – was – no – letter,' he announced clearly. 'Now get out of here.'

*

By evening's end, Andy sat on the pavement in front of the store, clutching his grandpa's watch. That's all I wanted, he told himself, the watch – not all this. His eyes stung from crying.

The front doors kept opening and closing before a crowd of onlookers. Word travels fast in a small town. First the ambulance trolley had come out, a white sheet covering the body. They moved quickly, through the open doors to where the ambulance had backed up to the entrance. Lonesome stood guard by the doors, Sergeant Adams coming and going, his eyes briefly making contact with Andy's throughout the turmoil. But the message was clear: *You're a part of this, aren't you?*

20

If I'd known Red had his suspicions, I might have done something earlier. But thinking back to those days with an adult's mind, it's difficult to remember how deep I wanted to bury that chapter of my life. I was only a kid, and sometimes, we lose touch with the child within.

SERGEANT Adams sat in the front seat of the police car, passing the last of his sandwich over his shoulder to Lonesome. The smell of dog wash from Lonesome's bath that morning filled the cab, leaving Red wondering which smelt worse: dirty dog, or clean one? He finished his Coke and let the empty bottle roll into the dip of the passenger seat next to him. Watching the Broughton boy's funeral from where he'd parked at the cemetery gates, he let a bubble of gas escape his lips. He wiped them with the crumpled napkin. Funerals were always sad, but the funeral of a child … The word *sad* didn't cut it.

He took his notepad out of his breast pocket, almost a ritual now, as he licked the tip of the pencil. First he flicked through his personal notes, not just on Toby Broughton's suicide, but anything relevant, always looking for a connection. Then his eyes fell on the last entry. *Andrew Walker … That same look … Greenways.* He circled the word *Greenways* heavily with the pencil until the lead broke under the pressure.

It made him wonder. Why did the Broughton boy end his life at Greenways? Why in Tucker's office? When someone takes their own life, the method and location are often significant; a message. And why leave no suicide note? Not on the body or back at his house. Something wasn't quite right.

Red clearly remembered the look in the Walker kid's eyes. Not so much for the expression that was there, but for the expression that was lost, that absence of innocence. And that manifestation was no stranger to Red, seeing it on other boys of the same age over the years. There was only one thing for it. Go back to the loose ends file. Check how many of the boys on his list worked at Greenways, or had a connection to it.

He started the engine, keen to drive away before the mourners did. Lonesome whined at the sound of the engine, squatting firmly on the back seat and resting his head on Red's shoulder.

Reflections

21

I remember first seeing Kyle's steamer chest on the day of my interview. I don't recall thinking anything sinister about it at the time, only that it reminded me of Ellie's glory box. Her future was stored in that camphor box, hopes and dreams neatly folded and stacked; but hopes and dreams played no part in Kyle's old trunk.

THE key turned in the lock with the protest of age. Kyle's grandfather had carried his meagre belongings in it from England to begin a new life in this country at the turn of the century. The trunk said more about the Tucker history than anyone outside could know. First his grandfather's, then his father's, and now his. He studied the imprints of time in its features. The rust, born of the Atlantic sea mists in its passage, all but dominating the flaking metal on the locks, edges and hinges. The leatherbound handles, worn and peeling from miles of cartage, the sweat of generations stained deep into the tattered hide. Each dent and scratch in the painted wooden panels, a mark in time, a milestone, a reminder of long journeys passed.

Kyle ran his fingers across the lip of the locks. 'Who's the big bad wolf now?' he whispered before opening the lid, drawing in the musty smell of secrets. He took Toby Broughton's suicide letter from the top drawer of his desk and placed it inside, on top of a bundle of newspaper clippings. He felt betrayed by Toby, his letter of lies painting him as a monster and wanting to tell the world. Staring into the chest, his heartbeat quickened, his breath shortened, the palms of his hands became moist again. Each item stored in the chest had its story, its history, each piece defining who Kyle Tucker had become; Toby's suicide letter was simply another chapter.

He sighed, closing the trunk and turning the key with a sense of resolve. Maybe that was the trunk's significance: not just a place to hide the truth, the trophies and mementoes, but a place to keep the very weight of the truth off his own shoulders.

Then why do I feel so tired of it all?

22

The act of rowing didn't come naturally to me, not right away, but the need to row did. I once saw a bumper sticker on an oarsman's car. It read: 'I row, therefore I am.' I didn't understand it at the time, but I do now.

SOME days were better than others after Toby's death. Andy read about the Blackwater Rowing Club's open day in *The Greater Western*. Held on the Sunday after the funeral, Andy made sure he was there. Following years of observing the crews on the river, now, more than ever, he needed to embrace something new, something he could call his own.

The building had a warm feeling about it. It had been there all his life, perched on the steep banks of the river above its dock, but he had never been inside. Perhaps it was that sense of belonging he'd been craving, he decided; of history and tradition. He lingered at the photographs on the wall, of champions past and present; at the trophy cabinet, reading the generations of names on each shield and plaque. There was a feeling of family here.

After exploring the clubhouse, he walked down to the registration desk in the boathouse, where a silver-haired man sat shuffling papers beside a small sign displaying the membership fee. Andy reached into his pocket and pulled out what money he had, barely making it with a shilling to spare. *That's it*, he thought with a sense of relief. Not because he had it, but because it was the last of his Greenways money. It felt good to get rid of it, like shifting blood money, like dumping something dirty.

The man glanced at Andy's fistful of coins and smiled, deep crows-feet wrinkles etched at the corners of his eyes from years of squinting at crews through the sun's glare. 'Welcome aboard, son,' he said. 'My name's Sam. Sam Mitchell. I'll be looking after you novices.'

*

Sam Mitchell watched the boy walk away; noticed the broad shoulders. A rower's build, he thought, and smiled. But there was more, that look in the kid's eyes that told Sam he wanted this badly. Why? It didn't matter to Sam. The whys always sort themselves out in time. His judgment of character had proved accurate over the years, and he could spot a natural born rower at a glance. Here was a kid who would benefit from the sport; a perfect platform for Sam's one perfect trick: building oarsmen.

He sat back into the rickety old chair and folded his arms, nodding his approval.

*

By the end of winter 1962, Andy had his regular crew.

There was Col Edwards, the oldest at eighteen, his stark blue eyes staring out from beneath sun-bleached hair and a tanned face, reminding Andy of the square-jawed characters in surfer movies. Col had his own car, a black 1941 left-hand-drive Dodge he claimed General MacArthur had driven during the war. Col had rowed for Kings College in his senior year. A solid build, he sat in the boat's two seat in front of Andy.

Sandy Thomas and Jock McMillan were friends outside of rowing. Andy liked them because they were funny. Jock was a stocky Scottish kid with a gruff wit and considered a sentence without a curse in it as incomplete.

Because of his height, Sandy sat in the three seat, usually humming under his breath while Jock called the shots from the stroke seat in front of them all. Despite his age, Jock had a good mind for tactics, timing and the big picture. Both boys were fifteen years old, leaving Andy – at fourteen – as the youngest oarsman in the club. Yet the baby of the crew remained their coxswain, Willy Jenkins. Under the official weight, eleven-year-old Willy had a sparrow's build that required him to carry compensation weights on race day.

Eventually the boys were issued a boat of their own. As rookies they didn't expect a new one, as the better crafts went to the senior crews. The boat's name, painted in faded gold along the bow, was *The Lady Beaumont*, in honour of a previous mayor's wife. The boat, old and heavy, had a wide keel that leaked until the timbers swelled in the water. But it was just the boat for a new crew, its wide girth allowing it to sit straight and balanced beneath a novice's unsteady oar.

With every mile rowed it was as if Andy's past drew further away. He still had the same issues with his parents, the badshit drifting in and out, yet every minute on the water meant another he didn't have to spend thinking about anything other than the pain in his arms and legs. He felt his confidence building. As the months rolled by, the boys' skill and technique improved, and by mid-season they were training with the main squad. Andy knew they weren't the most graceful crew on the river, but their times were improving every day.

Their boat hugged the bank during training as they desperately tried to row down the crew over their right shoulder. Andy manned the bow seat, at times glancing across to check their progress against the others. Being the last training race of the day, Jock raised their rating from twenty-eight strokes per minute to thirty-two.

'Come on, ya load of nancy boys, give me thirty-two, for fook's sake,' he cried, his accent stronger the louder he yelled.

The coxswain responded by counting off the strokes as Andy drew on strength he never knew he had, *The Lady Beaumont* running square in the water, reacting with groaning timbers to the boys' leg drive, each stroke running the boat smoothly across the surface. Andy looked over his shoulder once more, confident they were gaining on the others.

'Give me ten of your strongest strokes!' cried Willy from the coxswain's seat, counting them on. 'One! – Two! – Three!'

Each oar stroke, each push of the legs, burnt through their muscles to the bone.

'Four! – Five!' Their bow began to draw level with the opposing boat's coxswain.

'Six! – Seven! – Eight!' The old boat lifted slightly out of the water, gaining a foot or two ahead.

Andy looked over his shoulder again, but this time something else caught his attention, a patch of dark water where the riverweeds brushed the surface, reaching up for him. The dead man's fingers.

'Nine!' cried Willy.

Andy never heard ten … He was back at Frenchmans Basin; his breath caught in his throat, despair washing over him as Kyle whispered *I'm sorry*. He was in the water again, the weed brushing his skin, the imagined corpses reaching up for him. Andy felt his breath squeezed from his lungs. As panic set in, he no longer knew where he was. At racing speed, his oar caught at the finish of the stroke – *crabbing* – Sam called it, the blade burying itself in the water long after the other three had left the surface. The handle smashed into Andy's chest, catching him under the arms and lifting him over the gunwales into the river. Although he resurfaced quickly, Sandy's blade clipped him above the left eye, rendering him unconscious.

23

I didn't think I'd ever tell anyone about what happened to me. About the Game. But then I'd never met anyone like Sam before. I guess he was the day to Kyle's night.

ANDY began skipping both school and training, a depression smothering him after the flashback on the river. He sat in the ruins by Riverchase Lane, the direct afternoon sunlight causing the sandstone walls to blush in the orange hues of dusk. He recalled the summer days spent here with his best friend Butch, his index finger running lazily through Butch's carving in the wall from so long ago. His chest tightened when he realised how long it had been since he last saw Butch, but ever since the Game, Andy had put a barrier up, the only way he knew how to keep his secret.

He looked out through the doorway to the weathered jetty reaching out over the Pond. Movement in the long grass caught his attention and he saw a cat march out into a clear patch of ground. She stopped to sniff the air, then strutted off, her kittens behind her. They were scrawny and skittish, except for the hefty white one that looked just like Mother, standing to her right with that same look of vigilance in her eyes.

He heard a faint noise, assuming it was the cat and her brood. No one else came out here except Butch. Even when Andy heard Sam Mitchell's voice, it didn't register, sounding more like a memory than anything tangible.

'Hi, Andy.'

He turned.

Sam paused in the open doorway before stepping in.

'I called into your house. Your mother said you might be out here.' He sat on a pile of bricks next to Andy. 'I'll bet this was quite a home in its day, huh?' He patted the sandstone wall next to him with his big hands. 'Some afternoons I look at this place from out there on the water and wonder who owns it.' He brushed his grey hair back.

'Why aren't you out with the squad?' Andy asked.

Sam broke off a stalk of fennel growing through the window frame and smelt the aniseed aroma. 'I gave them the afternoon off,' he said. 'The training season's nearly done. Time to slow things down a little, I reckon.'

'Sorry about this week,' Andy said. 'I – I just wasn't up to it.'

The two stared across the water and listened to the steady hum of the sand quarry machinery beyond the wall of she-oaks on the opposite bank: trucks growling, the crusher's long conveyor belts piling sand in stockpiles that often peaked above the oaks.

'Don't worry about it,' Sam said. 'We've managed okay.' He chewed on the fennel seeds and spat their remains from his teeth. 'We're banking on you turning up Monday though.'

Shifting his gaze to the ground, Andy slowly shook his head. 'I – I just don't know.' His voice broke.

'It's funny,' said Sam, 'but I've learnt more about you this last week than in the whole rowing season.'

'Oh?'

'Jock told me about the Greenways suicide. Toby Broughton, wasn't it? I know it happened last year, but Jock said he was a friend of yours. Said you were the one who found him. Is that true?'

Andy remained silent for a moment. The last thing he wanted was for Greenways or the Game to infiltrate his rowing life any further. Rowing was his escape; his new beginning.

'Yes,' Andy said. 'He shouldn't have died like that.'

Sam spat the remaining seeds from his lips. 'There's nothing sadder than a troubled soul so young.'

Andy shook his head again, briefly feeling the anger surging inside. 'You have no idea, Sam.'

Sam shrugged, watching as a plover picked insects from the sandy shoreline. 'I don't like that Kyle Tucker fellow,' he said. 'Never have.'

Andy made eye contact with him for the first time that day.

'That *Kyle* fellow,' Sam continued. 'I can't put my finger on it, but there's something …' He searched the waters for the right word. 'False. Yeah, that's it. He's hiding something. Seems to have the rest of the town fooled though, prancing around like God Almighty in his bowties.'

Andy suddenly wanted to tell Sam everything. It rose from the pit of his stomach, as if escaping from a deep well, craving the light, but then choked in his throat. He bowed his head. 'You're right.'

'Right?'

'About Kyle,' Andy said reluctantly. 'You're right. He shouldn't be trusted.'

Their attention was drawn back to the plover, the afternoon sunlight casting a warm-coloured hue over the sandbank it scurried along, the bird stopping only to pick its fill of insects before nightfall.

'Did Kyle have something to do with your friend's suicide?'

A tear ran down Andy's cheek, betraying his emotions. 'He might just as well have put the cord around Toby's neck,' he said.

'Did he … hurt you, Andy?'

'I really don't want to talk about it. I'm sorry but – I can't.' He walked over to the window frame facing the river, his back to Sam. 'I don't think you'd understand.' Like Toby, he realised he was harbouring a secret he didn't feel he could reveal.

The plover cried out, launching itself from the sandbank, its wingtips contacting the river surface and leaving a trail of rippled circles, the *pat-pat-pat* echoing off the water.

'You know,' Sam said softly, 'I don't believe I understood anything until I had a ship blown out from under me back in the war. Maybe it was that. Maybe it was my time in Changi prison camp in Singapore. I don't know.' He stood to stretch, then shifted to where Andy stood. 'Oh, the Japs at the camp were bad enough all right, but their rules were very simple. Do as you're told, when you're told, the way you're told. Three things, that's all. To do it meant seeing another sunset. Don't do it, and they had more ways to kill a man than I knew how to die. That was the easy part, get through those three simple rules and it left you time to fight the dysentery, malaria and starvation. Those things could kill you too, but there wasn't much you could do about them. That was just God's will.'

'How can you believe in God after all that?' Andy asked.

'It doesn't matter what I believe now, but back then you had to believe in something. To think no one was caring for me, to believe there wasn't a better place waiting for me if I got killed, was unimaginable.' Sam picked a fresh stalk of fennel and began chewing the seed husks again. 'I didn't fight in the war, I was in the merchant navy, but I still knew what it was to stand by my brothers. As it was, some of them turned out worse than the stinking Japs.' Sam turned up his nose, the fennel seeds were old and bitter, so he spat them out. 'Jesus wept, Andy, you don't know what your fellow man is capable of until – until his back's to the wall. It brings out the beast in all of us.'

'I know about beasts,' Andy said.

'So tell me.'

Sam's directness made Andy feel trapped. His blood rose and his hands began to tremble, the badshit stirring. He wanted to run, unnerved that Sam could get so close to the truth so easily. Then a weight lifted. It came as a trickle at first, general details about Kyle and the store, but soon became a stream, and finally a torrent. The sun had slipped behind the mountains by the time he'd finished, the long shadows turning the riverlands cold.

'Jesus wept,' Sam whispered.

'I hope he's weeping for me,' Andy said. 'For me and Toby and every other kid.'

'I knew there was something about that bastard,' Sam said. 'Bloody hell, Andy, we've got to get the police involved. Red Adams needs to know about –'

'*No!*' Andy cried, grasping at Sam's arm.

'But, Andy, there are other kids at risk, we have to think about them too. Someday he might kill one of them.'

'Sam, please, I'm not ready. Don't you think I know about the risk the others are in? Don't you think it's on my mind every day? If all that came out right now, I'd die.'

Sam turned and began to walk back toward the lane. 'Come on,' he said, deep in thought, his eyes focusing on the ground ahead. Andy followed. 'It's okay,' Sam finally said, 'I think I understand.' He rubbed the day-old stubble on his face. 'There's more than one way to skin a cat.'

'What do you mean?'

'Well, here's what I'm thinking. An anonymous letter to Tucker.'

'I couldn't do it,' said Andy, his eyes wide.

'Not you,' Sam said. 'Me. We'll keep the police out of it for now. A step at a time. I remember Changi – sometimes the smallest action could set in motion the downfall of the most evil bastard. Maybe letting him know he's being watched will be enough to stop him. Enough to shake him up, make mistakes and expose himself … let justice deal with him before anything worse happens.'

Andy shook his head. 'I swear, Sam, some days I don't know what to do.' He wiped a tear from the corner of his eye.

Sam handed him a handkerchief from his pocket. 'I'd say you worry too much.' He ruffled Andy's hair. 'Your problem is you give no thought to now.'

'What do you mean?'

'Life's like rowing, Andy. It's the oar in the water that counts.' He considered his words a moment before continuing: 'It's no good worrying about the next stroke, because it hasn't happened yet. And it sure as hell doesn't pay to worry about the last stroke. It's gone and finished, just a ripple behind you. But if you focus on nothing but the oar in the water, if you make every one count, every stroke as perfect as you can, then the next and the last can be nothing but your best.'

'The oar in the water,' Andy whispered.

'The secret of life,' Sam smiled.

24

We all have our demons to live with. Some more than others.

KYLE sat in the dim light of his office. The door closed, the sound of the wall-mounted air conditioner humming in the background. He stared up at the timber beam where the boy had hung. His navy blue bowtie was unravelled, his white shirt unbuttoned at the neck. He drew on the filter of his cigarette, the ashtray on his desk full of twisted butts. The air, a haze of stale smoke, was cool, yet a thin beading of perspiration covered Kyle's top lip, and the taste of salty sweat lingered in the corners of his mouth. A glass and an open bottle of Johnnie Walker rested before him where a cluster of glass rings stained the wooden desktop.

'Fuck it!' he whispered to the shadows swimming around him.

A cautious knock came at the office door. Kyle twitched, biting his lower lip at the intrusion. Taking a deep breath, he finished his scotch, wincing slightly at the drink's heat.

'Who is it?' he said, pouring another measure.

'It's Ray.'

Kyle tried to recall the new kid's face. 'What do you want?'

'You said you wanted to see me before I went home.' There was a pause. 'Well, it's after six, Mr Tucker, everyone else has gone.'

Kyle glanced down at the handwritten anonymous letter, anxiety pressing at his chest as he crushed out another spent cigarette. Taking the next Chesterfield from the packet, he noticed his hands were shaking. Clenching them into fists, he broke the cigarette between his fingers and cursed under his breath. But still they shook. He drank the next shot of scotch in one go, his eyes watering. The same feelings of betrayal that he had felt reading Toby's suicide letter washed over him in a wave of anger and despair.

'Mr Tucker?' Ray called. 'Mr Tucker, are you okay?'

'I'm fine, Ray,' Kyle lied, trying to control his voice. 'Go home. It wasn't important. Just … go home.'

'Okay.' There was a pause. 'I'll lock up then?'

Kyle didn't answer. Alone again, he read the letter once more.

My reasons for not exposing your secret are mine alone, but if you touch one more child in this town, then I promise, the police and newspapers will be notified. Remember, I have the proof.

He tipped the pile of butts into the waste bin as he crumpled the letter in his fist. With an unsteady hand, he flicked open his Zippo before placing the note into the empty ashtray and setting it alight. As good as it felt to destroy the letter, Kyle knew it wouldn't fix the problem. What *was* the problem? *Who* was the problem? 'Who the fuck *are* you?' he whispered, stamping out the flames with the palm of his hand.

He called on the wolf to turn this around. *Think!* What did the note really tell him? If the author knew so much, why not turn him in? Who are you protecting? *Proof?* If he had proof, other than a testimonial, why not show his cards? Because all you have is someone's word … someone who would struggle in court to state his case. He thought of Andy. Of course – the last to play the Game. But this wasn't Andy's handwriting.

'I'll find you,' he said.

He flattened out what was left of the note, his eyes drawn to the first letter of text: *M.* The script was large and confident, a free-flowing style that suggested it was an adult's. But this particular *M* was familiar, unusual, looking more like a capital *H.* He placed it in his desk drawer. Sitting back in his chair, he felt the wolf's blood surge through his veins in a rush of adrenalin.

The letter changed everything. He needed to lie low. Kyle grabbed the ashtray, his knuckles white, then threw it against the office door, smashing it in a burst of porcelain and ash.

25

The Greenways building is still there today. A new name.
A new owner. But those same ghosts haunt it for me.

THERE he was – the Murphy boy. Andy stepped aside, breathless. He must be four years old now. Old man Murphy was struggling with shopping bags in one hand, his limbless son under his arm like a Christmas ham. The boy looked at Andy as they passed, his three-fingered stump poking out of his T-shirt, working up and down. *Was he waving?*

Old man Murphy stopped, setting down the bags while he adjusted his grip on his boy. 'What are you bloody looking at?' he said to Andy.

'Sorry,' Andy said. 'It's just –'

'It's just *what*?'

'It's just that you're carrying him like a football.'

Old man Murphy spat on the pavement, sneered, lifted his bags and walked on. Andy felt compelled to watch, the boy looking over his father's shoulder, his little flipper still waving. Andy turned toward home, walking into someone coming out of Holloway's Building Supplies.

'Sor – ry,' he stammered when he realised it was Kyle Tucker.

Carrying a small brown parcel, Kyle stared into Andy's face. As much as he wanted to turn away, Andy couldn't. Whether it was fear or anger that made him hold his ground, he couldn't say. Mindful of Sam's anonymous letter, he sensed Kyle searching his eyes, but made sure there was only revulsion staring back. He wanted to hurt Kyle, wanted to let him taste the badshit spawned at Frenchmans Basin.

But as the stalemate passed, Andy stepped aside and let him by. Neither looked back.

*

Like the river, time flowed on. By the end of the winter '63 training program, Andy, Jock, Sandy and Col had *The Lady Beaumont* cutting the water as fast as her old timbers would allow. The new rowing season opened during the first weekend of November with the Blackwater Regatta. The boys' racing times were adequate, considering their antiquated equipment, but Sam made it clear they would have to prove themselves before being assigned a better boat.

Sam entered them in the heavyweight fourth-grade fours, a novice event and the first race of the regatta. Andy noticed a crowd setting up picnic rugs and collapsible chairs under the riverbank's jacarandas as he and the crew readied the boat on the dock.

With no regatta experience, the boys played it the only way they knew: by the book – Sam's book. There were four boats in the race: theirs and three city crews. Andy's crew anticipated the gun and built their reach with every stroke. With the coxswain counting down the first fifteen sweeps of the oar, the crew settled at thirty-two strokes per minute. Yet, with the start won, their heavy boat only managed to get a yard ahead of the Mosman crew.

The river was like glass, reminding Andy of early mornings fishing, of watching the boats. Willy steered a dead-straight course, frequently checking their rating against his wristwatch. Andy focused. They knew to maintain their length in each stroke, making them count as their muscles protested with each drive of their legs. But the Mosman crew began rowing them down with two hundred yards remaining, and Andy felt their advantage slipping away.

Undeterred, Jock cried, 'Give me forty, ya pack of nancies,' and raised the rating even further. Though having never rowed over thirty-six before, they had no choice but to follow their stroke man. Their rhythm and timing fell away momentarily, but Willy brought them back into line over the next ten strokes. Muscles ached and lungs felt like exploding, but they persisted as their rating climbed and *The Lady Beaumont* bow arched from the water. The sprint home paid off, breaking the city crews' spirits, and when they crossed the finish line it was by a full boat-length.

The boys stopped rowing the second they heard the gun. Oars skipped across the top of the water as they fell back into the boat, lungs drawing air, muscles burning. The win hurt, but it hurt so good.

I row, therefore I am, Andy reminded himself.

*

Sam Mitchell watched the race through his binoculars from the clubhouse. This race, he knew, this moment, belonged to the boys. He watched their faces beam as *The Lady Beaumont* regained her lost dignity and glided over the line in first place. Right now no one could say what these boys might achieve in the future, but nothing would ever top the sensation of their first win. Sam knew the feeling, as had every oarsman smiling from the photographs on the clubhouse wall.

26

*I should have recognised the evil in the eyes of the wolf
tattoo on his arm. It must have meant something for
him to have it engraved in his skin like that – a forever
statement.*

KYLE was spending more time in his office, hitting the bottle and
neglecting the business, neglecting everything.

'I need to go home,' he told himself as he poured another shot
into his glass.

The room smelt musty. He could smell something else too –
fear. The grey flicker of light from the new TV in the corner
cast shadows across his desk, the TV's sound turned down to a
murmur. It was the late movie, Lon Chaney Jr's *The Wolf Man*.

Kyle raised his glass. 'To the wolf in us all,' he toasted. 'That's it,'
he said, swallowing the liquor. 'The curse of the wolf.' He poured
another glass, spilling over. He licked his fingers. 'Once bitten, the
disease is in your blood. Just ask good ol' Lon Chaney there.' He
raised his glass to the TV screen once more, winking at the images.
The werewolf howled at the moon over its shoulder in a close-up.
Kyle mocked a howl back, laughing.

Who's afraid of the big bad wolf?

That was the question Kyle answered for the last time on the day he turned sixteen – the last time his father tried the Game on him. It had begun when he was five. Even today, he could recall the initial sense of fun in the Game, a betrayal in itself – fun and fear.

'Who's afraid of the big bad wolf,' his father would cry from the other room, giving his son time to hide. Although he didn't know it then, Kyle would discover it was as much about the chase, the hunt, as it was about the kill. The game of hide-and-seek eventually turned one night, when his father came home stinking of beer and whisky. At the game's end, he found Kyle in the linen cupboard, his new hiding spot. He was angry at how long it had taken to find his son, and his hands slipped around the boy's throat, yelling, shaking, squeezing until Kyle passed out.

Kyle realised now that the reason he let his father hurt him, the reason he told no one, was for the attention. He was scared at first, but grew to feel that the control was the only thing his father needed from him. And the attention was what Kyle needed from his father.

But why his sixteenth birthday was different, Kyle couldn't say. Perhaps it was because his birthday fell on his father's payday that year. Perhaps it was as simple as feeling strong enough to fight his father for the first time, the aching need for his attention gone.

Kyle waited in his room until late. Waited in bed with his face to the wall until his father stumbled home. Until the bedroom door creaked open. *Who's afraid of the big bad wolf,* his father chanted, *the big bad wolf, the big bad wolf.* The old man slowly pulled the covers back and slipped his calloused hands around his son's throat. *Who's afraid of the* – his son rolled toward him – *big bad wolf* – and held the ten-inch kitchen knife against his ribs.

He recalled how he sat on the edge of his bed, his face a breath away from his father's, the hallway light reflecting off the blade, displaying its brand name near the handle. *Forge.* 'No more,' he told his father in a calm voice, calmer than it should have been. Kyle pressed the knife against his chest, cutting the fabric of his shirt, amazed at the fear in the old man's eyes. He relished the sudden reversal of power, the rush of control strangely exciting him, empowering him. 'Get out of my room, you sick bastard, or I'll kill you where you stand.' He could hear the words coming from his mouth, unrehearsed, yet perfect: everything he'd wanted to say.

His father backed away, a small circle of blood oozing through his shirt. 'I'm your father,' was all he could say.

'I'll still kill you,' Kyle replied, the clarity in his eyes confirming the statement. 'Who's the big bad wolf now, Dad?' That was when he realised the passion behind the power, satisfying his own inner wolf with the transfer of authority. He'd had the wolf's head tattooed on his arm soon after.

He winked at the TV screen again, remembering the curse. 'Once bitten by the wolf,' he whispered, 'the disease is in your blood.'

Reaching into his desk drawer, he took out the parcel he'd bought from Holloway's Hardware the day he ran into Andy.

Slowly peeling the brown paper wrapping away, he revealed the long kitchen knife, the *Forge* brand name stamped into the blade. When he'd seen it in the display cabinet, it took him back. It helped him then, and it could help him now. Kyle placed it next to the charred letter and smiled. He took a cheque from the top of the accounts pile and held it next to the letter, noting the similarities to the handwriting in the signature.

Now I've got you.

Kyle took the knife by the handle. 'Sam Mitchell,' he whispered, plunging the blade through the cheque and into the desktop.

The Oar in the Water

27

Sometime in 1964 things went from 'God Save the Queen', to 'God Bless America' almost overnight. It was the same year my father found me a job with Ashley Klein, a man he served with in the army.

KLEIN owned the regional newspaper, *The Greater Western*. He showed Andy around the small one-press plant touting printing as if it was the world's noblest trade, but Andy only saw a mass of heavy paper rolls and black ink that covered everything like dust in a coal pit. The odours were familiar – ink, paper and solvents – reminding him of the smells from the newspaper star charts he'd once collected and the comic books beneath his bed.

The environment was new to Andy, completely different to the fresh, air-conditioned supermarket. The pressroom was a corrugated iron building devoid of windows, a steady mist of warm oil drifting to the fluorescent lights in the high ceiling. Everything vibrated as the Goss Urbanite printing press clattered, threading its reel of newsprint through hungry impression cylinders. Andy's after-school job was to clean around the presses, the compositor's room and the loading dock. It was good money for easy work. Klein spoke of his father with fondness, but Andy reminded himself that Klein had probably never seen the badshit.

*

Andy met Dana Morrows on the cusp of a storm, when her family moved into town the same weekend that a flash flood took away half the rowing club's dock. They met at the dance to raise money for the repairs. She looked at him from across the room and smiled. He smiled back, watching as she talked to a group of girls from his school, her dark hair cascading over her shoulders, framing her olive-skinned face. Courage didn't play a part in asking her to dance, it was an impulse, one he knew he'd regret forever if he didn't give in to it.

He turned sixteen in July, and although Dana wouldn't reach that milestone until September, her parents allowed him to take her to the pictures to celebrate. They watched Jerry Lewis' *The Nutty Professor* and were back at Dana's by five o'clock, the taste of popcorn still in his mouth, and a Coke stain on the leg of his jeans. Dana grinned at his clumsiness the whole afternoon. She guided him behind the porch post and kissed him out of sight of neighbours and passers by. A faint moan escaped his lips, the tenderness in Dana's attention welcomed, his clumsiness ebbing away.

'That's for your birthday,' she said, smiling.

It was his first kiss. 'Oh,' was all he could say and kissed her again.

They stood at the top of the stairs holding each other against the cold July afternoon, Andy wishing they could stay like that forever, keeping the cold at bay. Her closeness made his heartbeat heavily. He watched over her shoulder as a flicker of lightning illuminated the cloudbanks beyond the mountains.

'I'd better go inside before Dad dusts off the shotgun.' She laughed.

'Sure,' Andy agreed. 'There's a storm coming, and I've got to be somewhere.' He kissed her one last time and walked away, hoping her taste, her memory, would stay with him forever.

28

It would be a while before I knew what Kyle was fully capable of. Before I knew what a truly cold heartbeat within that chest.

THE night carried no thunder, the storm too distant for the sound to carry so far, but the clouds flashed with spasms of lightning beyond the mountains. Kyle sat behind the wheel of his car, the engine cooling beneath the hood with an occasional metal tick, his palate dry as he waited in the dark, a strange taste lingering in his mouth. He had parked across the road from the rowing club, away from the streetlights, and waited for two hours, watching as Sam Mitchell parked and entered the boatshed below. The radio played low, crackling with static each time a flash of lightning lit the distant storm clouds. He checked his watch in the dashboard light. It was nearly eight o'clock.

'Sam Mitchell,' he mouthed.

Kyle's hands began to feel clammy again. His legs were numb with pins and needles when he moved after sitting too long. Then he saw the police car cruising toward him, its blue and white sign bright against the night. Kyle slid down in his seat as it passed. It was driving too slowly for his liking. This wasn't how he preferred to do things. This was reactionary – passive. As the police car passed, it briefly lit the interior of his car, the knife reflecting silver-white on the passenger seat beside him, his eyes fixed on the *Forge* symbol.

He listened for the car to leave, suddenly aware of his heartbeat. Could he do this? *I have to! I've waited long enough*, his mind reminded him. *I've been patient. Lain low. Kept the everyday face firmly in place.* He couldn't have anyone out there threatening his way of life.

Switching off the radio, he opened the door and stepped out, his breath steaming in the night air. He held the knife blade flat against his leg as he looked both ways along Main Street. It was quiet for now, and he walked across to the riverside park next to the clubhouse. Approaching the bank, he hugged the shadows, staying close to the wall of brush and ghost gums dividing the park from the rowing club. Finding a small clearing, he sat at the base of a tree where he could see into the open boatshed and gym. He saw Sam Mitchell closing his toolbox, standing beside one of the racing shells and wiping his hands on a rag.

So close. Four, maybe five paces away. A slash of the knife across his throat, deep, firm and even. One action from behind. Sam wouldn't even know his killer.

Kyle took a deep breath as Sam turned his back to him, ready to make his move, when Andy Walker stepped out from between the boat racks. Kyle froze before dropping to the clearing, hugging the dirt. *Too close! Too fucking close!* He could hear them talking about the boats, about the training and upcoming regattas, about the boy's birthday, but none of it made sense to Kyle – he'd been certain Sam was alone for the entire time he'd waited in his car.

His fist clutched the knife handle. He waited, then the sound of the river, deep and dark, whispered to him as he backed out of the brush and returned to his car.

He threw the knife to the floor and fumbled in his pockets for the keys as he got in. Starting the car, he drove, his hands moist and shaking on the wheel. It took all his might not to speed away, not to draw attention. His palate was dry again, and the strange taste was back. The taste of fear.

He slammed his fist into the roof, wanting to cry out in rage. His eyes caught a flash of lightning in the west, and he felt as one with the storm's raging heart.

29

*It had been a long winter, and I was glad to see summer
so near, mostly for the distraction that the rowing season
offered, but I was also looking forward to the Olympic
Games – something positive. But you don't always know
how close tragedy comes sometimes. It can pass by so near
you feel the air brush the hairs on the back of your neck.
However, sometimes it can leave a premonition in its
wake. For me it manifested during the Tokyo Games –
1964, the year Dawn Fraser won gold in the pool.*

ANDY watched the delayed telecast of Dawn's race. Watched her
poised on the blocks in anticipation of the starter's gun, watched
her plunge into the pool, surfacing quickly, each stroke taking her
closer to the finish, each kick driving her clear of the field. He
imagined the embrace of the water and the taste of chlorine. The
crowd cheered over the commentator's excited voice, and it was
over, one hundred metres and a lifetime of training. *Gold!*

His parents rose from the sofa, laughing. 'You little beauty!' his
father cried.

Andy watched as his parents held each other and looked happy
for the first time in so long. That's when he realised how special

this was. Not for its rarity, but for its sincerity. He wondered how they would react if he ever made the Olympic rowing team, and suddenly it seemed possible.

Staring at them, he wished the moment could last, and attempted to burn the image into his mind. Then a thought washed over him, clear and brutal in its absoluteness: *My mother's going to die.* The weariness in her smile said it all, knowing that for all the joy of the moment, it would not last. Here was a woman who lived her life in the shadow of the badshit.

As the thought struck Andy, his mother looked over his father's shoulder and their eyes met. *I know,* they told him, and her smile faded.

30

*On a late November evening, cool for that time of year, I
watched my parents leave the house on their way to the
Lounge Bar at the Quarryman Hotel. I'll always regret
not saying goodbye.*

IT was almost ten o'clock when Andy arrived home from Dana's, a
light rain still falling. Goose bumps formed on his exposed arms,
the showers arriving with a cold front from the south. He was on
edge, a strange weight building with every step, the only comfort
being a hint of Dana's perfume on his clothes.

Rounding the last corner, he paused to stare ahead at his house.
Something was wrong. Every light was on, his father's car idling in
the driveway, the passenger door open, the interior light blinking
with a faulty circuit. The rain beaded on Andy's face, gathered at
the ends of his hair and ran down the back of his shirt. His every
sense heightened and his nerves strained as he drew closer. Then
he saw the blood: watercolour droplets of red on the steps, pooling
along the veranda's timber boards at the front door. He held his
breath, skin bristling.

'Mum, Dad,' he whispered, his breath returning, his hands
unsteady as he fumbled with the door handle.

The light inside was offensive, like it didn't belong.

His eyes began to water as he followed the crimson trail along the hallway. He opened his mouth to call out, but his throat was so dry no sound came. It was too quiet, the air heavy. Terrible, brutal images, filled his mind as the trail led him to the lounge room where the badshit seemed to hide in every shadow, hissing obscenities. He stared at the spot where his parents had held each other after Dawn Fraser's win, a pool of blood now soaked deep into the carpet. The stain of violence was everywhere: blood-soaked towels draped the couch, the beeping of the telephone hanging off the hook.

Andy tried to call out, but his voice betrayed him, his legs and arms numb. The trail of blood led to his parent's bedroom door. He stood silently, his tears running freely. He felt helpless. Would his legs carry him any further? He considered turning to leave. To call the police. To leave it all to them, but – but he forced himself closer.

The brass handle felt cold as he turned it, ready to nudge the door open. But his heart thrashed as a heavy hand came down on his shoulder, making him cry out. He turned to see two men standing behind him, his mind taking time to recognise the ambulance uniforms. The tallest wore black-rimmed glasses and carried a leather bag with a red cross on the side. 'Come away now, son,' he said, 'and let us do our job.'

'Did you make the call?' asked the other. Andy was drawn to his eyes, pale blue and kind, younger than his partner. He guided Andy away.

Andy looked back at the telephone handset. 'No,' he replied, wiping his face with his shirt sleeve.

The tall paramedic brushed past them, flinging open the bedroom door with a sense of urgency. 'Jesus Christ,' he whispered, pausing in the doorway as he turned to his partner. 'Get the boy out of here.'

Andy's body felt weak, his legs unsteady before he found his balance against the younger paramedic.

'Come on,' the ambo said. 'What say you show me where the kitchen is, huh?'

Andy saw his father on the edge of their bed, weeping as he held a folded white towel to his mother's temple. She was motionless, her eyes closed, blood smeared across her face like a mask. It soaked down into her summer dress and the roses on their bed cover. Andy felt the bile catching in his throat, fighting the nausea and shock with the only weapon he had – anger. His eyes darted from his mother to his father as the rage built.

'I can't stop it,' his father said between tears, his own voice broken. 'I can't stop the blood.'

The tall ambo opened his bag and pulled on surgical gloves before taking Mary's pulse. He frowned.

Tugging at Andy's arm, the younger one tried to guide him into the kitchen.

'What have you done?' Andy murmured, annoyed at the jerking at his arm, but it was as if no one heard him.

'I can't stop the blood,' Frank repeated.

Helping Frank off the bed, the paramedic took the towel from him. 'Leave it to us now.'

Andy exploded, shoving the hand from his arm, tearing away. 'I said, what the fuck have you done?' He lunged toward his father, only to have the tall ambo step between them, peering through his glasses, his face red with frustration.

'Shit!' he cried to his partner. 'Get the police over here!'

'You've finally done it, haven't you?' Andy cried.

Anger burned in Frank Walker's eyes. 'She fell!' he shouted in response, bracing to face him. 'She fell … in the rain … on the steps. She fell!'

'You killed her!'

'Listen to me,' the tall ambo shouted at Andy. 'I can't help your mother if I'm playing referee to you two.' He adjusted his glasses. 'She's alive, but every minute is one you keep me from my job. Go into the kitchen and wait there, son. It's the only way you can help her right now.'

Andy looked at his father, seething, but all he saw was the badshit staring back.

'Go!' cried the officer.

Andy backed out of the room, taking one last look at the roses on the bed.

31

*My mother's death, the funeral, were some of the toughest
days of my life. The questions over how she died; seeing
Ellie again. It was like treading water: working hard,
but getting nowhere. Trying to make sense of everything,
even Kyle Tucker. He will forever affect the things I do,
even today. One of the most difficult things to come to
terms with is this. He will always be a part of me.*

KYLE treasured his time in the wilderness. There was a washed-clean
feel about the place after yesterday's rain, the waters of Frenchmans
Basin partially silty. The new kid sat beside Kyle in *Night-Mare's*
front seat, his hair speckled with yellow sand from the beach. The
cry of a circling eagle echoed into the thermals. Kyle smiled, at ease
with the river's gentle cradling effect as the boat drifted.

'You know,' Kyle said, brushing sand from the corner of the
boy's mouth, 'I'm sorry about what happened back there. Most
kids think I'm not, but I am.' He paused. 'But it didn't have to
be like that,' he continued. 'I mean, I don't know what you boys
expect will happen up here. I've looked after you haven't I? You
enjoyed the privileges you've earned, haven't you?' He shrugged.
'Well, what about *my* privileges, huh? I seem to give you boys

hours, weeks, *years* of my life, and when I ask for a little time …
Well, you force me to *take* it. Not once have you boys willingly
played the Game. I mean, would it kill you to just *give* me what *I*
wanted once in a while?'

Realising what he'd said, Kyle chuckled. 'I guess it would, huh,
kid?' He leant forward and drew the boy's blue eyes closed with the
tips of his fingers. 'I really am sorry it turned out this way.'

He contemplated the lifeless body before him; studied the
river stones packed into the shirt and pants as he searched for
his cigarettes. Contemplated the thick tape around the boy's
wrists and ankles. He flicked open his Zippo to light the cigarette
between his dry lips. These were the times he remembered the
others, living and dead. It had been so long since he had lost one
like this.

The cigarette tasted bitter. Pulling a face, he threw it over the
side and spat into the water after it. Clearing the fishing rods
from between the seats, he found enough leverage to roll the boy
over the side. He was gone quickly with little splash, almost like
he was never there at all, the water taking yet another secret. He
would call the boy's mother when he returned. Tell her that her
son wanted to walk home from the ramp. The wolf snickered over
his shoulder, and for the first time in his life, Kyle wondered if the
wolf was laughing at him. His jaw clenched, remembering how
his father used to laugh at him. Was the wolf turning, preparing
to abandon him after all this time? Suddenly, there was a real and
pressing feeling that the tidy threads of his life were unravelling.

32

I finished school in '65 with little in the way of ceremony. After all, it was a time in my life I'd rather forget. I guess I saw it more as the beginning of something rather than the end. Ashley offered me a full-time job as a reel hand at the newspaper. The pay was reasonable and the hours suited, leaving my afternoons free for training at the club. However, it seemed every time I saw the way ahead, the past had a way of catching up.

IT was late June in Andy's seventeenth year, a cold winter. The Friday edition of *The Greater Western* ran the cover story on the Murphy boy's first day at school, a picture of him smiling at his desk, propped up in a special wheelchair, a pencil clutched in his three-fingered hand. Andy couldn't help but smile back, remembering the time Robert Murphy waved to him over his father's shoulder. This was the first time Andy didn't feel sorry for him, realising the meaning behind the smile. Murphy didn't miss his limbs, because he'd never had them. He was simply happy … Happy just to be.

Then he saw a small story on page three. The headline, *Local Teenager Missing*. Andy couldn't place his name. According to the story the boy was an only son from a one-parent family who worked after school at Greenways.

A sense of dread overpowered him, his silence feeding the guilt. He wanted to believe the boy had run away like the story said, wanted to believe he fled before he was forced to play the Game. Andy had felt a sense of peace fall over Blackwater since Sam's letter. A sense that Kyle had stopped. That feeling was gone now. The Urbanite press rumbled like a steam train at full throttle, the concrete beneath his feet vibrating with every impression. And he wondered, where was this train taking him?

*

Kyle Tucker read the article. He sat in his office, the door closed, with a handwritten, *Do Not Disturb* sign hanging off the handle outside. He eased back into the worn leather chair and sighed as his eyes wandered to the fishing rods in the corner.

His lips pursed as if forcing back a tide of curses, the taste of his last whisky still in his mouth. Fear had always turned to anger, usually resulting in acts of violence, always steered by the wolf, his dark guide. He slapped the newspaper onto the desk and stared at his open palms. The grey newsprint ink on his thumb and fingers looked like a smear of blood from an old black-and-white film. He wiped them on his pants, but the mark remained.

Everything he knew was changing, his confidence waning along with his drive to control the problem of Sam Mitchell and the missing boys, which he knew must eventually lead the police to his door. His most primal fears were smothering him.

The fear he'd spent his life trying to mask had broken through, reminding him of the child he once was, the scared boy in his father's Game. But lately the fear wasn't so quick to evolve into anger, and he questioned his trust in the wolf's words. Only the wolf protected him as a child. And only the wolf could protect him now. But he was beginning to realise something unsettling – the wolf lied.

Sergeant Red Adams locked the police station doors and drew the blinds. Burrows had finished his shift and gone home. The constable's interest in Blackwater declined the closer he came to his transfer date. Adams noticed that not even a missing kid could pique his interest, the mother's statement devoid of his usual detail. Adams didn't blame him. Blackwater wasn't the place for an ambitious rookie like Burrows.

Lonesome slept in front of the counter, and the sergeant had to step over him to get to his desk. Placing his hat beside his pipe, Red grabbed an apple from the drawer, took a bite and reopened *The Greater Western* at the article about the missing kid. *Police aren't treating it as suspicious yet.* He spat a seed into the waste bin at his feet, before taking another bite. A drop of juice splashed the newsprint and he wiped it away. Taking a pen from the empty coffee jar on his desk, he circled the word *Greenways* before cutting the article out and clipping it to Kyle Tucker's statement. He recalled the police interview, how Tucker was keen to answer the questions, seeming concerned, a careful mix of empathy for the mother and worry for the boy. Not a tremor in his voice or an unsteady hand to warrant suspicion. But Red felt his instincts telling him otherwise.

'Tucker,' he whispered.

There was still every chance the kid might turn up, but Red didn't have the resources to conduct a wide search of highways, bus depots and the usual haunts, that duty taken by the regional station at Haywood, but to be thorough, Red made his notes. As much as he wanted to apply pressure to Kyle Tucker, he knew he had to be careful, because the boy had run away before, and until he had something other than a folder full of circumstantial evidence, such pressure could be viewed by any lawyer worth his salt as harassment. Frustrated, Red knew he had to keep building the case and following the evidence while his instincts argued with protocol.

He threw the rest of the apple into the bin, then flicked through the documents and began writing a list of names from the folder, anything linked to these disappearances. But the deeper he dug, the more frustrated he became, knowing that without a body, none of this mattered. Without a body, it was just a missing person case.

33

*My first journey outside Blackwater without my parents
was through rowing. A trip to the Emerald City, where
the bays and inlets hosted warehouses and mangrove
woodlands, where expensive houses peered down from
the hills, and the office towers of Sydney stood tall.
Perhaps more symbolic than anything else, but that was
the day I first realised the bonds of the past weren't as
firm as I'd once thought.*

LETTING go was always difficult. Sam watched the boys push
off from the pontoon, a part of him not wanting them to win
this race. It was the selfish part, the one that didn't like to give
things away. Then he remembered his one perfect trick and smiled
reluctantly as they took their first stroke into deeper water.

'Good luck, lads,' he said softly.

It was the first regatta of the new season, hosted by the Sydney
Rowing Club on Hen and Chicken Bay, the boys' inaugural second-
grade race. Although his boys had few problems winning their
lower divisions on the flat Blackwater course, Sam knew today's
race would prove tougher, the senior grade competing against a
stronger field over a longer venue. They had a new boat, lighter

oars and enough spirit to drive a ship's turbine. But second grade was the turning point for any crew. Sam's job was to recognise potential, hone technique, build a foundation and then – pass them on to Keith Morgan, the senior coach. His one perfect trick.

Sam swore under his breath as he walked back to the Sydney clubhouse where he could see the course better. Just once, he'd like the opportunity to follow through. Just once, he'd like to take one of *his* crews to the nationals. He studied the boats out on the starting line manoeuvring for position before the gun went off.

Maybe he was getting crabby, or perhaps he just wanted one lousy photo on the clubhouse wall with *him* standing next to the state or national champions instead of Morgan. Right now he'd do just about anything to stop the senior coach seizing glory yet again, but not at the expense of his boys. Aside from being a member of the board, Morgan was an ex-national champion. And what was Sam?

Some days, his one perfect trick felt more like a curse.

He watched the race to the end. In view of what he was about to lose, it was difficult to feel pleased when the boys' boat slid across the finish line two lengths in front of the rest of the field. The race marshal's gun blew a small plume of smoke in the air and the delayed crack vibrated across the water. Sam winced as if the shot went through his heart.

'Sam Mitchell?'

He turned, not recognising the voice or the face. 'That's right,' he replied.

The man was short with silver-grey hair beneath a white Panama hat. 'They tell me you coach the Blackwater crew.'

'Right again,' Sam said. He looked out across the bay with pride. 'It's their first senior race.' He turned back to the stranger. 'What can I do for you?'

'My name's Roy Wilson,' the man said, extending his hand, 'and it's more about what I can do for your boys.'

*

As the last boat was tied onto the Blackwater trailer, Sam met the boys and stretched his arm across Jock's shoulders. 'Good work today, lads. You made it look easy.'

The four gathered around.

'Couldn't have done it without you,' Andy said.

'Well,' Sam began, 'this is a whole new league you're in now. It gets serious from here. Important people are going to take notice. Things are gonna change.'

The boys searched each other's faces, shuffling nervously until Col said what was on all their minds.

'We're not rowing for Morgan,' he said bluntly.

Sam remained silent, caught off guard.

'We've already talked it over, Sam,' Col added. 'We know the score, and we don't want to row under anyone but you.'

Sam bit his bottom lip. 'That's a fine thought lads, but it doesn't work like that. You all know my place in the club.' He turned away, staring out over the water to avoid their eyes. 'Keith Morgan is a fine coach with the experience and connections to take you *all* to the next level.'

'We can get there without him,' Sandy said.

'Yeah,' Jock added, 'we want *you* as our coach, Sam.' He looked to the others for support. 'We started this with you; we want to finish it with you.'

Sam turned back. 'I can't,' he said bluntly. 'This is a whole new grade you're stepping up to. More hours, more training, more travel. You need to think about the rest of my squad, everyone from novices to third graders. That's what I do. To dedicate the kind of time with you guys would take me away from the others. That's why Keith's senior squad is so lean. He handles the best Blackwater has.'

'It doesn't seem fookin' fair,' said Jock.

'I'll tell you what's *fair*,' Sam said. '*Fair* is that you boys get the best training and opportunities the club can provide. I know what you're trying to do, lads, and it makes me feel ten feet tall; but remember, no matter how far this sport takes you, I'll always know that a good part of *me* took you there.' Sam's voice broke. 'I swear, if any one of you boys ever made it to the Olympics, no matter where, I'd be right there in that boat with you.' He placed a hand over his heart.

There was a moment of silence. 'The Olympics, huh,' said Andy, breaking the lull.

'You bet,' said Sam, 'and you may have taken that first step today.'

'What do you mean?' asked Jock.

'A man named Roy Wilson from the Rowing Federation introduced himself to me today. He asked a lot of questions about you lot; in fact, he's been watching your progress with interest all season.'

'What's he want with us?' asked Andy.

Sam smiled. 'Wilson's a state selector. He wants you to try out for this year's Colt Squad. One, or all of you, may be representing the state this year, boys. And that's the first step to the national team, to the Olympics.'

Crossroads

34

Nothing stays hidden forever.

THE river was running low, the water flowing slower so more people in smaller boats made their way upriver to chase the better fishing grounds normally reserved for bigger boats and braver hearts.

Bryce and Darren Jackson were twins, Bryce three minutes older and never letting Darren forget it. They'd turned seventy a month ago, and still lived together in an old weatherboard house by the boat ramp. They could sit in a room for hours without speaking; communicating with no more than a glance, a nod of the head or gestures only they could decipher. They never argued, because they always seemed to know the other's needs, and would finish each other's sentences or speak the same words in unison.

Bryce stared out from under the brim of his hat, wiping sweat from his brow. His brother steered their outboard through Frenchmans Basin to where other boats were fishing the deeper water there.

'Looks like they beat us to the bass,' Bryce announced.

'Won't catch nothin' but a cold out there,' Darren replied.

The twins had been trawling off the steep river bends with little luck other than catching an eel two miles back – it was already stinking up the boat.

Bryce pulled in one of the lines to check the homemade lure. It looked fine. 'Can't see why …'

'… they're not biting,' Darren finished.

'Must be too much food around.' Bryce threw the lure in behind the boat as the sound of the outboard bounced off the cliff walls.

'Slow down a little,' said Bryce. 'Let the …'

'… lure run deeper.'

As Darren eased off the hand throttle, the two silver lures fashioned from the tops of old soup tins sank deeper.

'Don't know what could be more appetisin' than a Jackson lure dipped in fennel sap and maple syrup,' Darren said with a dry chuckle.

Both lines suddenly pulled taut, almost stopping the boat.

Darren eased the throttle back against the strain and switched the engine off. He and Bryce kneeled either side of the motor while each pulled their line in, heavy on a dead weight; evidently they'd snagged the same object.

'Must be a tree branch or somethin', the twins said together. They pulled on the lines until it broke the surface. Only, it wasn't a branch.

✳

Monday's newspaper ran the story. Andy was working the presses when he read about the body found by the Jackson twins, the ink still wet on the paper. He ran outside, fighting the sensation to be sick.

Kyle! Andy told himself, the taste of bile burning his throat.

It added up. The boy was young and worked part-time at Greenways. He came from a single-parent family. The body was found at Frenchmans Basin. Andy knew that there were only a few boats in Blackwater capable of making it through the Narrows when the river was high, and one was Kyle's.

Blame and anger burnt deep, a cocktail of rage and sadness, his body trembling, the air around him thick with revulsion.

That boy died because of my silence, he told himself.

Andy ran into the admin building, where he found an unattended room with a telephone. Panting heavily, he closed the door behind him and dialled Sam's number. The mouthpiece smelt of cigarettes and it seemed to ring forever. He was about to give up when Sam picked up.

'It's Andy.'

'Andy, how are you?' Sam's voice was cheerful.

'Not so good, Sam.' He leant across to lock the door. 'The paper is running a story on that missing kid.'

'Have they found him?'

'He's dead.'

A brief silence fell on both ends of the line as if the world had held its breath.

'Where?' Sam finally asked.

Andy's voice was unsteady. 'The basin. His hands were bound with tape, his clothes weighed down with river stones. Sam, this … This is –'

'Tucker,' Sam finished.

Tears formed in Andy's eyes, guilt weighing down his soul. He didn't know how long he could justify his silence, but knew speaking out would kill him. 'I don't know what to do. Even after this, I can't go public. No one would understand … I –'

'It's okay, Andy. It's okay.' Sam paused, and Andy prayed he wouldn't force him to go to the police, prayed he would find another way. 'Look, we can work something out, but … if it is Tucker, we … *someone* … has to stop him.'

Andy suddenly heard Toby's voice. *The real monsters in this world are right out there in the daylight.* 'I don't know *how* to stop him.' He slapped the desk, the badshit surfacing. 'Why me! Why is it on *my* bloody shoulders to stop him? I … I didn't want *any* of this!'

'Andy … Andy,' pleaded Sam. 'Stop. Take a breath. Don't worry, maybe we can do this without implicating you, but …'

Andy took that breath, deep and settling. 'But what?'

'But the main link in this whole thing is Greenways and Kyle Tucker.'

Someone outside tried the door handle, startling Andy. 'Shit!' he hissed. 'Sam, I've got to go.'

'Andy!' Sam said before he could hang up. 'Do you trust me?'

'Yeah, of course.'

'Then go back to work. Leave this to me.'

35

I was eighteen and disillusioned ... afraid ... alone ...
Then, after my phone call to Sam, I came to realise that
disillusionment would pass; fear was a part of life, and
I wasn't alone after all. Yet only Sam could know the
weight of guilt on my shoulders back then. And only Sam
could know a way forward, whatever the cost.

SERGEANT Adams tapped the head of his pipe on the edge of the waste bin beneath his desk, picking out the last of the ash and placing the clean pipe on his desk beside his tobacco pouch. A hint of the tobacco's port wine aroma remained in the air. Before him was the open copy of the dead boy's file, the pictures taken of the body in the bottom of the twins' boat not for the faint-hearted. For now, the boy was still in the town morgue awaiting the coroner's report, but Adams had already made up his mind. *Tucker.* Yet he still needed evidence, not simply suspicion.

The Haywood detectives had made a preliminary investigation, interviewing the twins, the boy's mother and Tucker, but were waiting on the coroner before continuing. Red made sure he was present for Tucker's interview, noticing he had a lawyer with him this time. Tucker had less to say, but maintained his calm demeanour, his lawyer suggesting the case against Tucker was circumstantial, that the boy could have been taken back up the river by another boat and, as Red anticipated, was quick to throw allegations of police harassment on the table. Circumstantial or not, the court ordered Tucker's boat to be impounded for testing, but Red presumed Tucker was too thorough to leave any incriminating evidence on board.

Meanwhile, Red placed a half-page notice with a photo of the boy in the local paper requesting anyone who may have been at the boat ramp on the same day to come forward. He also discovered that the tape binding the boy's hands and feet was sold at Holloways Hardware in town. It was a common brand, yet the link remained. Still, he could hear the lawyer's words echo in his mind. *Circumstantial.* He knew the first rule was to follow the evidence, but his instincts were telling him that it wasn't enough.

Distracted, Red heard Constable Burrows talking with someone at the front counter. He looked at his watch – it was a little after noon – when Burrows appeared in the doorway.

'Hey, sarge? Sam Mitchell wants a word with you.'

Red hadn't spoken with Sam for two years or more. 'Send him through.' He took the moment to close the file.

Red stood, extending his hand. The man hadn't changed a bit. 'Sam. It's been a while. Everything okay?'

They shook hands across the desk. 'Don't suppose you get too many people coming here to tell you everything is fine, Red.'

He gestured for him to sit opposite. 'You've got that right. Seems like nothing but bad news out there.' He shrugged. 'A copper's lot, I suppose.'

'Yeah.'

'You okay?'

'Maybe I've got some good news after all.'

Red raised his eyebrows.

Sam glanced over his shoulder toward the doorway leading out to the counter. 'Can we talk somewhere a little more private?'

Red stood, stepping over to the door, his eyes fixed on Sam. He tapped on the wall, catching Burrows' attention. 'Sam and I need some time. No interruptions, huh?'

'Sure thing, sarge. I'll hold your calls, too.'

Red grinned. Burrows was wet behind the ears, but he was eager to please. 'Thanks,' he said, closing the door behind him. He walked back to his desk. 'This is fine here,' he told Sam. 'As private as it gets.'

Sam shifted in his chair. 'It's about that body the twins found.'

'I'm listening.'

'I know who did it.' Sam leant forward, elbows on the desk, his voice low. 'Or rather, I know someone who knows.'

'So why isn't that someone here with you?' Red never considered Sam the type to play games. 'Hearsay won't hold any weight in court. I'm going to need a statement from this person.'

Sam took a moment to compose himself, resting back in his chair. 'He's only young, Red. He's been hurt, and doesn't want to be implicated.'

'What do you mean, hurt?'

'He's lucky not to have shared the same fate. I promised him that his name would stay out of this.'

'I'm not sure I can honour that, Sam. If you know who did this, then I want that statement.'

'I can get what you need to prosecute, but it won't be from my source.'

'I don't understand.'

'Red, I'm telling you Kyle Tucker murdered that boy, and it may not have been his first.' The two stared at each other, Tucker's name suddenly binding. 'You know as well as I, men like Tucker know how to hide behind the law. They know how to twist a witness's words until they choke on them. Sometimes you have to take that away from them.'

Red thought about Tucker's conduct. 'What are you proposing?'

'A lie, Red. In the name of justice. I can tell you everything my source knows, and what you do with that information is your choice. But I'll take the stand; swear the oath; and tell the judge that *I* saw Tucker heading upriver that day with the boy in his boat. I'll also testify that I saw him coming back … alone.'

'That's perjury, Sam.'

'Perhaps perjury is the cost of justice in this case.'

Red took up his pipe and pouch, pinching a portion of tobacco and filling the chamber. He studied the ivory bowl as he considered Sam's proposal, balancing the shank between thumb and forefinger like his father used to. The word *justice* lingered in his mind joining the lawyer's word, *circumstantial*. With his free hand he wrote on a blank piece of paper. 'That's the estimated time of death. Your statement needs to reflect that.'

Red noted the relief that overcame Sam, and scratched a match to light his pipe.

'Give me pen and paper,' he said. 'I'll write the statement now, then give you my source's information.'

'His lawyer is smart,' said Red. 'You'll need a reason why it's taken so long to come forward.' He watched Sam pause from writing.

'Your plea in today's paper – the boy's picture. It jolted my memory.'

Red nodded, feeling better about their unlawful alliance than he should.

✳

It was Friday afternoon and Tucker told his boys they wouldn't be having drinks that night. He told Ray to lock up the store when he'd finished sweeping, then retired to his office. He wasn't feeling well. Ever since the body was found upriver, ever since those out-of-town detectives started asking questions. Lawyer or no lawyer, he knew he was on the brink. He took the time to look around the office, whisky and cigarettes ready on the desk, the air conditioner's steady hum comforting.

Sanctuary, he breathed.

But any feelings of safety dwindled when he saw the afternoon edition of *The Greater Western* crumpled in the bin by his desk where he'd thrown it earlier. Kyle eased himself into his leather chair, opened the scotch, and poured. He went to loosen his bowtie, but noticed he wasn't wearing one for the first time in years. Rubbing his face, he realised he hadn't shaved either. He once found comfort and refuge in this office, his private place for private matters. Now, it was as if the walls were closing in on him. He began to feel trapped, the confines reminding him of past indiscretions, cord marks on the ceiling beams and his grandfather's steamer chest testament to them. The trunk was locked and the key safely hidden, but that didn't stifle the memories inside. History – *his* history. Someone once told him there's a difference between pleasure and happiness, and that what gives us pleasure doesn't always make us happy. He was beginning to understand.

Kyle lit a cigarette, thinking about his father. 'Reap what you sow,' he whispered, raising his glass in a toast. 'To the wolf in us all.'

A knock came at the door. 'Mr Tucker?' came Ray's voice.

Kyle closed his eyes before answering. 'What is it, Raymond?'

'Um, there are some men here to see you.'

He downed the last mouthful of scotch, hiding the bottle and glass in the top drawer. Kyle opened the door, a hint of muzak drifting in, but remained mute. Standing there, dwarfing the boy, were two policemen.

'Sergeant Adams.' He attempted to smile, to put on his everyday face, but sensed it looked pathetic under the circumstances. Then, he realised his instincts had failed him, the wolf sleeping as the hunters moved in.

Red stepped into his office, brushing past Kyle as he spoke: 'Mr Tucker, I have a warrant to search these premises and the premises of your abode. I'd appreciate it if you'd wait outside with my constable until the Haywood detectives arrive.'

'What? No!' said Kyle.

Adams handed him the warrant as Burrows guided Kyle out through the door. Kyle glared at Adams as he passed. 'Red,' he pleaded. 'You – you can't do this. I want to call my lawyer. This is harassment … You were warned!'

Red paused. 'You take that up with the judge this time, Tucker. Oh, and you can tell that fancy lawyer that we've just moved beyond the circumstantial phase.'

Kyle's eyes grew wide and unblinking.

'We have a witness.' Red grinned.

Streetlights flickered to life as the detectives began carrying items from the office, packing them into the rear of the Ford paddy wagon by the main entrance. There were boxes of books, photo albums and plastic evidence bags. Last of all, Kyle's steamer chest, its brass lock forced open.

Red Adams, his head held high, led Tucker into the street. A woman with blue-rinsed hair drew breath when she saw her grocer wearing handcuffs. Then, startling everyone, came an explosion of light as a flashbulb went off.

History would ultimately judge Kyle Tucker, but *The Greater Western* would record it.

*

The cover picture on *The Weekend Western* was of a frightened Tucker gaping into the camera as he was led to the police car. Andy watched the image repeating off the press at thirteen thousand impressions per hour.

It took weeks for the complete story to unfold. Briefly interviewed by police, Andy was never asked to testify. Thankfully, few witnesses were called due to the evidence in Tucker's office and Sam's statement in court. He followed the story closely each day, the *coup de grace* being Toby's suicide note found in the steamer chest.

You did it, Toby! After all this time you nailed the bastard!

36

*I can only imagine what it was like for Kyle Tucker
to walk into Long Bay. I used to think about it often,
wondering if my own prison was any different. We were
both left damaged by his actions; both left alone to make
some kind of sense from it all. After all, it's more than
high walls that make a prison.*

THE guard towers and ramparts of Long Bay Gaol cast their
afternoon shadows to the cliffs beyond its cold stone walls. Seagulls
circled the shoreline, their squawking echoing off the rock face,
some breaking ranks to dive through the sea spray for baitfish and
refuse from the sewage outfall. Kyle's first night here was so close,
and Blackwater so far.

His jaw was clenched tight, the muscles aching as the two
prison guards escorted him past the row of closed cell doors.
Head high, shoulders back, he attempted to maintain an air of
confidence, while inside, terror gripped him. His senses bristled,
the new prison greens feeling sterile and over-starched against his
skin, every step closer to his cell stripping away the person he once
was. He could hear a radio playing music, the sound faint and
distant. Kyle carried two folded blankets, a set of sheets and a roll

of toilet paper – all he owned now. The guards stopped outside an empty cell, its door open, a steel-framed bunk along one wall. His heart racing, he realised this was it. *Life.* A waft of urine and sweat met him, but he could also smell the ocean. The shorter of the two guards, Dawson, a man with a callous expression, placed his baton in the middle of Kyle's back and nudged him forward.

As the heavy door slammed shut behind him, fears he hadn't felt since childhood welled up. His shoulders dropped and he allowed the moment to foster those fears, knowing he couldn't display them outside his cell. Out there, he would have to be the wolf. The two guards walked away, but Kyle heard, 'We'll be burying this one before the end of summer, you wait and see.'

What could he do? *Adapt,* he told himself, *or die.* He had to take control. Find his place here, somewhere between the meat-axe muscle and the smarts he had seen while being processed, become someone who had something to offer the system, on whichever side of the bars that might be. But the guard's parting words echoed in his mind, taunting him.

Nearing the end of his first week inside, he learnt what the guard meant. He kept the wolf close, his job in the laundry demeaning but easy. On day six, and in a haze of fog from an opened steam press, a flash of steel came from his right, the shiv slashing his cheek then striking his lower back three times before he fell, buckled over in a torrent of pain. His face, bloodied, was pressed into the concrete floor, a voice over his shoulder whispering, 'Child killer.' A fist, grasping his hair, lifted his face and plunged it back to the concrete, and he heard his nose break before the pain registered. A series of kicks was delivered to the ribs, maybe one man, maybe two, hiding in the curtains of steam. Then it was over, the wolf no match for prison justice, consciousness waning until everything faded to black.

When he woke, it was to a morphine daze, a doctor in a white coat standing over him, his fingers probing the gauze on his cheek.

Kyle groaned, the pain raking his body when he tried shifting his weight in the bed. He winced, the stitches in his cheek pulling tight.

'Take it easy,' his physician said. 'You're in the prison hospital.' Then, as an afterthought: 'You're lucky to be alive.'

'No shit,' he said, allowing his body to relax, his hands exploring the dressings over his nose and cheek, the fire in his ribs becoming unbearable.

'Yeah,' said the doctor, 'most child killers don't live through a hit like that.'

'Who did it?'

He laughed. 'Nobody.' He picked up the chart on the end of the bed and began writing. 'That's the way it goes in here.'

'What's to stop them doing it properly next time?'

He raised his eyebrows and replaced the chart. 'Relax,' he said. 'That little attack earned you a place in the protection wing.' He began to walk away before adding, 'With your own kind.'

37

With Kyle Tucker in prison, I felt a strangeness fall over Blackwater; a quiet sense of denial about what happened. How could a community let their own succumb to such a monster? I suppose Dana was my way of filling that vacuum.

ANDY was eighteen, and Dana seventeen when they married. She wore her mother's wedding dress, while Andy hired a black tuxedo, forgoing the usual bowtie for a paisley cravat. Butch Dugan, childhood friend and best man, wore the same, constantly tugging at his sleeves and collar, the big man never having looked more uncomfortable. The reception was in the rowing club's upstairs auditorium, the wedding party arriving from St Stephen's Church as a brilliant sunset reflected off the river's surface. Andy looked into Dana's eyes when they stepped out of the car, the red hues of dusk bathing her face with a gentle glow. She turned his attention to the clubhouse and his heart soared when he saw their honour guard, eight rowers, oars crossed blade to blade at the entrance. He noticed Sam Mitchell in the crowd, and his coach gave him a wink. After the speeches, he tracked Sam down by the bar.

'Hey,' he said, speaking over the music.

Sam smiled, raising his beer in an informal toast. 'To the groom,' he said taking a sip. 'Great night, Andy.'

'Yeah,' he said looking around at the guests dancing and chatting, singling out his old crew settled at a corner table with their girlfriends. 'Thanks for the crossed oars ceremony when we arrived. Dana loved it.'

'Don't mention it,' Sam said. Then, patting his coat, he added, 'I bought you something.' He reached for the envelope in his inside coat pocket.

'Sam, the fondue set was plenty.'

'Yeah, well that was for the happy couple. This one's just for you.'

Andy opened the envelope, taking out a two-inch silver oar attached to a chain.

'That's to remind you.' Sam's voice faltered. 'Remember …' he said.

Andy finished the sentence for him. 'It's the oar in the water that counts.' Loosening his cravat, he placed the chain around his neck. 'Thanks, Sam.'

'Take another look in the envelope.'

There was a letter folded inside.

'It's a copy of the Olympic selections, and your name's on it, Andy. All the state squads get a crack at it.'

After showing the letter to Dana, Andy found a moment to himself by the open window overlooking the river. The lights had been dimmed for dancing, but there was enough cast over his shoulder to make out the letter's words, and he read them again with pride.

He wished things were different with his father; wished he could be here to share it, but the rift between them had grown wider after his mother had died. There were too many questions, and he was afraid of the answers. Looking out over the water, he wondered about his sister Ellie. He didn't even know where she lived. But none of that mattered now. He looked over at Dana, remembering the first time he saw her, here, in this very room.

'I bought you a beer, man.'

Andy turned. Butch's shirt was hanging over his pants and the cravat was now tied as a headband. Andy smiled and took the beer. 'Thanks, but I think I'm actually paying for the drinks tonight.'

Butch took a mouthful, the head leaving a rim on his lips. 'It's the thought that counts.' He slapped Andy's back. 'What are you doing over here all alone?'

'Getting some air. A little peace and quiet. Until you came along.'

'You'll miss me when I'm gone, man.'

'Aren't you scared?' Andy asked.

'Of what?'

'There *is* a war on, you know? Vietnam.'

Andy noticed Butch's expression sober slightly as his attention was drawn to the full yellow moon, their Blackwater moon staring back at them.

'I don't know,' Butch continued. 'The guy at the recruiting office told me the draftees were more likely to go before the regulars. Anyway, we're over there in a support role, that's all. You know, supplies and stuff. Shit like that.'

'You're kidding aren't you? What about the shit-fight last August? Long something.'

Butch's face lost all expression. 'Long Tan,' he said. 'That's what they called it in the paper.'

'Eighteen Aussies were killed in that stoush, with twenty or more wounded. That's not just a supporting role.'

Butch smiled unconvincingly. 'Well, my piece of paper tells me to report to Kapooka next week, not Vietnam. Anyway, man, the whole thing will probably be over before I get through basic training.'

'I wouldn't count on it,' Andy said.

'You scared of the draft?' Butch asked.

Andy thought about it. 'I guess … A little.'

'What scares you most?'

'Messing up my life, I suppose.' He unconsciously laid his hand over the envelope in his coat pocket. 'You know, getting in the way of what I want to do.'

'And Dana? What does she think about the draft?'

Andy shook his head and watched a pale cloud drift across the Blackwater moon. 'Don't get her started about the war, Butch. She doesn't think we should have anything to do with it. She's joined some group over at Haywood, writing letters to the government and local papers. Can't say I approve.'

'This war of ours,' Butch said. 'It's not like our father's war, huh?'

'What do you mean *our* war?'

'Well, you know, it seems every generation gets to have a war. My grandfather had the First World War, my father had the Second, and we get Vietnam. Shit, they don't even call it a war. They call it a police action. Doesn't seem fair. I bet the world forgets all about it in ten years.'

38

On the 9th of January 1967, the same day Ronald Ryan was hanged, I received word that I made the Olympic Eight.

ANDY stood with Dana in the observation lounge of Sydney Airport while a Qantas jet taxied toward the runway, the whine of its engines barely audible through the glass. It was bound for Saigon, South Vietnam. On board, along with ninety other young soldiers, was Butch Dugan.

Andy was aware Dana felt torn, betraying her principles by being there, any support for the war seeming to question her moral judgment. He knew it was a fine line he walked, because his refusal to get involved in politics made Dana more resentful. The war meant little to him, and he couldn't understand why Dana had become so anti-war so quickly.

On the train back to Blackwater, she raised the issue again. 'I can't believe today, of all days, you don't see a need to get involved in the movement.'

He rolled his eyes. 'What do you mean, *today, of all days*?'

'You just saw your best friend leave for Vietnam. Doesn't that do anything to your conscience?'

'My *conscience* has nothing to do with the war, Dana. *I* didn't start it! *I* didn't send Butch.' He stared out the window, frustrated. 'Anyway, I thought your problem was conscription. Butch joined of his own free will and volunteered for duty abroad. It's just … a job.'

'A job?' Dana said. 'Show me a job description that requires you to kill children?'

'Jesus Christ, Dana! Why are you hitting *me* with this shit? I go to work and I row at a national level! I have few vices, so tell me, how is *that* supporting the bloody war?'

'Sometimes the greatest crime is doing nothing,' she said quietly. 'How many Butch Dugans will it take before you stand up and do something?'

'What do you suggest I do, Dana?' he said. 'Even if I wanted to, how many hours do you think there are in a day? Should I give up my job? Be like those limp-dicked hippies in your movement and live off welfare while I smoke pot and protest the war? Christ, Dana, be practical.'

'Priorities,' Dana said. 'It's all about priorities. God forbid that you give up rowing for a while. Maybe then you could help us at the committee *and* see me a little more.'

Andy laughed. 'Dana, a few years ago I was a novice rower spending more time *in* the bloody water than on top of it.' He was looking her square in the eyes. 'I now row for my country. Don't you understand that? Next year I'll be representing Australia in Mexico. It's what we've dreamed of.'

'No, Andy, it's what *you've* dreamed of.'

He shook his head. *What in God's name is wrong with you?*

Dana looked away. But Andy's eyes stayed fixed on her, annoyed, still not believing what he was hearing. He watched as her hands twisted the buttons on the front of her dress. Watched how her chin quivered just before she cried.

'Dana, what is it?' he asked, softening. 'What's wrong with you today?'

'I'm frightened,' she said.

He reached over to hold her. She rested her face on his chest.

'Frightened of what?' he asked.

'Yesterday I watched the draft on TV. I watched the balls roll out and I suddenly felt frightened. The man called out the numbers, then the birthdays. I thought it was your birthday at first, but it wasn't. I should have felt relieved but I felt scared, then angry, then – oh, Andy, for that split second I thought I was going to lose you to the war. I don't want our lives to be changed by a stupid lottery. It's not fair.'

Andy held her tighter, stroking her hair and tenderly kissing her cheek. 'You should have told me, Dana,' he said.

'I'm sorry. I was confused, that's all … I can't lose you now … I – *we* need you.'

'We?' asked Andy.

She smiled and cupped her stomach. 'Me and our baby.'

Private Edward (Butch) Dugan,
3rd Royal Australian Regiment,
Australian Task Force,
Nui Dat, Phuoc Tuy Province,
Republic of South Vietnam.

Dear Andy,

Vietnam isn't what I expected. I imagined storming the beaches; instead, we flew in-country on a commercial airliner, our duffle bags clinking with duty-free scotch. We've been with the Task Force at Nui Dat for three weeks, and I still haven't seen much of the war.

I feel so fresh-faced. The grunts call us cherries. Last week we were assigned our duties and I think I struck gold. After months at the School of Infantry and weeks of jungle warfare training up at Canungra, the army decided to issue this over-trained jungle killer a set of car keys instead of a gun. Probably just as well.

Yesterday, I accompanied my lieutenant on an ordinance audit to Vaung Tau. That's the dock where our ships drop new men and supplies. It's also the closest Leave-In-Country destination for *the Australians. There's a lot of French architecture, and lots of beaches. I think that's what the Aussies like most about it. The bargirls probably have something to do with it too. The area is divided into the front beach and the back beach. Our guys drink at the front, while the Viet Cong drink at the back just yards away.*

Anyway, back behind the wire now, safe and warm — the thermometer just topped ninety degrees. Between the rain and the humidity, I don't think I've been dry since I stepped off the plane.

Give my love to Dana, and I'll write again soon.

Butch

*

Fridays were dropped from the training program, so Andy began accompanying Dana to her committee meetings, and noticed how the anti-war movement had begun to attract more radical people. Fewer concerned parents and more dropouts, their hair long and their tie-dyed shirts stinking of dope. Andy felt he didn't belong, and wondered why Dana thought she did.

He was running the Gestetner duplicator, printing flyers for a weekend letterbox drop the night Steve Holloway first arrived. Why people assumed he knew how to run the damned thing, just because he worked at a newspaper, was beyond him. He had ripped four stencils that night already, and the blue ink had ruined his third shirt in as many weeks. 'There's more ink on you than the darn flyers,' Dana pointed out.

Holloway's father owned the hardware store in town, but Andy didn't care for his assertiveness. Holloway told Andy he had dropped out of a law degree at Sydney University to help at his father's store. If university taught Holloway anything, Andy thought, it was how to organise an effective protest rally.

But Andy kept his feelings to himself; easy, until Dana announced that Holloway's father had offered her a cashier's job. The jealousy rose, trying to drag the old badshit up with it. He didn't want her anywhere near Holloway. 'I just don't see why you have to work *there*?' he said.

'I don't see too many other offers coming in.'

'You haven't been looking,' Andy said. 'In fact, I'm surprised you can find time to work at all with everything you do for that damned committee.'

As soon as he said it, he realised he'd crossed the line, and tried to rein the jealousy in. 'I'm sorry,' he said, 'that's not what I meant. It's just ... Well, jeez, Dana, in another few months you'll be quitting to have our baby anyway.'

'We need the money *now*, Andy. Besides, Steve's father said I could come back part-time after the baby is born.' She rolled her eyes. 'Maybe we won't have to rent forever.'

'I don't like it, Dana.'

'All right, fine.' Her face flushed. 'Give me one,' she said, holding up her finger, 'just *one* good reason why I shouldn't earn us a little extra money?'

Andy looked her in the eyes and melted. He hated confrontation. It was only an argument, but it still flicked that switch, reminding him of his parents at their worst.

'I don't suppose I can give a good reason,' he answered tenderly, staring at the floor, the fight gone. 'But … It's Steve Holloway.' Looking back into her eyes, he felt determined to tell her what he thought of him. 'I don't like him! I don't like the way he takes control of everything, the way he belittles people who can't do things the way he wants them done. And I definitely don't like the way he looks at you.'

There was a brief silence as her expression softened. 'Oh, baby, you're jealous,' she said wrapping her arms around him.

Private Edward (Butch) Dugan,

3rd Royal Australian Regiment,

Australian Task Force,

Nui Dat, Phuoc Tuy Province,

Republic of South Vietnam.

Dear Andy,

One of the men I came over here with was killed last week, and I have no doubt we're at war now. I felt so bad about it that I requested a transfer back to the 3rd Battalion infantry, but my request was knocked back. Every time I hear about 3 RAR going outside the wire, I feel I should be there with them.

I recently had my first encounter with the Americans. My lieutenant and I had to deliver documents to Saigon. We flew in a US chopper. Man, you should see this country by air. It's beautiful. The mountains. The checkerboard paddy fields. Even though the Noggy villages look peaceful below, our door gunners got nervous whenever we flew over them.

I was kicking around Saigon airport while the chopper made ready to return. There was a problem with one of the parked transport planes, because the truck doing the sullage pumping *had broken down. The driver tried to fix the pump, but was too slow for the Guam-bound plane. The captain came out of the aircraft telling him he would have him 'severely reprimanded if this plane isn't back in the air in ten minutes.'*

The driver threw down his tools, spat and looked the Captain square in the eyes. He said, 'With all due respect, I have no rank, it's ninety degrees in the fucking shade and I'm stationed in Viet-fucking-Nam for a year pumping shit out of airplanes. Just how are you planning to punish me?'

Sums it up nicely.

It's late afternoon as I write this, safe inside the wire. There's a saying here: 'We own the day. Charlie owns the night.' The base was mortared yesterday on the northern perimeter, the usual hit and run, but by the time I got there it was over. I think my biggest fear is going home without any war stories for my grandkids.

I'm approaching my tour's halfway mark now and think of home a lot. I miss everyone. Give my love to Dana, and have a happy birthday. Wish I was there to celebrate.

Butch

Dana had been working at the hardware store for a month. The day before his birthday, Andy walked into town to meet her for lunch, but as he crossed Main Street his stomach tightened.

He could see Steve Holloway with Dana through the store window, could make out his wife's smile. She began to laugh at something Holloway said, cupping the little mound that was their child. A sense of rage grew as Andy watched them. The jealousy rose, feeding the badshit, raising it from its dormant state. He'd forgotten the strength it gave him, suddenly remembering all the things in his life that nurtured it. The badshit, there to fuel his father's rage; there to witness his mother's demise; there to watch the Game. Always there … always. Now it drove him, his heart thumping blood to muscles that wanted to tear flesh and take the bastard down.

Holloway brushed a hair from Dana's cheek as a car sounded its horn and Andy found himself standing in the middle of the road, staring down a Mercedes. He placed his clenched fists on the bonnet, his eyes fixed on the windscreen. The driver, a woman, appeared frightened, and Andy caught his reflection, the rage staring back with his father's eyes.

No! He would not become the badshit's medium.

Andy took a last look at his reflection, relieved his father was gone. He stepped back to wave the car on, and when he looked up, Dana was running out of the store to meet him, her smile filling his soul and sending the other emotions cowering back into the shadows. Holloway was gone, but the pain in Andy's gut remained, the muscles in his jaw aching with the tension. He met Dana on the store side of the road and kissed her softly, hoping Holloway could see them.

'Hey, Andy,' she said, 'you're squashing our baby.'

'Sorry,' he said, hoping she didn't recognise the residue of hate in his eyes. 'You ready for lunch?'

'Yeah. Cinema Café?'

'Great,' he said, smiling. He kissed her again, this time a little gentler, but lingering, still hoping Holloway could see them.

Dana pulled away, glancing at her watch. 'Save it for tonight, birthday boy. I only get thirty minutes for lunch.'

*

Andy watched Dana sleeping as he fell in love all over again.

He lay restless. It was warm inside the loft, but the wind rattling a window reminded him of the cold night outside. Turning off the bedside lamp, he let his eyes adjust to the darkness. Dana's perfect form reappeared, lying naked on her side, one arm curled under her chin. He smiled, but felt a wave of anxiety roll over him.

What if I ever lost you? he thought.

The clock showed 12.30. It was official: he was now nineteen. He drew a deep breath and held it before slowly exhaling, the knot of anxiety still tight. He rolled toward his wife, placing the palm of one hand gently on her stomach. Perhaps it was his imagination, but he was certain the baby moved. Dana opened her eyes and smiled, then rolled over and pulled the blankets across her body.

Andy rested on one elbow. Through the window, the star Antares, the red heart of Scorpius, slowly descended behind the mountains.

NUI DAT
SEP 3
1967
VIETNAM

Private Edward (Butch) Dugan,
3rd Royal Australian Regiment,
Australian Task Force,
Nui Dat, Phuoc Tuy Province,
Republic of South Vietnam.

Dear Andy,

*The grunts here say Vietnam is 99% boredom, and 1%
adrenalin rush. That's okay when you're treading deep jungle for
days, but I don't even get to do that, stuck in an office. When I first
got here, I thought the only danger was getting a paper cut, and
they don't send you home for that.*

*It seems the closer I get to going home (three months to go), the
more anxious I become. When I arrived in-country, I didn't give
a shit, but I'm that bloody jumpy at shadows now it's not funny.
It's like every Noggy is hell-bent on making sure I don't make it
home alive.*

*The base was attacked again one night last week, badly
wounding a sentry (I even managed to fire a few shots off
myself). Charlie tests the perimeter every now and then to
see where our machine guns are placed. I saw a mass of trace*

in-bound, then it was over. The best thing we can do is resist firing back. There's another saying here: 'Trace goes both ways.' That's how Charlie marks our defensive lines, so we change positions every night. A patrol came back in the next day without a body count, but they'd seen where Charlie had been.

The next day I woke to find a bullet hole an inch above my head in the wall next to my bunk. Can't tell whether it was a friendly stray or one of Charlie's, but either way, I realised how quickly life can come to an end here. Three months is a long time in the Nam. I can't remember what it's like to feel safe any more.

I'll see you soon. Maybe we can go fishing when I get back. Give my love to Dana; hope the pregnancy's not too hard on her.

Butch

*

JOSEPH Edward Walker was born on 3rd October, 1967. Immediately, his name became Joey. The next day, Andy received notice that he had to register for the draft. He didn't tell Dana – how could he?

And on 5th October, the war finally came home when Andy learnt Butch had been killed. Andy went alone to the ruined sandstone cottage. He ran his finger through the inscription Butch had carved in the wall all those years ago:

Butch & Andy
Legends
1960

39

Red Adams had been Blackwater's law for as long as I could remember. The day the police station closed, the sergeant looked relaxed and content, driving out of town with Lonesome's head stretched through the passenger's window, his wet tongue trailing from the corner of his grey-whiskered mouth. Red looked me in the eye that day. That's when I realised he knew everything about my involvement with Kyle. I nodded my thanks, and watched him drive over the bridge.

AFTER dusting the photo of him and his father, Red placed it in the cardboard box on his desk with the rest of his personal belongings. Constable Burrows had left a week ago for his posting in the city, leaving Red to wind things up at Blackwater. He stepped over Lonesome, sleeping on his side as usual, his legs twitching, whimpering every now and then. Sitting back in his chair, Red wondered if he'd ever find another so contoured to his body. He then wondered the same about Blackwater: would he ever find a town more contoured to his soul? He considered the office, dustcovers over everything except his own desk, every inch a memory. Closing his eyes, a murmur of traffic and the ticking of the wall clock were the only sounds he could hear. He didn't know how to say goodbye, so quiet contemplation would have to do. Red smiled, deciding he could move on, a new beginning, with no loose ends.

The Lottery

40

December 1967. The month Prime Minister Harold Holt disappeared off Victoria's Portsea. On the other side of the world, the first transplanted heartbeat inside the chest of a human courtesy of Dr Christian Barnard. Yet, in Blackwater, my future collapsed in a ballot on national television. First the numbers tumbled out, the birthdays they represented read aloud like the prize in some morbid lottery. I was drafted. My whole life – father, husband, national oarsman – on hold while I served my country.

BATHED in the TV's blue light, Andy closed his eyes. 'Christ, no,' he whispered. He looked across to Dana, her tears already beginning.

She cried for days, pleading for Andy to challenge the draft. 'It's not draft dodging,' she cried. 'They're called conscientious objectors, and they have lobby groups out there right now trying to make a legal argument against the draft. There's nothing morally wrong with refusing to kill.'

The argument was becoming tedious, and it broke his heart that Dana felt this way, but he wasn't about to go to prison for someone else's convictions. 'I just don't think I can. It's running away, and you're asking me to do something that's not in my nature.'

'It's not *running*. It's – it's standing your ground.'

'Yeah, standing my ground in a prison cell, or on the run like some criminal.' He couldn't help raising his voice. 'Do you think I'm happy with the timing? I'm supposed to be rowing in next year's Olympics, for God's sake.' He could feel the badshit rising with his blood pressure, clenching his fists. 'Maybe they'll let me off because of that, but if they don't, I'd prefer to do my service rather than spend years on the run.'

She slapped his face. 'If not for you, then for *us*,' she cried and ran into the nursery to Joey.

The sting in his cheek snapped him out of the rage.

'I'd prefer you were alive in prison than dead on the battle field,' she yelled, and Joey responded with a cry of his own.

The weeks that followed grew difficult. As hard as he tried to convince himself that time would mend the conflict, it wasn't so. The holidays were filled with disappointment. It was Joey's first Christmas, and the final countdown toward the Mexico Olympics began. Andy became the invisible man around the house, fits of depression only ever a breath away. Although these episodes never lasted long, he'd learnt how to mask them.

Alone, he picked up the photo of Dana and Joe – the one with them playing beneath the jacarandas by the clubhouse. His whole world was right there, and he didn't realise he was crying until the first tear splashed the glass.

When he phoned the national coach with the draft results, Andy knew that it was the end of his Olympics. A week later, the Australian Rowing Association formally dropped him from the crew. He was empty inside, everything he had built had fallen.

41

I thought about Kyle Tucker often before leaving for the army, wondering whose prison had the higher walls – his, or mine.

TESS Jansen sat alone in the meeting room at Long Bay Gaol, the metal benches and table bolted firmly to the floor, cold to the touch. Although just thirty-six, the cold made her finger joints ache lately, and she worried that the early arthritis her mother suffered might be hereditary. She rubbed her hands together for circulation, then adjusted the comb holding her honey blonde hair off her face, taking the opportunity to review her appearance in the compact mirror she took from the briefcase at her feet. This wasn't her first case study in the prison system and she knew perception was everything inside. She felt she needed to project a grey image of neutrality. Her hazel eyes stared back at her, bright and clear behind little make-up. She knew to play down her looks when interviewing in prison, and had removed her wedding ring, though aware of the ten-year groove left in its place.

Although a qualified forensic psychologist, her current work was limited to the clinical area, with the legal cases going to her male peers in either the Prisons Department or those close to the State Coroner. Her practice was small but busy, on the edge of the city, just her and Jody her receptionist. The request to act as expert witness for the prosecution in the recent Kyle Tucker case had surprised her, because it had been seven years since she'd completed the criminal profiling studies for the Goulburn Prison Psychiatric Board.

She was proud of her Goulburn work, even though the outcome left a bitter taste in her mouth. She'd put in the hours, many unpaid, and written the report of her career, only to have the credit go to Davis, her supervising psychologist. While Davis' career received a healthy boost, she was left to linger back in the world of clinical practice. But it wasn't all bad, because when the prosecutor in the Tucker case couldn't locate Davis, he looked up the second name on the report – hers.

Profiling Tucker for the trial reawoke something she thought she had left back at Goulburn, a branch of Baron-Cohen's 1955 concept *Theory of Mind*, spawned from studying the ability to attribute mental states. Tess had chosen to target the criminal mind, calling her theory Associative Recognition. This time around, she wouldn't let anyone else take the credit for her work. Having Tucker land in her lap was the opportunity she needed to advance her career and she planned to clutch it with both hands.

She could hear prison officers on the other side of the steel door, locked after she'd been escorted inside. Putting away her compact, she took Tucker's file from her briefcase and placed it on the table. She fingered through the correspondence to the Prison

Psych Board, wincing at how difficult it had been to get them to cooperate with the research she wanted to carry out, particularly on a prisoner she'd helped convict. There were so many conditions attached, peer reviews and total disclosure to the board being the most onerous. But here she was.

It was getting colder in the room, despite the summer heat outside. She rubbed her aching hands together again as the door's peephole cover slid open and a guard announced, 'Tucker's on his way, Miss Jansen.'

'Thank you.' She didn't bother correcting him, but looked down at the groove on her ring finger.

The peephole closed with a clang.

*

Kyle stood inside his cell door, his hands through the access hatch while the guard outside put the handcuffs on his wrists. When the cuffs tightened that extra notch, Kyle knew it was Dawson. Kyle had recognised his cruel streak on day one.

'Step away, Tucker.'

Kyle stepped back as the latch fell and the door swung open to reveal Dawson's familiar smirk, the ill-fitting uniform, the greased-back hair.

'Let's not keep your date waiting.' With his baton resting at his shoulder, Dawson stepped around Kyle to follow him out. 'You know the way.'

'Thank you.' His voice was measured and calm, but the wolf within cried silently beneath the ink, *I know you, Dawson! You and I, we're not so different.*

Stepping out into the hall of the protection wing, Kyle felt the claustrophobia of his cell lift, drawing air to acclimatise.

'What's with you and this Jansen woman?' asked Dawson. 'Isn't she the one that sent you here?'

Turning a corner on his way to the interview room, Kyle considered the question. 'Something like that.'

∗

Tess stood as Tucker came inside. A knot of trepidation tightened as she held out her hand. 'Hello, Mr Tucker. Thank you for seeing me.'

He held out both cuffed hands, cupping hers gently in his right. 'As it turned out, I wasn't all that busy,' he said. His eyes stayed focused on the handcuffs as he let her hand slip from his.

'Are the restraints completely necessary, Officer Dawson?' She returned to the bench, gesturing for Kyle to join her on the opposite side of the table.

'I'm afraid so, ma'am. Governor's orders. If you want an unsupervised meeting, then the cuffs stay on.' He was walking out of the door.

'It's okay,' Tucker said. Resting his hands on the table in front of him he added, 'Rules are rules.'

'If you need anything, I'll be right outside.'

'Thank you,' she said as the door closed and locked. She made eye contact with Tucker, realising she felt less comfortable than she thought she would. Tucker had lost weight since the trial, and seemed to have fitted into prison life.

'It's been a while,' Tucker said matter-of-factly.

'I'm a little surprised you agreed to meet with me at all.'

Kyle shrugged. 'I hold no grudges. You were only doing your job.' His shoulders dropped, relaxed. 'Truth is, I was impressed with your profile of me, regardless of the lies it was built on. It kind of opened my eyes. You know ... Seeing things through someone else's perspective.'

She tapped the file with her index finger, aware that the right words didn't necessarily make it the truth. She knew Tucker's ability to lie. 'That's why I'm here, Mr Tucker. I'd very much like to explore your profile further. Dig a little deeper.'

'Why?'

She sat back, considering his body language carefully. 'Did you understand the concepts in my profile?'

'Kind of,' he said.

Tess leant forward, arms resting on the table. 'You're extremely perceptive, Mr Tucker. And that's something that sets you aside from most –' she stopped herself.

'Psychopaths,' he finished for her. 'Or would you consider me more of a sociopath?'

She straightened, composing herself. 'They're both just clinical names, Mr Tucker.'

'There's no need to sugar coat it. I'm sure you'll want to label me with something', Kyle shifted in his seat. 'Where is this going?'

'I have a theory I'd like you to help me with. I call it Associative Recognition. Where someone like you, someone with a particular condition, can recognise that same condition in others.'

Tucker immediately thought of Officer Dawson standing outside the door. 'I think I understand,' he said. 'You want a hound dog. Someone to sniff out other psychopaths for you.'

'Associative Recognition,' she corrected him dryly. 'A chance to turn your condition into a gift.'

'A gift?' He laughed. 'For who?'

'For the kid out there who doesn't have to go through what you were capable of doing to them.' She knew this was the turning point, where he would accept her invitation or reject it outright. 'For the parents who won't have to bury their child.' She studied his expression. 'This is a chance for you to do some good, Mr Tucker. To identify potential killers *before* they can kill.'

Tucker took a moment to reply, his expression sober. 'What's in it for me?'

'I'm not in a position to offer favours, Mr Tucker. But I may be able to arrange certain privileges in here.'

Kyle smiled, his gaze falling to his hands.

'What's so funny?'

'I know about privileges. It's a system of reward, of manipulation, but at what cost?'

She leant forward, her expression stern. His eyes rose to meet hers. 'I know you do, Mr Tucker.' She tapped on the open file again. 'I wrote your profile, remember.'

'Can I think it over?'

*

The door to Kyle's cell closed with a familiar clang, the guard's footsteps on the concrete outside disappearing up the line with an echo. Kyle collapsed onto his bunk as a wave of anxiety surged through his body. He had managed to keep his cool throughout the meeting with the psychologist, but only just.

Her motives were clear to him. *Never lie to a liar*, he thought. Proving her theory was her way of getting ahead. A means to an end, and he sensed it was more important to her than she made out. He lay on his back, staring at the ceiling, the anxiety ebbing away. Maybe he could use this to his advantage. Find his place in this stinking prison. Maybe even – a way out. He closed his eyes as the walls pressed in.

42

Confirmation of my draft arrived in a manila envelope. Shortly after, I reported to the recruitment centre in Sydney, having to push through a crowd of chanting protesters to enter. One placard read, 'Stop the Draft!' Another, 'Say No To Vietnam!' It pissed me off. After all, not all conscripts were sent to the war.

IT was the platoon's third night out. The jungle's humidity had extracted what little energy Andy had left, leaving him slumped against a tree, his pack digging into his shoulders, rifle heavy in his arms. A trail of sweat ran between his shoulder blades. Then it began to rain again, heavily, relentlessly. The sound on his poncho hood made it difficult to hear anything else. He felt for the condom over his barrel's gas suppressor, a trick he'd learnt to keep the rain and mud out of his weapon. His eyes had long grown accustomed to the night, and he was aware that his section leader was crouched beside a tree ten yards to his left, but the rain had since obscured his view, leaving no chance to read the corporal's hand signals.

Then *pop*, a parachute flare burnt bright above the tree canopy, its phosphorous fuel defying the heavy rain, yet falling faster than usual due to the soaked chute. Andy pressed himself against the tree trunk, his heart pounding, careful not to look directly at the light, knowing it would only take longer to adjust to the darkness that followed. The swaying flare broke through the canopy, casting undulating shadows across the jungle floor. Once again he could see the others scattered around him, his corporal crouching, wiping rain from his face, his eyes wide and weary. There was no instruction to move.

Wait. Like always. Just wait.

The flare hit the ground, burned a moment longer, and then extinguished in a bed of mud. He let his body slump against his cover, legs weak beneath his own mass, spread before him as the mire contoured to his weight. The rain stopped as quickly as it had begun, and Andy slipped the poncho hood off. It was only a temporary relief, since the mosquitoes would soon venture out to feed again.

This was only his second week at Canungra's Jungle Training Centre. How on earth would he survive a year in Vietnam?

He remembered the day he stepped off the bus with the other national service recruits. Back then there was still a chance that he wouldn't see the war; that he could do his time at the National Training Centre and get a posting closer to home. For Dana, it was a compromise. For Andy, the prospect of not missing the first year of Joey's life was still a real possibility. He'd felt certain that their marriage could survive those terms.

Reaching beneath his poncho, Andy patted his breast pocket, feeling Dana's letter crumple beneath his fingers. Only a few ounces of paper, yet it seemed to weigh heavier than his pack and rifle combined.

'Oh, Dana,' he whispered.

The first mosquito buzzed past his ear, reminding him of summer nights in his backyard, watching the stars and listening to the sounds of Blackwater. He stared beyond the crown of trees. No stars tonight, no moon. He slapped at the sting of a mosquito on his neck, just as another flare exploded above them. He looked toward his corporal. And again – wait. He had become an expert at the art of lingering. Like waiting for Dana to reply to his last letter.

Everything had changed when he was posted to the Fourth Royal Australian Regiment. Andy knew it was bad enough being dispatched so far from home to 4 RAR's base at Enoggera, but it grew even worse when his intake of Nashos was assigned to make up the numbers for the regiment's deployment to Vietnam. He recalled how his stomach tightened when his mob received word, how it took him three days to tell Dana.

There was limited access to phones on the base, and Dana grew more agitated with every call. But since Andy's final placement to Canungra's Jungle Training Centre, she'd stopped taking his calls, instead writing to him, leaving him no choice but to write back. He pressed at her letter again as the flare died. She was using their savings to take Joey away, to London. It was crazy, the badshit rising with the suspicion that Holloway had something to do with it. He felt the heaviness of the rifle in his arms, his finger inching toward the trigger at the thought of Holloway with his wife and child. But he couldn't let it eat him away here, the anger only fogging his mind.

A sound startled him from behind, his finger tightening on the trigger. He'd never seen a boobook owl here, but had heard plenty at night. The sound brought him back, his eyes drifting toward his corporal. Something was happening. The corp had his right arm raised in a fist, beckoning the machine-gunner forward before turning his attention to Andy's rifle section, signalling to stand by. Andy reared up, leaning his weight against the tree, his pack trying to drag him back to the mud. He thought about the stories he'd heard of soldiers shooting themselves in the foot over in the Nam to get a ticket home … *Could he do that to save his marriage?* His hands, wet and slippery, gripped his rifle as the corporal signalled for him to move forward, and his muscles protested at the first step.

The heavens opened once more.

*

The rain had stopped, the sky a brilliant blue, its heat drawing moisture from the soaked ground to cook a soup of humidity in the valley. Andy's platoon had been back at the Jungle Training Centre's Kokoda Barracks for three days. But after just two nights in a bunk, they were on their way out again. Andy still had no reply from Dana. Still had no leave approved. It was a private hell, one he kept from everyone except his commanding officer.

'If I sent home every man who received a Dear John letter,' his lieutenant told him, 'we'd only ever be at half strength.' The statement was like ice through Andy's heart.

The evening was drawing near as they mounted the covered trucks, Andy sitting by the tailgate, thankful for the fresh air. They were headed to the live firing range, not far from the barracks, the sunset painting a bank of distant clouds in the west like the sunsets over Blackwater. He reached for his dog-tag chain, clasping Sam's silver oar, trying to draw strength from it. *It's the oar in the water that counts.* But it wasn't helping. He needed more than a stupid trinket to get through this.

Word was they would sleep under canvas, performing a night shoot. The firing range was dug into the valley's foothills, and the humidity dropped slightly as they drove closer, rendering it bearable. Andy took out the photo of Dana and Joe he carried. It was dog-eared and shabby, but it was all he had.

Around midnight, the air thick with the smell of cordite, a cool weather front rolled in from the south. Andy sat with the others, cleaning their rifles beneath the arc lights, the generator humming. His shoulder ached from the rifle butt's impact after hundreds of shots, his ears ringing, his eyes still seeing tracer rounds whenever he closed them.

At least the event was classified low-tact. After the weeks of intense training, Andy looked forward to low-tactical events, the pressure eased, some of the men almost making it a party atmosphere. They gathered wood for a fire, despite the time of year. But with the southern breeze rolling in, Andy found the fire comforting, the flames hypnotic, the crackling soothing, just like the bonfires of his youth.

In ten days he would be on a ship destined for Vietnam. *But Dana and Joey?* He took her letter from his pocket, the ink running in places from his sweat and the rainy nights. He read it again. *Jesus, they could be on their way to London by now.* Andy's eyes were drawn to the empty ammunition boxes, *7.62mm*, stencilled on the sides. Tomorrow was a daytime shoot. Could he fashion an accident, just like those boys in the war? *An accidental discharge,* they called it. *A ticket home,* he called it.

He stood from the rock he was sitting on, screwing up the letter as he approached the fire. When he felt the heat on his face, he cast the paper to the flames and watched it burn.

'Heads up, Andy,' one of the men said, dragging a log toward the fire. 'This is a heavy one. Should burn all night.'

Andy stepped back, and a shower of sparks shot skyward as the log was pitched into the fire. He returned to his rock and the fire exploded. There was a shattering pain in his right leg and a burning sensation in his neck before he fell unconscious.

43

*Not long after Kyle Tucker's trial, I remember a dream,
recurring. At the stroke of midnight, I would hear the
growl of a car's engine driving past the house, always
gone when I got to the window. Until the night I waited
up for it, seeing Tucker's cherry red Holden prowling
past, turning into the driveway, driverless, its chrome
grille turned up in a sneer, its tinted windscreen staring
at me through my window.*

KYLE sat in the recreation room, his attention drawn between the
clock on the wall and the TV screen in front of him. Because of his
status as a protected prisoner, he was allocated time in the rec room,
exercise yard and library when the general population was in lockup.
It was May, four months since his last meeting with Jansen, and this
afternoon he'd agreed to meet her again. It felt good to have control,
as limited as it may be. He dragged it out as long as he could to gauge
how badly she wanted this, and to work out the advantage. But he
knew she would be aware of any ploy. If she guessed his tactics, then
she would also know not to come empty-handed. The clock ticked.

Dawson came into the room, turning the TV off. 'Your
girlfriend's here, Tucker. On your feet, before I let in some of them

other inmates.' His laugh was more like a wheeze. 'And you know what they'd do to you given half a chance.'

Dawson was always quick to remind Kyle of the power he had over him.

'That won't be necessary.' He held out his wrists for the handcuffs he knew would be waiting. He'd learnt to clench the muscles in his wrists before Dawson pulled the cuffs tight, relaxing them again to lessen the pinch.

*

Tess Jansen stepped forward and extended her hand. 'Good to see you again, Mr Tucker.'

'Thank you,' he said with a polite smile. He walked around the table and sat at the bench opposite.

'Can I get you anything?' Dawson asked.

'I'm fine for now,' she said, sitting. She took her files from her briefcase, avoiding Dawson's stare, before adding, 'I'll call you if I need anything in the meantime.'

Dawson turned his attention back to Kyle, a smirk lying just below the surface. 'You behave yourself, Tucker.'

Kyle nodded, holding up his cuffed hands for all to see. 'Of course,' he said dutifully.

Dawson stepped outside and locked the door behind him. 'Four months,' she said, her eyebrows raised. 'I had assumed you'd decided to decline the board's offer.'

'Time is all I have,' he said. 'Have you given any time to *my* request?' He leant forward to mirror her posture.

She maintained eye contact. This was new. Tucker's confidence had grown since she last saw him, and she couldn't help but smile.

'Something funny?' he asked.

'I'm a psychologist, Mr Tucker. You have to understand, my powers to provide the kind of privileges you're after are limited.'

'You're a very good psychologist,' he replied. He leant lazily away from the table. 'I don't believe you would come here today without something to offer.'

Tess was aware of her pulse, of the flush that she knew Tucker would take note of. She lifted a letter from the file, the Prisons Department logo at the top. 'This is what's on offer,' she said, sliding it across to him. 'But the department wants to see some results first. I understand how badly you want out of maximum security, but unless you embrace the spirit of what we're trying to do here, I'll be honest – you won't be going anywhere.'

Her cards were on the table. Kyle drew the letter closer, reading the two paragraphs carefully, showing little expression.

Tess hoped the department's offer was enough. A deal to consider transferring him to the medium-security prison at Grafton if he complied with the board-sanctioned trials.

He nudged the letter back, making eye contact again, frowning. 'Grafton is an old prison with high walls … just like here. I was hoping to see a horizon.'

'I don't think you realise the limitations on this study. The board is being very generous to both of us.' She paused. 'Grafton is a start, Mr Tucker, and a darn good one if you ask me.' She leant forward to engage him further. 'Look at it as a stepping stone. A few years of good service there while we work on my hypothesis, and who knows where you could end up. You have to be patient,' she reminded him. 'One privilege at a time.'

She noticed him wince at the word *privilege*.

'I'm not a very patient man, I'm afraid. Too used to having my own way.'

Tess knew she had to close this. 'Well, unless we can show some firm results, I don't think I can negotiate anything better than Grafton right now.'

His expression bleak, Kyle walked to the window and looked down into the exercise yard. 'Do you see that man standing alone by the shelter?'

She stood. 'I see him,' she said.

'His name is John Smith,' he said. 'A fitting name, don't you think? Just as common as Jones or Brown. He's in here for manslaughter, drunk driving. He's in protective custody because he was a prosecution lawyer on the outside. He's scared every day, and not just because he could die in here if any of those animals got to him, but of something much deeper. That primal fear sown years before.'

'Primal fear?'

'Yeah, I've been reading up on it since our last meeting. Mr Smith's fears were founded long before he became either a lawyer or a killer. And I can predict that the fear that drives him to survive in here is the same fear that will drive him to kill again. Accidently or otherwise.'

'How can you be so sure?'

'Because, everyone has focused on the manslaughter charge. When asked *why* he killed, the natural answer was because he was drunk behind the wheel.'

She stepped closer to the glass to see Smith more clearly. 'But isn't that the answer?'

'Partially. But no one has considered the *root* cause. No one has asked, *why* does he drink?'

'I'm with you so far.'

'Smith drinks to kill the pain, and I didn't have to talk to him for long to find that out. But he can't drink in here, so what is a man to do when he can't kill the pain?'

'Are you saying he'll murder someone in here?'

'I'm saying he'll dig deeper to protect himself from the spectre of who made him like he is. He's not that different to me.' He paused. 'Maybe not that different to you.'

Tess didn't know if that last statement was meant to shake her up. Although she hated to admit it, the pattern Tucker was painting was not uncommon. Whether he got it from a book or not, if Tucker was correct, she was on the right track, and the prospect excited her. 'So what should I do?'

'You're the expert. Maybe take a look at Mr Smith's file. Look for the reason behind the crime, and spend the time to prevent it.'

Tess was so aware of his presence next to her that she felt her flesh crawl. She had to remind herself that he was a convicted child killer. Yet, here they stood, side by side, Tess wondering why she felt more like his equal than his psychologist.

'This,' she said cautiously, 'is what I meant by embracing the spirit of what I'm trying to do here.'

He turned to her and stepped far closer than she felt comfortable with. She was aware she needed to stand her ground and not step away.

'So let's both embrace that spirit,' he said. She could smell the last cigarette on his breath. 'If I'm right – if I can help prove this theory of yours – I want to go home. I want a transfer to the minimum-security prison farm near Blackwater.'

*

Tess sat in the car park outside Long Bay, realising her hands were unsteady on the steering wheel. She felt foolish for letting Tucker gain control – and not for the first time – but was also excited about the potential of her program. What she hadn't realised until now was how badly she wanted this. At thirty-six, she thought her ambition had died with the Goulburn experience, thought she was content with her small practice of depressed housewives and middle-aged men seeking anger management. But no ... This was the turning point, her last chance to gain the career she always wanted. Yet after today's session, her only concern was how far she would go to achieve it.

She reached over to John Smith's case file protruding from the top of her briefcase. Tess had had to do some slick talking for the prison to release it for twenty-four hours. If her analysis matched Tucker's intuitive profile of Smith, then she knew Associative Recognition was possible. It would give her the foundation she needed to build a working model. A model to train damaged people like Tucker to seek out others like themselves. From this would come the basis of pre-emptive therapy and allow her to make her mark.

44

You can't begin to imagine what it's like to wake up and think: I'm alive.

ANDY woke clean, between white sheets, to hear quiet voices murmuring nearby. A ceiling fan moved the air across his face as nurses drifted past like angels. One of them smiled at him and he wanted to cry.

The morphine did what it could, but the pain in his leg fought through, attacking the peace he knew only in sleep. And more than anything, he wanted that peace back. Sleep took the pain in his body and heart away, if only for a short time. He sometimes heard someone screaming, and desperately wanted the nurses to stop them, unaware they were his own screams until he felt the familiar jab of a syringe.

∗

On the morning of 21st December, Andy woke to the voices of astronauts. He sensed it was daylight, but had no desire to open his eyes, content to lie in bed enveloped by the comfort of darkness. He could smell bacon from the kitchen, sense the ceiling fan's breeze on his face. Although his leg was uncomfortable, the pain was a moderate ache now. He wondered how long he had been at the mercy of the morphine, glad suddenly to be feeling anything, even pain. Content with the foggy solitude, he kept his eyes closed like a child faking sleep, happy to listen to the astronaut's voices.

'Oh, we're doing just fine, Houston …' *pip* '… We have a stable orbit and will be in the moon's shadow in approximately four minutes …' *pip.*

'We copy that, Apollo 8 …' *pip* '… Capcon suggests you'll be off the air for a little while over on the dark side …' *pip.*

'Roger that, Houston. We'll see you on the other side …' *pip.*

'And that was Commander Jim Lovell, who, along with his crew, will be spending this Christmas on the return leg from that historic first manned flight around the moon in preparation for the landing scheduled for Apollo 11 later next year. We'd like to thank NASA for the audio today …'

Christmas! How long had he been here?

'Well, if they can send one man to the moon,' came a nurse's voice, 'why not send them all, I say.'

Andy opened his eyes, cringing at the light. The nurses had decorated the ward in red and green crepe paper. *Christmas.* A doctor stood at the end of his bed, white coat open, revealing the nametag above the breast pocket of his army greens, *Captain M. Lorenzo.* He looked up from his clipboard, surprised to find Andy awake.

'Ah, Private Walker,' he said, 'good to see you're conscious.' He stepped around to the bedside and felt Andy's pulse. 'How are we feeling today?'

'We're feeling ...' Andy felt washed out, his mouth dry, his lips parched as he swallowed. 'We're feeling like shit, doc,' he said, his fingers exploring the gauze taped to his throat.

'Considering what you've been through, son, I'm not surprised. It was quite an explosion, they tell me.'

Andy searched the ward for a face from his platoon, but didn't recognise anyone. 'How long have I been here?'

'Almost four weeks. You started drifting in and out of consciousness last week.'

He attempted to sit up, a spasm of pain in his leg deterring him. Dana ... Joey ... Four weeks. 'I need to go home.' He tried clearing his mind, thinking of what he needed to do. 'Where am I anyway?'

'Townsville.'

'What?' Andy spat, fighting through the pain to sit up against the bedhead. 'What the fuck am I doing in Townsville?'

'Relax, private.' The doctor's voice rose as he placed a firm hand on his shoulder, reminding Andy of his senior rank. 'They operated on your leg and neck down at Brisbane while you were still comatose, then flew you up here to the repatriation hospital.'

Andy fell back into the bed. His mind began to swim. 'What the hell happened to me?'

'There was an accident on the Canungra range. An unexploded shell was lodged in a log used in the camp fire. The ordnance could date back to the Second World War when the range was used to train tank crews. Apparently they would use the trees as aiming points to zero their sights.' He shrugged. 'That's how it was explained to me.'

'How long before I can leave?'

'When you can walk on that leg.'

The reality of his situation seeped into Andy's mind, defeat filling every pore.

'Have I had any visitors?'

'No, but we've notified your father. There are some letters in your bedside drawer.'

'My wife?'

The doctor's expression softened. 'No,' he said. 'Although listed as next of kin, we haven't been able to contact her, I'm sorry.'

'What happens now?'

'You get better and you go home.'

As Andy studied the other faces on the ward, the doctor returned the clipboard to the foot of his bed.

'Who are all these other men?' He spoke in a whisper.

'Soldiers … Vietnam.'

Andy sank deeper into the bed, feeling like he didn't belong, like he hadn't earned the right.

45

I didn't much care for earning privileges, a legacy of my time at Greenways. To me, they were just another form of blood money.

A week after their last meeting, Tess Jansen sat opposite Kyle Tucker in the interview room.

'Do you know why I'm here?' she asked.

'To discuss John Smith's suicide,' he said.

She was aware her voice was wavering, and she didn't mind. It made her sound like she was upset. But the fact remained: right or wrong, she was excited. After studying John Smith's case file she recognise traits of possible violent tendencies, but his addictive shortcomings overpowered him, enticing him to drown his fears in alcohol rather than face them with the conflicting responses of reason or violence. Take away self-medication, and his other characteristics would surface. His was a dual personality, *reason* serving him well in the courtroom as a prosecutor, but in here, as a target, *violence* would be the stronger attribute. The truth is, at face value, she would never have diagnosed Smith as a threat. Yet Tucker had.

'Smith killed a guard before he committed suicide, Mr Tucker,' she reminded him. She waited for a response, and Tucker shrugged. 'You were right.'

'Thank you,' he said.

Tess considered his lack of expression, and wondered why he wasn't pushing his request to be transferred to a minimum-security facility.

'How does that make you feel?' she asked.

Tucker smiled. 'The classic shrink's opener,' he said. 'How does that make *you* feel, doc?'

'I'm a psychologist, Mr Tucker, not a psychiatrist. There's no need to address me as *doctor.*' She knew she had to be as brutal with her honesty as Tucker was with his. 'The loss of any life is tragic. But what happened yesterday was always going to happen while you kept this gift to yourself.'

'Are you blaming *me* for their deaths?'

She thought about the chain of events before answering. A simple shiv carved from a plastic toothbrush. Smith stabbed Officer Dawson twenty-seven times, quietly, deliberately, quickly, as Dawson performed his weekly inspection of Smith's cell. Smith then closed the door and hanged himself from a wire cord he'd bartered. An hour later, both bodies were discovered.

'No, I'm not blaming you, Mr Tucker,' she said. 'But you can understand why you now have our attention.'

'So give me what I want,' he said. 'My *privilege.*'

She maintained eye contact. 'Although unfortunate, it's my duty to salvage what I can from this incident. I can't ignore that the Smith case gives great basis to my hypothesis and certainly lays the foundations for an empirical study. And the board agrees. If we can start work immediately, Mr Tucker, I've been assured that we can come to a suitable arrangement.'

And that's when she first saw it in his eyes. From her profile at the trial she knew that the wolf was a manifestation of the power his father once held over him. But the look she saw in his eyes, beyond any clinical name, induced a spasm of fear.

The Long Way Home.

46

*It was the year the bats came to Blackwater; thousands
of them, flying in from the northeast. I watched them
pass overhead, an endless cloud, from the window of my
room above the Quarryman Hotel.*

THREE days, and Andy hadn't set foot outside the room. He told
no one of his homecoming, instead slipping into town under cover
of night like the bats. Since leaving Townsville, life had become a
circus of feverish dreams while he tracked down Dana and Joey.
They had left for London, just like her letter said. A new beginning
where the war and its politics played no part in their lives, she
wrote, leaving no return address. Andy realised that the drive the
badshit once delivered had abandoned him, his body too weary to
pursue Dana, his mind too muddled from the painkillers to think
clearly. After a series of compulsions to board a plane and find
them, in the end he realised that he needed to mend first, needed
to give them a reason to come back. Yet the river still flowed and
life in Blackwater went on.

He drew the curtains and fumbled for the pill bottle on the
bedside table. He was supposed to take two, but swallowed four
with a mouthful of bourbon. Sitting on the edge of the bed in

his underwear, he moved the half-empty food containers from the covers to the waste bin. He had ordered Chinese every night, never able to finish a meal. Propping up the pillows, he lay back, reached for the bourbon bottle again, and prayed for sleep.

Tomorrow I'll let them know I've come home. Tomorrow.

Andy smirked at the thought, aware he'd been telling himself the same thing every night. He lay waiting for the drugs to take effect. *Tomorrow.* Waited for reality to glide on by. *Tomorrow.* Just like the bats. *Tomorrow …*

*

Andy woke with a start, rubbing the week-old whiskers on his face. His fingers explored the shape of the beard, pulling at a few hairs just to feel the pain.

The ceiling fan stirred the air as the ache in his leg returned, reminding him of his fuck-ups, past and present. He hated the mornings, never knowing where he was. Needing a drink, he rolled over and sat on the edge of the bed, the mattress creaking beneath him. As was his morning ritual, he inspected the scars below his right knee.

Andy stood unsteadily, staggered, then limped to the bathroom. After washing his face, he stared at himself in the mirror. He was so thin now, his rib cage prominent, and hospital pale, his close-cropped hair making his face appear gaunt. Maybe he would grow his hair long, like the others his age. Turning his neck to the light, he traced the white scar beneath his stubble with a trembling finger.

'Come on, boy,' he said to the mirror. 'It's tomorrow. Time to go home.' He pictured his father at the house, and his nerves strained at the thought of going back there after believing he would never return. His father had called his ward at the repat hospital, but Andy never spoke to him. What was there to say?

Opening the wardrobe, he considered the army uniform hanging there pressed and clean. It was the only decent clothing he had, but he didn't feel worthy of it. Andy took his dog tags from the breast pocket, his attention drawn to Sam's silver rowing blade. He placed the chain around his neck and closed the door. After a shower and shave, he dressed in the civilian clothes he'd worn when he went to basic training six months earlier. Today the clothes floated over him, making him look even more unwell. Leaving the room at noon, he left his uniform hanging in the hotel wardrobe. He was done with the army. If he needed a reminder of his service days, the dog tags would do – the dog tags and the scars.

He closed the door and placed the key in the lock, noticing his hands shaking. It was Sunday. He wondered if his father would even be home.

47

In those first few days home, I wanted to find solitude from the memories that refused to leave me alone. I wouldn't discover until later, however, that while I sought places to hide, Kyle Tucker sought the opposite.

GONE were Kyle's handcuffs and Tess was allocated an office in the administration wing, with lounges, coffee pot and a view over the car park. She felt pleased. All because of Tucker's cooperation and the positive results she'd been reporting to the Prisons Department's psych board.

She sat in the corner chair as she always did, her notes spread out on the coffee table in front of her, leaving the lounge vacant for Tucker. Routine was important, reinforcing the sense of familiarity she knew put Tucker at ease. He would be escorted in, greet her, have his cuffs unlocked, make a strong black coffee and sit on the lounge. Give her his usual opener, 'So, where were we up to?'

Tess picked up her notes, feeling anxious at how close she was to making a slice of history.

The door opened, and Tucker was escorted in by one of the guards. Tess stood to greet them. Kyle smiled at her as he raised his cuffs so the guard could unlock them, rubbing his wrists when they were free.

'Good morning,' he said, walking past her to the coffee pot at the kitchenette.

Routine, thought Tess with a wry smile. 'Morning, Mr Tucker,' she replied, before nodding her appreciation to the new guard, one she didn't recognise.

'You can call the desk when you're done, ma'am,' the guard said quietly. 'Thank you.' She turned her attention to Kyle as he stirred a sugar into his coffee. *That's different*, she thought. The door closed, and they were alone. She relaxed into her chair, watching him as he sat opposite, waiting for his usual opening comment, but nothing was offered. Instead, he looked past her toward the window as he sipped his coffee.

'You seem distracted,' she said.

'Why do you say that?'

She nodded toward his coffee mug. 'Sugar?'

He stared down into his cup before placing it on the table. 'It was a little bitter. Thanks for noticing.'

'It's my job to notice.'

'Don't read too much into it. I don't have much opportunity to change things in here beyond adding sugar to my coffee.' He gestured to her notes. 'What have we got today?'

'I thought we'd recap what we've established so far.'

'Sure.'

'Well, we've established that Theory of Mind, or Associative Recognition, is plausible. However, I'm still having trouble tapping into your methods outside of the current clinical data. What I need to identify is the *Kyle Tucker-specific* method. For that we need to identify the link binding you and Smith. What it is that allows you to recognise elements of your own make up in a complete stranger.'

Tess kept evaluating Tucker's body language and expressions. Looking for reactions to certain words. But today he was flat and unreceptive.

He sighed, picking up his coffee cup, sipped and toyed his fingertip around the edge. 'Nature?' he queried, putting down the cup again. 'Nurture?' He stirred in his seat. 'I'll be honest, I'm starting to get a little bored with all this.'

She kept calm. 'Bored? But we've made such good progress.' She gestured around the room. 'And surely this is better than handcuffs and a cold interview room.'

'You know it is,' he said, leaning forward, demanding her attention. 'But it's not exactly what we discussed as far as privileges were concerned, is it?'

She met his gaze. 'Then help me find what I'm looking for. Give me a reason to argue a place in a minimum-security facility.'

His frustration rose to the surface. 'You're looking for a silver bullet! A miracle cure! A fucking gene pool that may not even exist!' He stood, pacing the room, his brow furrowed. 'I don't believe this is something you can put a neat little label on.'

Tucker's pacing slowed until he returned to the lounge. He cupped his hands over his face, rubbing his eyes. 'For me, it goes back to my father's attacks, but you already know this.' His hands fell to his side. 'Those attacks left me so guarded that I had to learn to think like him, like a predator, in order to protect myself, to stay one step ahead. But you have to understand, sooner or later, that shit sticks. The predator's persona, which I had to embrace as a matter of survival, stayed with me until it was just as much a part of *me* as it was a part of *him*.'

'Like a parasite?'

'Yeah,' he said calmly, his hand unconsciously brushing the wolf tattoo beneath his sleeve. 'Like a parasite.'

'Surely we're talking about conditioning, though.'

'Perhaps,' he conceded. 'I guess I conditioned myself to recognise the predator wherever it may be. Sooner or later you have to ask yourself, do I remain on guard all my life, or do I reverse the order of things? Armed with what I'd discovered, I had a choice. Do I become the predator over the prey? The hunter over the hunted?' He made eye contact with Tess, his expression showing the closest thing to remorse she'd ever seen in him. 'I can't paint you a picture of what someone like me is supposed to look like, because the picture that society sees is different every time. I can't say whether we're talking nature or nurture. For me, everything I do is instinctive. Surely nature only provides the foundation of humanity, but the evil you're trying to identify and label is nurtured from that humanity – it's not born.'

Tess stifled her own frustration. 'After all this, are you suggesting we can't present a definitive model?'

He tested his coffee, deciding it was too cold. 'I'm saying I can't teach someone how to be me. Not without having them walk around in my skin for a while.' He smiled sarcastically. 'And who would want to do that?'

Tess realised he was right. Associative Recognition couldn't develop any faster than the field of criminal profiling. Profiling's only fault was it was passive, from the outside looking in, data necessarily captured after the fact, based on details left following the crime. What she was looking for was inside knowledge: active over passive. A method of prevention over cure.

'Okay,' she said after some consideration. 'What do you think about utilising your gift first hand instead?'

She had his attention. 'What do you mean?'

'I mean planting you as an observer in a known –' she paused, careful to choose the right word, '– suspicious environment.'

'Do you think that might work?'

'It worked with Smith. We just didn't react in time. With your cooperation, I've convinced the board it's worth testing further.'

He stood quietly. Tess watched him walk to the window, his hands touching the glass. 'Do you see that out there?'

'It's the car park,' she said.

'It's open space, a horizon beyond.' He turned to look at her. 'I can do what you want. I can be your hound dog and sniff out every psychopath you put me down wind of, no matter how clever they are; no matter how dug in they may be. But I want my horizon. I want minimum-security.'

'And if I can't arrange that?'

'Then all you have is a theory.'

48

Coming home, with the mess my head was in, I thought
about Toby frequently, wondering where his breaking
point was before he decided to take his own life.

AS much as he tried to settle, the past continued to haunt Andy,
every shadow in Blackwater shimmering with memories. Joey,
Dana, Toby, Butch ... and his mother. He realised that the accident
at the Jungle Training Centre was the crossroads, leaving layers of
guilt. Guilt at not doing enough to save his marriage; guilt at not
serving his time in the army. It wasn't enough that he couldn't have
things both ways. Now, he was left with nothing, climbing the walls
of his father's house, trying to remain civil, but the bridges had
burned between them long ago. Every time he opened a newspaper
or turned on the TV, there was the war, taunting him, as if he should
be fighting in Vietnam rather than cringing here in Blackwater.
Whenever he looked in the mirror, it was the guilt that stared back.

His father had left for the quarry, and Andy sat on the front
steps, rubbing the ache in his leg, watching the postman on his
bike, the cars on their morning routines, the cycle of suburban
life. Leaves were burning somewhere, the smell of eucalyptus
smoke drifting over the fence. He held the bottle of bourbon to the

morning sun, the amber light reflected on his face. *I am my father's son*, he told himself as he took another drink, contemplating the long night that had passed.

The term 'dreams' wasn't appropriate for the images sleep delivered to him, the explosion, the pain, months of rehab while his family abandoned him. He thought of Holloway, and the badshit stirred. Holloway had disappeared, and Andy hoped he had crawled back under the rock he came from rather than joined Dana in England. There were times when he would say his son's name to the wind and hope it might reach him some day. When Dana had stopped writing, he'd considered hiring a private detective to find them, but the remainder of his service pay wouldn't cover it, which confirmed his need for a job. Something normal back in his life.

Returning to *The Greater Western* wasn't easy; smiling at Ashley Klein and asking for his old job was even harder. All Klein really wanted to know was the one question Andy never wanted to answer.

'So,' he said, leaning back in his leather chair, 'what happened to you up there? Went and hurt yourself, I'm told.'

Wrong fucking place! Wrong fucking time! he wanted to scream.

'Oh,' Andy replied, hoping Klein couldn't smell the bourbon on his breath. 'Training was tough. I wish I could have gone on with the men I trained with but … An accident.' He patted the side of his injured leg. 'An explosion on the range put an end to my fighting days.'

'Do you have any plans to pursue rowing again?' Klein asked with an air of suspicion.

Andy remembered Klein's frustration with the time he spent training when he made the Olympic squad.

Sorry, Ash, but haven't you noticed the fucking wince on my face every time I take a step?

Andy smiled politely. 'No, Mr Klein, I'm afraid my rowing days are over.'

He was due his painkillers, and his hand was unsteady as Klein offered his own to shake. 'Welcome back, Andy,' he said simply. 'We missed you around here.'

✱

Kyle Tucker sat in his usual place on the lounge, coffee in hand, looking across at Tess. He knew something had changed in their relationship, her expression colder than usual, the professional mask she normally wore gone. And he knew about the masks people wore. He felt the wolf stir, suddenly guarded.

'So,' he began, offering something of normality back to the morning, 'where were we up to?'

A faint smile creased the corner of her mouth. 'Let's go straight to *your* agenda this morning, shall we.'

'I refuse to feel bad about wanting to improve my lot in life. Everyone,' he said, leaning forward to place his coffee on the table, his eyes focused on hers, 'and I mean *everyone*, has an agenda.'

'I'm close to finalising your transfer to the prison farm, Mr Tucker.' She broke eye contact. 'It's in the hands of the Prisons Department right now, but based on the results from my – *our* work, and your conduct here at Long Bay, I'm told it's looking positive.'

'That's wonderful.' He sat comfortably, feeling he had control again, masking the sense of relief. Yet there remained a tension between them as Kyle took up his coffee, sipped, and asked, 'So what of *your* agenda?' If she wouldn't tell him what was wrong outright, perhaps he could tease it from her.

'My agenda has never changed, Mr Tucker.'

He nodded. 'Of course,' he said. 'Using a killer to spot a killer. The, "It takes one to know one" theory.'

'Let me ask you a question,' she said bluntly.

Kyle paused. *Here it comes*, he thought.

'If a man like you possesses the ability to recognise evil in another, wouldn't he also possess the ability to manipulate another, let's say even manipulate him to kill another?'

Kyle felt his face flush, felt the control slip away, an image of Smith coming to mind. Was she testing him, or was she throwing down what she'd learnt through her clinical tests? Either way, Kyle decided that she needed him as much as he needed her. But did she want it enough to turn a blind eye for her career's sake? 'You're talking about murder by proxy,' he said.

'I know what I'm talking about, Mr Tucker.'

'Then we're both aware the answer is yes.'

She took a deep unsteady breath. 'Did you manipulate the murder-suicide between Dawson and Smith?'

His expression broke into a smile, and for the first time in months, he felt the blood of the wolf surge in his veins, sensed the tattoo ink shift anxiously under his skin. 'Really,' he said calmly, 'would it make any difference now?' He laughed, standing to pace the floor. 'It's the elephant in the room, isn't it? We both know what happened between Smith and Dawson, but conveniently ignore it because it suits our respective agendas. A smart woman like you must have suspected I had an influence over Smith's actions inside, yet here you are with your deal for a transfer. And why? Because proving your theory is more important than an inmate's life.' He paused by the window overlooking the car park. 'And do you know something, *Mrs* Jansen?'

'Tell me,' she said, uncertain whether the disgust she felt was for Tucker or herself.

'You're right.' He turned to face her again. 'Smith was going to die in here anyway, his own fears would've made sure of that. He wasn't wired for this place.' Kyle resumed his place on the lounge, briefly considering his coffee before pushing it away. 'And Dawson was a man with a black heart and a darker past. You may refer to what I have as either evil or a gift, but I recognised these things in those men, and you know it. You need no more proof of your theory because you know I possess it, even if we had to fabricate that truth.'

Kyle could imagine how she felt, having compromised her professional and moral integrity for her theory, her career.

Tess hastily gathered her files from the coffee table and slipped them into her briefcase. 'I think we're done for the day, Mr Tucker.' As she walked to the door, she added, 'You should hear word of your transfer shortly.'

Tucker guessed he had his answers.

It was 20th July 1969. The alarm chimed six a.m. Stirring from his usual restless sleep, Andy sat awkwardly on the edge of the bed and placed his dog tags around his neck. He rose, cooked enough bacon for two and ate breakfast with his father as they drank tea and listened to the morning news on the radio. At six forty-five his father left for work with little said between them. During the summer months, the quarries started at five a.m., and his father was much happier with the winter starts in sunlight. At seven, Andy called in sick to *The Greater Western*. Ashley sounded pissed off, but Andy didn't care; he was beyond caring. Walking out to the front steps, he sat until the morning sun was high in the sky, the winter air brisk.

Do it! he told himself.

The decision was liberating, and for the first time in months, he felt no pain, just calm and in control, his whole body relaxing, tension falling away. A tear ran down his cheek, and he knew it was happiness. *All over soon*, he told himself.

He stepped back inside to get his father's Lee-Enfield rifle – a souvenir from Frank Walker's own war. It was heavily oiled, the residue sticking to his fingers, the smell strangely sweet. He wiped his hands on his pants and placed a round in the chamber before closing the bolt, and wrapping the weapon in a grey blanket. Stopping at the kitchen radio, his finger had paused over the power button, but he decided to leave it on.

He walked to Riverchase Lane, where the sandstone ruins overlooked the Pond, feeling at home there for the first time since returning to Blackwater, recollections of his youth seeping into his soul with the winter sunshine. His eyes were drawn to the jacaranda tree by the water's edge, the family of feral cats in its branches, a slight breeze rustling the leaves around them. Their numbers had dwindled, perhaps due to foxes, and the matriarch was looking weary with age, but her white princess looked strong, its face to the breeze.

The place was more overgrown than he remembered, the lantana and fennel embracing the building's walls. Inside, Andy rested on a pier in front of the window cavity. He sighed, his gaze caught by the old warped jetty. His finger traced over Butch's carved words in the sandstone, the smell of fennel bringing with it memories of fishing here with his best friend. He missed him.

The she-oaks whispered in the breeze as he unwrapped the rifle before leaning it against the wall, feeling an exaggerated chill pass behind him. He glanced over his shoulder, but no one was there.

'I'm just so fucking confused, Butch,' Andy whispered, trembling. 'I don't think I can go on.' He shook his head and rubbed his temples. 'I'm in a lot of pain, man. In my body – and up here.' He gently tapped his forehead. 'It's all gotten away from me, you know.' He shook his head again and drew a deep breath. 'I don't like what it's doing to me. I can't sleep. I'm angry all the time. And now … Now I'm hitting the bottle just like my old man.'

He looked out over the water and wondered how his best friend would respond.

'I want the pain to stop,' he told Butch. 'I want to sleep without nightmares. Without wondering whether I'll ever see my son again.'

Andy cupped his face in his hands and wept. At first moderately, then uncontrollably. 'I'm sorry,' he pleaded between his fingers. 'I'm so fucking sorry, Butch – Toby – Mum.'

Emotionally exhausted, Andy slumped, lost for words. He felt alone again, and his eyes were drawn to the rifle, his thoughts drifting to his son. And it was clear. He could never know what might happen in the future. Perhaps he needed to give Dana and Joey more time … And make sure there *was* a future. He waited, composed, by the river he loved.

Raising his face to the sun's warmth, he looked at a near-full moon in the noon-day sky, brilliant against the blue, bringing with it a surge of melancholy for his nights under the stars as a boy. He headed home, but not before throwing the Lee-Enfield out into the deep water. The sound of the splash flicked the switch he was longing for, a reason to go on, and he recalled Robert Murphy: just happy to be.

On his way back, his attention remained on the moon, savouring that first gift after turning his back on suicide, unaware of how special it truly was until he stepped into the kitchen at home. Crackling through the static of space came a stranger's voice.

'That's one small step for a man. One giant leap for mankind.'

49

The moon landing in '69 will always possess a special meaning. The day was an opportunity to start again. Sam Mitchell's words, 'It's the oar in the water that counts,' never held more meaning. For others, too, it meant a new beginning.

'HEY, you think they've really done it?' came a voice from the next cell. The words carried through the cold, empty spaces of Long Bay, bouncing off the stone in a way that reminded Kyle how many walls were between him and freedom.

He lay on his bunk, flicking through an over-read copy of *Portnoy's Complaint*, the contraband copy especially popular once the book was banned in the country. Marking his place with a dog-ear, he rolled onto his side. 'Do I think they've done what?' he asked.

'Those Yanks,' came an excited reply. 'Some say the whole moon landing thing is a hoax.'

'So?' Kyle replied.

'So, so what do you think?'

Kyle smiled. 'I think they were right to lock you up.'

'Fuck you,' snapped the voice from the next cell. 'I was just asking your opinion, that's all.'

Kyle sat on the edge of his bunk and lit a cigarette. He shook the lethargy from his face and checked his watch.

Restless, he waited, listening for the footfalls of the guards. One thing he had grown good at was waiting. His anxiety heightened at the sound of the sea beyond the walls. It was so long since he'd first been driven through those gates and learned to survive and mark time.

Solitude, by its very nature, forced Kyle to face his misgivings night after night, to pause naked before a mirror and see what truly stood there. But prison wasn't without its philosophies and teachings either. It taught him patience; taught him caution and vigilance.

If only he'd learnt them earlier; perhaps things would be different and the Game might never have surfaced. With Jansen's help, he was beginning to understand why the childhood terrors of those nights left him craving the same control when he'd become an adult. He could accept the world didn't like his kind, yet he knew no other way to be. After all, the scorpion stings, the spider bites, and the wolf hunts. He checked his watch again. Then he heard the footsteps. The guard stopped at Kyle's cell and slid open the peephole. He carried a large manila envelope, rolling it into a tube before slipping it through the narrow opening.

'It's official, Tucker,' he said. 'You've been downgraded to minimum-security. This time next week, you'll be milking cows on one of Her Majesty's prison farms.'

The peephole slammed shut, and Kyle's heart soared beyond the walls.

The clock radio on the bedside table ticked over to midnight, the music cut short by the ABC beeps counting down to the hour. Tess turned the volume down so as not to disturb her husband, asleep beside her. The first story of course was the moon landing, and she was already sick of hearing about Neil Armstrong's one small step.

She slipped out of bed, careful not to wake her husband. Throwing on her robe, she walked out to the kitchen and put on the kettle. She'd known it would be a rough night when she'd discovered that Tucker would be notified of his transfer. How long would she feel like this, she wondered. Torn between ambition and guilt. But wasn't there also a sense of justice in this after the Goulburn chapter of her life?

She placed a teabag in a clean mug and waited for the water to boil.

Where were Davis' ethics when he gagged her and took the credit for her work? She shook her head in disgust. Perhaps promotion and advancement were paved in shattered ethics, she decided. Wasn't this simply the righting of a wrong? The universe finding its balance? Didn't she owe it to herself to seize this opportunity?

The kettle began to whistle. She took it from the stove and poured the water into her mug. She let it cool before taking a sip; it tasted good, but did nothing for her frame of mind. She could justify her actions all she wanted, but the fact remained: she would have to stay the course and hope that the course would be a short one.

50

*I found comfort in solitude during those early days of
1970, slowly coming to terms with my losses as I began
seeking ways to manage the depressive episodes. In time,
the pain in my damaged leg eased and I slowly weaned
myself off the painkillers, the addiction making me
consider my father's own failings, empathy for the man
seeping in with every serving of cold turkey.*

IT came as a revelation, Andy deciding he didn't need the
medication, even though the craving remained long after he
dropped his last tablet. He endured a week of withdrawal sweats
throughout long nights of broken sleep. But he knew that was just
the meds, substituting the bourbon for drugs.

Reading the article about Tucker's transfer to the minimum-
security prison farm near Blackwater didn't help matters
either. When he first saw the story streaming off his press the
badshit kicked in, the anger wanting to kill the man all over
again, stirring every other misgiving until a soup of rage boiled
inside.

It was the moon that helped him shake off the bottle. The
Blackwater moon. He wanted – needed – to stop drinking before

it became a real problem, before it took his soul. But he knew it wouldn't be easy; he'd still be on edge, still jump at phantoms.

Whenever the telephone rang, it left him wondering if it was Dana … but it never was. He ploughed through the mail each day, praying to see a postmark he didn't recognise, but it never came. That was the revelation. While looking at himself in the mirror one morning, he decided, *I can't let them see me like this.*

As a part of his self-imposed rehab, he walked most afternoons, drawn to the river every time. Walking past the Murphy house, he saw the boy on the veranda, sitting in his wheelchair, a book opened on the table across the armrests. He must be eleven by now, his boyish looks pale but bright, his eyes deep pools of blue. The boy spent a lot of time on the veranda these days. Andy nodded to him, but didn't keep eye contact; he never could.

'You know, I won't bite you, mister.'

It was the first time Andy had heard his voice. He stopped, turned. 'Sorry?'

'You always pass by, but never talk to me. We're neighbours.' He arched forward and turned the page with his stumpy hand. Looking back at Andy, he shrugged. 'After all, I'm armless.'

Smiling, Andy felt torn between pity and admiration at the silly joke. Then the Murphy kid smiled, and Andy laughed. 'You're right,' he said, resting on the fence. 'I won't let it happen again … I'm Andy.'

Murphy nodded, a faint smile breaking. 'I'm Robert.'

Andy pointed to the book. 'What are you reading, Robert?'

'*The Adventures of Huckleberry Finn.*'

Andy raised his eyebrows. 'Mark Twain, life on the river, huh?'

'Yeah,' Robert said. 'Third time. I read this, and I'm right there on the raft alongside Huck and Tom Sawyer.'

'I've got the Classic Comic version at home somewhere. You can have it if you want.'

'I tell you what. I'll arm wrestle you for it.'

Andy shook his head. 'No, something tells me you'd win. I'll bring it around later.'

They chatted for a while, then Andy walked on. It was his habit to rest in the shade of the jacaranda tree behind the ruined cottage after his walks. He looked for the old cat and her brood, but she was nowhere to be seen. Not without its own history, the tree's dense shadow kept him safe from the weighted memories whenever the rowing crews passed by, glimpses of Sam always leaving a stab of guilt. Sam had written to him while he was in hospital, but Andy had never replied.

It was late February, and the summer rains had subsided when he first noticed the *For Sale* sign outside the ruins on Riverchase Lane. At first Andy was amazed: he'd never considered that this place belonged to anyone other than his boyhood memories. Yet staring at the sign, an idea began to form, growing every day until he could think of little else.

51

I recall waking one morning and thinking, 'He's close.'

THE warmth of the morning sun through the windows and the steady hum of the bus' wheels on bitumen provoked a sense of calm. It had been years since Kyle had felt satisfied, and the deeper they drove into the country, the more satisfied he felt. The Prisons Department bus had left Long Bay two hours ago, and Kyle and a prisoner picked up from Parramatta were the only inmates on board, their destination the Goodridge Correctional Centre outside of Blackwater.

Kyle was cuffed to the seat in front of him, craving a cigarette, a coffee. The armed guard sitting at the back of the bus was slowly falling asleep while the second chatted with the driver up front, rarely checking on the condition of the two prisoners. Kyle rested his head against the glass, staring out at the flood plains of corn and fruit orchards as the familiar mountains drew closer. A waft of apple drifted in through the window and he smiled. *Such space,* he thought.

He rolled his shoulders, his muscles beginning to tighten, then leant toward the younger inmate across the aisle, who had kept his head bowed the entire journey, his long stringy hair falling over his face. Initially Kyle thought he was sleeping. Kyle could almost smell the fear.

'Hey there,' he said softly, 'you ever been to the farm before?'

The young man looked cautiously over at Kyle. He had a slim build and smooth face, his dark eyes bearing the scars of an institutional life. Kyle could see years of abuse in his lack of expression. *I know you*, thought Kyle. It was the same dysfunctional traits he looked for in his chosen boys back at Greenways, and he knew how to groom them.

'Nope,' the young man said.

'You're not much of a talker, are you?'

The man returned his attention to the cuffed hands in his lap. 'I talk plenty when I've got something to say.'

'You got a name?'

'Billy.'

'Just Billy?'

'Billy Bones Shepard,' he added.

'Interesting name,' said Kyle.

'My sister added the Bones part. Called me that after some character in a book.'

'*Treasure Island*,' Kyle nodded. 'Have you read it?'

Billy's shoulders sank. 'Nope,' he said softly. 'Can't read too well.'

'Maybe I could teach you,' Kyle offered. 'I'm sure there's a library at the farm.'

Billy looked up, brushing the hair from his eyes. 'You'd do that?'

'I've got nothing but time.' Kyle waited for the next inevitable question after divulging his sentence, but it never came. Kyle smiled. 'That'd be neat,' said Billy.

Kyle sensed the moistness rising in his palms. His mind drifted back to the Game. The wolf was hungry, despite the work he'd been doing with his psychologist. He clutched his hands together, squeezing, the pressure working up his arms.

'You okay there, mister?'

For the first time in years, Kyle found his everyday face. 'I'm fine,' he said. 'Call me Kyle.'

The bus soon pulled into the long drive of the prison farm, the tall Cyclone fencing with its crown of barbed wire seeming flimsy after Long Bay. He could see through to the other side. *A horizon at last.* His mind bristled with a keenness to get settled, to fit into the new system and earn his privileges. But more than that, he wanted to see where all this was leading.

52

*I worked solidly on the cottage and bought a 1960
Ford utility to haul timber and building supplies. I also
bought a rundown plywood caravan from a farmer in
Haywood, jacking it onto brick piers so I could live in it
while building. My toilet was a hole in the ground with
a modesty partition of hessian sacks. I was living like a
pauper, but felt like a millionaire.*

FOR a case of beer, the park ranger slashed the long grass from
corner post to corner post with the council tractor. Andy stood
back and surveyed the cleared land, feeling a sense of order.

Needing to define his boundaries, he erected a sturdy post and
rail fence. With the metric system creeping in, ordering materials
wasn't as simple as it used to be – inches and centimetres didn't
mix when it came to cutting timber. With the lantana cleared, he
gutted the original cottage, leaving only the walls and fireplace
before beginning the new framework in the autumn of 1971.
His life had become the rasping of saws and the smell of sawdust
and paint.

He knew he was in over his head the day he decided to
render the fireplace, the centrepiece of the home. Before doing

so, he decided to replace a broken brick from the hearth's arch. He carefully chipped out the crumbling mortar, pulled out the offending brick, and cleaned the cavity. He was holding the replacement brick when he heard a sound, a cracking, straining. Then the whole face collapsed, mantelpiece and all, a plume of dust and soot billowing in his face.

'What the fuck?' He spat grit from his lips, staring at the bricks piled at his feet, his gaze moving to the one in his hand.

∗

The season was born of a wet summer, the river swelling its banks as it did every few years, but the cottage remained high and dry. He guessed that the days of regular floods would soon be over when the new dam's spillway was complete upriver. Floods had always been a part of life here, but he wouldn't miss them. Using timber pallets from the newspaper's paper store, he laid raised pathways around the property to keep him above the mud.

As the seasons passed, the cottage progressed from its pine timber floors to the shingled roof. Jerry Sheldon, a veteran of the Korean War who sported a neat grey crew-cut and chewed an unlit cigar all day, became his builder. He hummed songs from the fifties while blinking constantly. They were comfortable talking of general army life, but neither spoke of details.

The cottage was structurally complete late in 1972, Andy having built a wide covered veranda to sit on and admire the views. There remained rooms to be painted and the jetty to fix, but the majority of the work was complete.

That summer, he sat in his armchair by the window overlooking the jetty, his fingers speckled with peach-coloured paint while he listened to the water lapping the bank, a plover calling to its mate and the wind in the she-oaks. The sound of home. He wore his long hair in a ponytail, drawing his fingers through his beard as he stared at Butch's inscription in the sandstone. At six o'clock, the sound from the prison siren drifted in from upriver. Andy checked his watch and adjusted the time. As always, the siren's wail reminded him of Kyle Tucker. Building the house had allowed him to shake most of the monkeys off his back. It had given him time to think as he worked, time for broken bones to mend, withered muscles to build and his mind to clear. It gave him time to come to terms with all that had happened, finding order again in his new-found solitude. But solitude was never without its price.

53

Ten years had passed since the Game. Ten long years, and I needed every day of that decade to fully comprehend what effect it had had on me. Sometimes I felt trapped, the old terror still there. As I cleared my head and body of addictions after my national service accident, it became evident that I needed to face the genesis of those fears. I needed to stand and face the man who created them in the first place. But was I strong enough?

THE next weekend, Andy drove his Ford across Queens Bridge toward the Goodridge Correctional Centre, the utility's loose exhaust pipe rattling beneath the floor with every pothole. Nervous, anxious, he grew more agitated with every kilometre, his hands white-knuckled on the wheel as he found himself craving a shot of bourbon for the first time in a year.

*

'Hey, Tucker! You've got a visitor.'

Bleary eyed, Kyle was hosing out the cattle pens after the morning's milking, the smell of stirred-up manure permeating his clothes. Turning off the nozzle, he stared at the guard with an air of confusion. *A visitor?* The only visitor he ever had was Jansen, and she wasn't due for another week.

'Who is it?' he asked, wiping his hands down the front of his overalls.

'How should I know?' answered the guard. 'The governor's office rang it through.'

'But I'm not expecting anyone.'

'Relax,' said the guard, taking out a smoke. 'It's probably some do-goodin' Salvation Army preacher come to save your soul.'

'Well,' said Kyle, scraping cow shit off his boots, 'they'll have their work cut out for them.'

*

The outside visiting area was a grassed compound with scattered picnic benches surrounded by tall fencing. Andy received his visitor's pass at the reception building and was escorted into the compound, where the guard left him, closing the gate with an unnerving clang. The sound reminded Andy he was on Kyle's turf now. Wolf country.

His eyes explored the compound, wondering how much Kyle might have changed, no more the man of white shirts and pens clipped to his breast pocket. No more bowties. The prisoners wore dark green overalls or sweat suits, family and friends sitting with them at the tables as guards wandered among the groups. Their chatter was constant but inaudible, a surge of laughter escaping from time to time. Andy studied each inmate's face, but couldn't recognise Tucker among them. He waited ten minutes and was ready to leave when another guard led a new inmate through the open gate on the far side.

Andy swallowed.

The face was Kyle's, but how it had aged. Andy stared, afraid to look away, the mere sight of Tucker taking him back, stealing air from his lungs.

I can't do this!

Tucker had lost his confident man-on-a-mission step, walking slightly hunched, almost with a shuffle. His hair appeared dirty and unkempt, slicked back over his ears with a single streak of grey above the right eye. His face was weathered and tired with a deep scar down his left cheek, his eyes wide, darting like a nervous animal.

Andy turned, facing the gate, clutching the wire mesh and calling to a guard. 'I'm sorry, but I have to leave.'

The guard looked bemused, no doubt sensing Andy's anxiety.

'Now!' Andy insisted. 'I have to leave now!'

He ran back to his car, his bad leg aching, causing him to limp, keys fumbling at the door before locking himself inside. *The real monsters in this world are right out there in the daylight.* He clutched at his hands to stop them shaking, needing a strong drink more than ever.

*

Kyle was escorted into the compound, trepidation in every move. This wasn't Long Bay, but it had its own rules, and he was still learning them. When the guard left him, he searched for the Salvation Army uniform. Scanning the area it was clear no one was waiting for him, most visitors at the tables talking to other inmates. At first a sense of relief came over him as he stepped deeper into the yard, but then he noticed a man just inside the opposite gate, his back to him, leaving the compound. It didn't really matter, because whoever it was hastily turned and ran back outside the gate, disappearing beyond the wire. Kyle tried to place him, but his only distinguishing feature was a limp.

He shrugged, a sense of uneasiness lingering, the wolf lying low.

*

Andy sat on the veranda, the noon sunlight reflecting in the Pond's ripples. On the way home he had swung into the drive-through behind the Quarryman and bought a bottle of Jim Beam. Twice he prepared to break the seal, and twice he placed it on the railing unopened.

'Fuck it!' he spat, reaching for it again, its weight comforting.

Grasping the neck firmly, he twisted the cork out and drew it under his nose. He inhaled the strong aroma of good whisky, closing his eyes to enjoy it. It was like welcoming an old friend. As if opening his eyes from a pleasant dream, he smiled, but tipped the contents out over the railing.

'Not this time, Tucker,' he whispered.

He pitched the empty bottle into the river, where it bobbed twice before disappearing beneath a trail of bubbles.

54

In 1972 the world's focus was on Munich and my mind drifted back to '68. Four years since my lost Olympics, I recall watching the boat race from my hospital bed, my old crew gliding across the line for silver. As I write this journal entry, my bad leg aches with the memory, and for a second I think I can smell the disinfectant air of my repat ward.

PRIME Minister McMahon committed the government to a gradual withdrawal of Australian troops from the conflict in Vietnam. *That should please Dana,* Andy thought. *Nixon's gone to China and our boys are coming home.*

On the morning of Saturday, 2nd December, Andy drove into town to vote at the federal elections. *It's Time* placards and banners were everywhere, posters of Gough Whitlam flashing the peace sign hanging in every second window along Main Street. Andy could sense something extraordinary on the wind – change. After voting, he drove back to the cottage and took out his toolbox to spend the rest of the morning working on the jetty. A new project for a new day.

Just off the bank, a man in an aluminium punt pulled relentlessly on the outboard's starter cord. Andy walked over to where his tools sat and watched. The man had his back to him, and almost fell out of the boat each time he heaved on the cord, the engine muttering with false hope just before it died. 'Jesus wept!' the man hissed.

Andy froze.

Sam Mitchell? He reached for the silver oar on the dog tags under his shirt, pressing it to his chest. His first instinct was to run, to put as much distance between him and the past as he could. And yet he also wanted to go to the man he once called friend and mentor, the man who coached him through life, love and rowing. *It's the oar in the water that counts.*

Afraid, he made his way back to the house, realising he was running again. He paused, uncertain, then returned to the scene playing out on the Pond as he negotiated the jetty's broken boards. 'Cursing won't get that thing started,' he shouted, hoping Sam wouldn't notice the tremor in his voice.

His old coach pulled the cord one last time. 'Don't tell me –' he hesitated mid-sentence, and glanced over his shoulder.

'Hey,' Andy said.

Sam's expression was a little less surprised than Andy expected. He scrunched his sun-bleached canvas hat in his fist and wiped the sweat from his brow, a smile breaking as he sat back in the boat. 'Well, well, well,' he said, his smile widening. 'Andy Walker, home at last.'

'Been home a while,' Andy said, diverting his eyes.

'I know,' said Sam.

'I meant to catch up,' Andy added, 'meant to answer your letters but …'

Sam waved the comment away as two rowing crews caught up, the oars breaking the water to stop nearby. 'Ah, time gets away,' he said. 'I knew you'd come see me in your own sweet time.' He shrugged as if it didn't matter. 'I heard you got pretty badly hurt.'

'You heard right.' Andy rolled up the cuff of his right leg. 'Bad enough to leave this.'

Sam winced at the scarring. 'I'm sorry, Andy,' he said. 'I truly am.'

'Yeah, well,' he said, gesturing to the cottage behind him, 'I'm doing okay.' He rolled down his pants when he realised Sam's boat crews were looking at his scars too.

'I'm sorry about Dana and Joey, too. If I'd known, maybe I could have stopped her. You know – talked her around.'

Shrugging. 'It is what it is, Sam.'

'We've missed you down at the club.'

'My rowing days are over.' Andy slapped his leg.

'Ah, get out of here. There's plenty to do down there without rowing. And besides, I can't do this forever. I was thinking of retiring soon anyhow.'

'This place and *The Greater Western* keep me pretty busy,' Andy said with a shrug. 'Maybe some other time.'

'Some other time, my arse,' Sam said. 'You'd make a great coach.'

'Maybe, Sam. But it's … It's a little more than I can handle right now.'

'Look, those crews out there are just the tip of the iceberg.' He gestured toward the boats. 'And besides, I'm dying here. I could do with a good number two.' Sam wasn't about to lie down on this.

'Look, I – it's harder for me than you think.'

'Okay, okay.' Sam held up a single finger. 'One day,' he said. 'That's all I'm asking for. Come out on the speedboat with me for just one training session. If you get nothing out of it, well, no harm done.'

Andy thought for a moment. 'One day?' he confirmed.

'One day.'

Andy smiled reluctantly. 'All right,' he conceded. 'I'll see you tomorrow afternoon.'

Satisfied, Sam nodded. 'Four-thirty sharp, on the water.'

'Sure.' Andy felt a surge of emotion for Sam, realising how much he'd missed him. 'Now,' he added, 'what say you throw me a rope and we take a look at that motor of yours?'

Sam grinned. 'Ah, I don't know. Let's just give it one more try.' He crouched at the engine, switched on the fuel line, primed the system and pulled the cord. It jumped to life first go. 'Look at that,' he said, scratching his scalp through thinning hair, 'I must have bumped the fuel tap off.'

On 5th December 1972, for the first time in twenty-three years, a Labor Party governed the country. In Whitlam's first official press conference, he announced the end of conscription and the release of all those imprisoned for resisting the draft.

Redemption's Shore

55

*When I first stepped back inside the clubhouse, it was
as if the walls stood in judgment over me. As I waited
for Sam to arrive, I paced the length of the auditorium,
reacquainting myself with the photographs, brushing
my fingertips across the sepia faces of those who rowed
before me.*

ANDY stopped, staring into his own face in the photograph.
Wearing his Olympic team blazer, the younger Andy smiled back
through eyes that had sought glory and honour in the quest
for gold. He stepped closer to read the caption: *Andrew Walker,
Original 1968 Olympic Team.*

'You've spotted the change, I see,' said Sam from behind him.
He placed a friendly hand on Andy's shoulder. 'It's just a small part
of your life, Andy. There's more ahead yet. And anyway, there's
plenty to be proud of in that statement.'

Andy held up his finger. 'I agreed to give you one day on the
water, Sam. Let's get out there before I change my mind.'

On the water, Andy found order. On the water, he found
freedom. On the water, he could gain control of his life again.
Sam's *one day* was drawing him back into the light. And that day

began a decade of making peace with himself, embracing rowing like an old friend, discovering a familiar joy in the faces of those he coached. He knew that a racing shell wants nothing more than to move as fast as it can through the water, unable to perform without a crew acting as one. One goal; one strength; one focused effort: *the oar in the water.*

*

Andy felt that the seventies were stripping away his values. Disco was killing rock-n-roll, while tie-dyed jeans and long hair made way for the glitter of an even more bizarre fashion era. During the early part of the decade, man walked on the moon twice per year, but Andy couldn't understand why people preferred to watch re-runs of *I Love Lucy* rather than another moon landing.

Prime Minister Whitlam soon came undone when the Governor-General dismissed his government. Many would argue the rights and wrongs, but Andy would always think of Whitlam with affection for bringing home the troops. He hoped Dana was happy.

56

1977, the year Elvis died, the year the ghosts walked out of the mist.

THE King had been dead for a month, but the local radio station was still playing tributes. Andy listened to *Heartbreak Hotel* with a sense of sadness, the car radio hissing waves of static from the morning fog. As his Ford crawled at thirty kilometres an hour, Andy moved his face close to the windscreen, his eyes squinting to pierce the white-out. It was a little after eight a.m., and he was travelling north along Haywood Road when he noticed the first little spectre walk out from the haze.

His headlights caught her for the briefest moment before the vapours engulfed the image. He was about to pull over when he noticed a boy in grey school colours sitting cross-legged in the roadside ditch. No tears, just a blank stare, then he was gone. Clutching the steering wheel, he swerved to the other side of the road. With the Ford barely moving, he watched as two older girls walked hand in hand along the road's double centre lines. One was crying, and her friend held a folded school blazer to a bloody wound at her forehead.

'Oh shit,' he whispered, standing on the brakes as the shadow of a truck loomed before him. He pulled to the roadside, stopping in a hiss of gravel before stepping out, staring bewildered at the quarry truck on its side in the eastern ditch, reeking of spilt diesel.

The driver was suspended in the cabin by his seatbelt, eyes open, mouth frozen in a scream, dead. Andy walked onto the bitumen listening for oncoming cars, but all he could hear were young voices. Another child shambled out of the white. The boy was around eight years old and cradled a deflated football under one arm.

'Hey,' Andy said, his voice shaky. Then louder: 'Hey, what's happened here? How many are hurt?' But the kid kept walking until Andy stepped in front of him. 'Listen,' he tried to reassure him, 'you're injured. You need to get off the road.'

'Can't,' said the kid, his eyes glassy. 'Football practice this morning … Can't be late.' The boy nudged Andy aside and kept walking.

The voices, some crying, were all around him. He crossed the road and walked past two more kids in the ditch, the youngest offering Andy an apple. Andy shook his head and moved on. Ahead he began to make out an orange glow flickering in the mist. He quickened his pace when he realised it was the turning indicator of a school bus.

Gagging on fuel fumes, Andy noticed the weather thinning enough to reveal a tear along the length of the bus from front wheel to back. The gutted vehicle appeared to have left the road and smashed into an ironbark, he could even smell a hint of eucalyptus from the tree's torn trunk. There were kids everywhere, some walking in circles, some sitting dazed, some lying far too still. Andy closed his eyes, seeking a release from the nightmare.

Regaining his composure, he began gathering the children from the crash site, guiding them from the road until a passing semi slowed to a stop. 'Oh, Lord,' cried the driver over the sound of his engine, crossing himself.

'The radio!' Andy yelled to him. 'Call for help! Police … Ambulance … Anything!'

He turned back to the bus, running its length, peering through the broken windows for anyone trapped inside. Many of the seats had crumpled in on themselves on impact, pinning one of the kids between the rows. Hearing his cry, Andy pulled himself through the nearest window and made his way up the constricted aisle. The boy was alone and dazed.

'I can't feel my leg,' the boy told him.

Andy crawled in beside him, where the roof had collapsed, leaving little space to manoeuvre. It was a blessing the boy couldn't see the damage. His leg was crushed below the knee, the steel frame of the seat in front pressed deep into the bone and splinters of white stuck out through the flesh.

'Help's on its way,' Andy said, unsure if the statement was true.

'Can you get my leg out, mister? It's stuck.'

'I don't think it would be a good idea to pull these seats apart right now. You could get sick if I do that.' Andy smiled reassuringly, uncertain of what he should do. 'It's the blood, you see. The bad blood building up behind the wound can rush to your heart and make you sick.'

An ambulance siren sounded in the distance, growing louder, but too slowly for Andy's liking.

'Hear that?' he said. 'That's the ambulance. They'll know what to do.'

The kid's lips quivered, his skin white. Andy held his hand. 'Hey, I'm staying right here until they tell me to get out of their way, okay?'

'Okay.' The kid tried to smile.

'You know,' said Andy, 'it's okay to cry if you want. Even the bravest men cry.' He brushed the kid's fringe from his eyes. 'And anyway, who's gonna see you crying in here?'

'My dad might see me,' he said softly. 'Dad says brave men don't cry.'

'Well, maybe so, but your dad's got to realise brave men earn their passage just like everyone else. And do you know where they earn it?'

'No,' answered the boy.

'They earn it growing up, a small piece at a time.' Andy frowned. 'At times like this.'

A tear ran down the boy's cheek, cutting a path through the dust. Andy wiped it away for him. 'That's it,' he encouraged. 'No one here but you and me. Your dad won't see a thing.'

'But Dad can see me from heaven,' the boy said through sniffles. 'My mum says he's watching over me all the time.'

'Look,' Andy said after some thought, 'whatever your dad told you, I'm sure he's mighty proud of you right now. I know I am.' Andy brushed the boy's brow again to keep the hair from falling back across his eyes. 'Hey, how old are you anyway?' He knew it was a lame attempt to change the subject.

'Eight.'

'I've got a little boy the same age.'

'Does he go to my school?'

The sirens drew closer.

'No, he lives with his mother.'

'What's his name?'

'Joey.'

'Maybe I could meet him some day.'

*

It took forty minutes to cut the boy out of the bus before they stretchered him away. Andy watched as the trolley was rolled into the ambulance, the morning fog having cleared. He felt his legs begin to give way, his own weight too heavy, his bad leg aching. Staggering to the ditch, he sat and watched the ambulance pull away, realising he hadn't even asked the kid his name.

The next day he read the story in the paper at work, searching for any names, but none were mentioned. He recognised his Ford in the crash site picture, but couldn't see himself anywhere. It was surreal, bringing with it a cloud of depression that he couldn't explain. Then, on page three, he saw a story on Robert Murphy. Now eighteen, he had won a scholarship to Sydney University to study law.

57

That damned prison siren haunts me still.

BILLY Bones had asked Kyle the question just as the morning muster siren began to wail. They both waited for it to end.

'What was it like?' Tucker couldn't help but repeat the question, a grin forming. 'Getting away from Long Bay was like being reborn. Do you have any idea what it's like to be reborn, Bones?' The tall corn husks rustled in the breeze.

Kyle and Billy were assigned to tend the northern fields, taking a break while their guard went behind the hayshed to pee. Kyle still had trouble with being left unwatched. This would never have happened at Long Bay. You were either watched or locked up. While waiting, Billy Bones sat whittling the end of a bent twig with his handmade shank.

'You wouldn't much like it in Long Bay,' Kyle said. 'It's a lifeless place. Colourless. Loveless.' He lifted his face to the sun and closed his eyes. 'Yeah, coming here was my rebirth. It's all about growing, I think.'

'Hard to grow this side of the wall,' said Bones. 'Even here,' he shook the wire fence, 'a prison's still a prison, even if you can see through the walls.'

Kyle opened his eyes, pressing his face against the wire. 'Yeah,' he whispered.

Bones threw the twig over the high fence. 'There,' he said, wiping his hands on his shirt and returning the shank inside his pants' waist band. The stick landed in the river and floated downstream. 'That twig's got more freedom than we do.'

Kyle watched as it disappeared around the bend.

'You're right,' he said. 'It's one thing to be born; quite another to grow.' He shook his head then bowed it. 'I can't grow in here can I, Bones?'

Bones turned away from the river, his back resting against the fence. He stared at the outbuildings across the fields, at the men working the tractor and plough. 'You shouldn't go thinking that way, Kyle,' he said calmly. 'You're a lifer: this is as free as it gets for you.' He shrugged. 'Don't go thinking of freedom, man. You break this place and they'll send you back to the Bay.'

Billy straightened when he saw their supervisor returning. The guard zipped his fly before adjusting the rifle strap over his shoulder.

Kyle stared into Billy Bones' eyes, his expression firm. 'I – *we* still have choices. Even in here.'

58

For more than a month, I noticed the boy who came to sit on the bench in the park by the clubhouse. He appeared around five p.m. most days, watching as the crews came in off the water.

IT was April. Andy discovered the blonde-haired boy wandering in the boatshed, running his hand along the smooth hull of a timber boat and humming a tune under his breath. Quietly watching, Andy noticed the slight limp. The kid was around twelve years old, and always wore oversized track pants regardless of the weather. With each uncertain step, his pants rode up to reveal a flash of metal from the calliper brace strapped to his ankle.

Then he remembered the boy trapped in the bus.

After wiping the grease from his hands, Andy discarded the rag and spanner into the boat he was working on and walked over. 'How's it going?' he asked.

'Fine,' said the boy.

'I think we know each other,' Andy said. 'You were in that bus crash five years back.'

The boy nodded, 'Uh huh.'

'Don't you remember me?'

The boy looked into Andy's face.

'I stayed with you until help arrived,' he added.

A smile broke the boy's lips. 'I remember.'

'You don't know how happy I am to see you standing.'

'Yep,' the boy said, tapping the metal frame through his pants. 'I'm just like Steve Austin, only I didn't cost six million dollars to fix.'

Andy laughed. 'Well, I'm glad to meet you under better circumstances,' he said, extending his hand. 'My name's Andy,' he added. 'Andy Walker. What's yours?'

The boy took Andy's hand and shook it firmly. 'Nathan Saunders.'

'Well, Nathan Saunders, I see you down here a lot these days.'

'My mum helps with the club's bookkeeping so I hang out down here until she's done.'

They talked away the afternoon, watching the boats come in at dusk, their wakes as straight as the river course, swirling pools remaining where oars left the water.

'So you like rowing?' Andy asked. 'I can tell by the way you watch the oarsmen out there.'

Nathan paused. 'I've never seen anything more beautiful.'

'Why not give it a go?'

Nathan looked away momentarily, his expression cooling as he pulled up the leg of his track pants. His left leg was firmly strapped to the metal brace. 'Mum says I need two good legs to row.'

Andy considered his reply, then rolled up the right leg of his own jeans to reveal his scars. 'Look at the two of us,' he said slapping his leg like a side of beef. 'Between us we have one good set.'

Nathan laughed, letting his pants leg fall back.

'Come on,' Andy said, lowering his jeans leg again, 'you can be our first bionic boy … Just like Steve Austin, only cheaper.'

'I don't know,' Nathan said sombrely. 'My mum likes to keep me wrapped in cottonwool these days. She's very protective.'

'Maybe I could talk to her.'

Nathan winced. 'No. I couldn't do that to you. She can be … Well, tough sometimes. Not tough like a mother, but tough like a grizzly bear.' He scratched his head, deep in thought. 'Maybe I'll run it by her tonight. You know, test the water.'

'Naathaaan …' His mother was calling from the clubhouse entrance. Andy saw an attractive woman with dark hair tied back in a ponytail. He guessed she was in her early thirties, but at this distance it was hard to say.

Nathan waved to her.

'Come on up,' she cried.

'I've got to go,' Nathan said and hobbled up the bank.

59

I know, now, that Nathan came into my life right when I needed him most.

ANDY spent his evenings toying with plans to incorporate Nathan's leg brace into a rowing scull. Using the fitter's workshop at the newspaper, the prototype took a week to make before he was happy to test it.

Nathan held it up, turning the frame over, considering it from different angles. 'How does it work?' he asked.

'It's simple,' Andy said, eyes beaming with pride. 'In your case, one leg is stronger than the other, right? Which causes you to twist your body whenever you apply pressure on the rowing machine. This brace –' he took it from Nathan and turned it the right way up, '– will attach above the knee of your good leg and be fixed with these –' He pointed to the two cross pieces attached to the frame, '– to the braces on your weak leg.'

'How will that help?'

'Because they're joined, it'll stop your body twisting at the hip, transferring the power from your leg down the centre of the boat where it belongs. No matter how much you favour your good leg, the two braces will transfer the power where it's needed.'

Nathan tested the finished product on the rowing machine, Andy taking notes, marking pinch points on the frame and adjusting the leather straps. The process was painstaking, but after several days, they saw results. Seamless movement, no pinching, no pain. Andy set the rowing machine to simulate a two-thousand-metre-course, and Nathan rowed his best time, the machine's wheel fanning the air with a strong decisive *whirr* on each stroke. After the session, Nathan sat on the machine, exhausted, forcing a smile.

'That … that felt … great,' he said, between breaths. He arched his back, working his lungs. 'I want to get in a boat, Andy – I want to compete.'

The statement caught Andy off guard. 'Well, I want the same thing, but …'

Nathan lowered his head in anticipation. 'I haven't asked Mum yet,' he said softly. 'I'm afraid she'll say no.'

'What if she saw you in action one afternoon, maybe then she'd –'

'No, trust me. That would just bring out the grizzly in her. There's every chance she'd ban me from the club altogether.' Nathan shook his head. 'She doesn't like surprises. Doesn't like me doing anything dangerous.'

Andy placed a hand on Nathan's shoulder. 'I understand her situation. Maybe we need to look at things from her side,' he said. 'Perhaps explain how we're approaching the whole thing, you know, get her involved.'

'Maybe, but –'

'But nothing, ya chicken shit,' Andy said, roughing up Nathan's hair. 'You need to tell her what we've been doing. You need to ask the question.' Andy detached the brace and helped Nathan to his feet. He threw him a towel. 'Come over here, I've got something to show you.'

Nathan followed him to the back of the boatshed. Andy let him catch up before sliding the canvas dustcover off one of the smaller boats resting on the far rack: a single scull, its finish dulled with age.

'Her name is *The Salesbury*, after the river.' Andy stared at the boat with a sense of pride. 'She was launched back in '59, quite a pretty thing in her day, but now used as a trainer.'

'She's amazing,' Nathan said stroking the gunwales. 'Beautiful.'

'And she's yours,' Andy finished.

Nathan paled.

Andy held up his hands in mock surrender. 'The club captain had her earmarked for sale next year so I made him an offer,' he confessed, lowering his hands. 'Now I'm giving her to you.'

A sense of anxiety entered Nathan's voice. He stepped away. 'I … I can't take it,' he finally said. 'Mum won't let me.'

'Don't panic. It can stay here in the boatshed. The old girl needs some work before hitting the water, maybe widen the gunwales to accommodate your callipers, but basically there's plenty of life left in her yet.'

'Oh, Andy,' said Nathan, his voice breaking, 'now I *am* scared.'

Andy shrugged. 'It's good to be scared from time to time. Listen, why don't you let me talk to your mother? If she's as tough as you say, then I'll handle it. Let's face it, we've got nothing to lose.'

'I've got plenty to lose.'

Placing a hand on his shoulder, Andy looked into Nathan's eyes. 'We can't go any further. Not until your mother's on board.'

Nathan knew that as well as Andy did. He approached his new boat, laying both hands across the timber keel. 'Okay,' he said cautiously. 'But don't say I didn't warn you.'

60

'If you live among wolves you have to act like a wolf.'
This was a quote from Nikita Khrushchev I read in
an old Newsweek, and it was probably the first time I
wondered why Kyle became the person he was. I cut this
clipping out to leave in the pages of my journal – the first
of many.

NONE of the inmates knew how old T.J. was, but Kyle guessed he was in his mid-seventies. He told Kyle that he'd been in prison most of his life, so long now he'd forgotten how to live on the outside. Yet, with his collection of *Reader's Digests* and carved toys, old T.J. appeared as content as any man. A part of Kyle envied him his complacency, though he didn't want to think of T.J.'s life as a preview of his own future.

'What are you making there?' Kyle asked. He straddled the bench opposite and studied the old man at work, turning his nose up as a gust of wind blew the stink of the fertilised fields their way.

'A bird,' T.J. said, making the final slice with a razor blade.

T.J. carved his toys from empty plastic bottles and containers from the kitchen trash. Today he was making a bird of paradise, the colours from mustard-yellow, tomato sauce-red and olive-black containers. He slipped the last tail feather into place with a dab of the glue he was so fond of sniffing. Smiling, he held up the finished piece in the sun.

'Not too shabby,' he said, his toothless mouth grinning.

'It looks so real it could fly out of here,' Kyle told him. 'Who knows, maybe it'll take us with it.'

T.J. rolled his shoulders and stretched before taking out his tobacco pouch. 'I'm afraid you'd be flying alone, Tucker.' He began rolling a cigarette. 'Ain't nothin' outside for me nowadays.'

'No family?' Kyle asked. 'Brothers, sisters, children?'

T.J. licked the tip of his smoke and rested it in the corner of his mouth while he searched for a light. 'Nope,' he said striking a match from his pocket. He drew on the cigarette and coughed. 'Had a brother once, long time ago, but he was killed in France during World War II. I never married, never had no kids.' He sighed. 'It's just me.' He spat a piece of tobacco from his lips.

'I'm sorry, T.J.' Kyle felt off guard. 'It doesn't seem right for a man of your years. You shouldn't have to –' Kyle realised he was thinking out loud now. Realised his only consideration was for himself.

'Shouldn't have to die alone?' T.J. finished. He waved Kyle's sentiment off. 'Don't kid yourself, Tucker, we all die alone.'

Kyle sat silently while the old man packed his homemade tools and coloured plastic into his shoebox. He watched the unhurried purpose in T.J.'s manner, listened to the wind humming through the wire of the high fences, hunting the sparrows from their perch. Then he had an idea.

'Here,' said T.J., handing the toy to Kyle. 'Let me know if it ever flies.' He stood with a groan and began walking back to his cell.

'Hey,' Kyle yelled after him, 'teach me.'

T.J. stopped and turned. 'Teach you what? To fly?'

'No,' said Kyle. 'How to make stuff like this.' He held the plastic bird up.

'Sure,' T.J. said before turning to walk away again. 'I got the time.'

'Me, too,' Kyle whispered.

61

I had looked into the eyes of the wolf and worse. But I'd never felt more afraid than when I looked into the eyes of an overprotective mother.

ANDY studied his features in the bathroom mirror. Patting his cheeks, he felt glad to see a little weight returning. But the beard had to go, he decided, scratching at his jaw as he felt for the scar beneath the whiskers. Since returning from hospital, he had embraced the anonymity of a beard, but nothing was forever, and cupping his cheeks, he tried to imagine how he'd look clean shaven. Then he reached behind his head to clutch his ponytail.

The next day he spent his lunchbreak at the barber's, and while waiting for a chair, he reread the story in last week's *The Greater Western* about an Elvis sighting in Blackwater and laughed. The man had been seen more times dead than when he was alive.

'Been a while since we've seen you round here,' said the barber.

Andy put the paper down and sat in the chair, the barber tying the faded apron around his neck. The smell of Brylcreem and hair lotion filled the air, and the radio was tuned to the horse racing station, reminding Andy of his days here as a kid.

'Let's make up for lost time then, Bernie,' Andy said. 'How about you give me the works. Short back and sides and a shave.'

Bernie Carlton whistled under his breath, tilting the chair. 'Must be a new woman on the scene.'

'Give me a break,' said Andy settling back. 'I just want to clean myself up.'

'Sure thing,' he said with a clean slice of the scissors. He held the ponytail up to the mirror like a trophy kill. 'You want to keep this for posterity?'

*

His shift at the newspaper over, Andy drove to the boatshed, cleaning out the storeroom until Nathan arrived.

'Wow,' said Nathan with a double-take at Andy's new look. 'You've … changed.'

'Thought it might help,' he said. 'With your mother, I mean.'

Standing outside the shed, Andy steadied himself, his eyes set squarely on the doors ahead. 'Right,' he said, sounding like John Wayne about to storm the beaches of Iwo Jima, 'I'm going in.'

'Good luck,' was all Nathan could say.

The administration office was located to the left inside the entrance. Knocking first, Andy stepped inside, but the room was empty. He walked along the hallway to the function room looking for Nathan's mother, finding her studying the photographs, a pen tucked behind her ear, sipping a Coke through a bent straw.

If she'd noticed Andy, she wasn't letting on. He saw Nathan's features in hers, except his blonde hair, which must have come from his father. Her own dark hair, shoulder length, was held back with a comb.

'That's me,' Andy said, stepping forward and pointing to the photo on the wall in front of her. As introductions go, he knew it was clumsy.

She turned, studying Andy's face before returning to the photograph, leaning forward slightly to better read the inscription. 'It says here you were an Olympian,' she said. 'Very impressive.'

'The Olympian that never was, I'm afraid,' he said. 'Made the crew in '68, but the draft got in the way.'

'I know what you mean,' she said, her expression sobering. 'The draft got in *my* way too.'

'You served?' Andy asked, thinking she might have been on the medical staff.

'No,' she said, 'my husband. Drafted in '69, made it through Vietnam without so much as a blister on his foot. Then – then the silly bastard volunteered for a second tour.' She finished her Coke, her nose turned up slightly from a rush of bubbles. 'He's buried up at Saint Stephen's,' she added, throwing the empty bottle into the bin by the door. 'We visit him on weekends.'

'I'm sorry.'

'Yeah, me too,' she said. 'Anyway, I've got work to do. Nice to meet you –' she glanced at the name under the photograph and added, '– Andrew Walker.'

'Actually,' Andy broke in, 'I was hoping to talk to you about Nathan.'

Her eyebrows raised. 'You know my son?'

'Well, yes,' he said nervously.

'How's that?' She appeared a little defensive, and Andy was reminded of Nathan's reference to grizzly bears.

His face flushed. 'Well,' he said, swallowing, 'I coach some of the kids here at the club and … And your boy began hanging around the dock in the afternoons you see …' This wasn't going well. 'And, as it turns out, Nathan and I began talking and he told me he was interested in rowing so I –'

'Now I know you,' she said rocking her finger toward him. 'I've seen you with Nathan.' She smiled, brushing Andy's smooth cheek with the back of her hand. 'You've cleaned yourself up.' She stood back, and shook her head. 'I'm sorry, but the answer's no. Nathan can't row. In case it escaped your attention, my boy only has one good leg. Last time I looked, you needed two.'

'That's not necessarily true. Nathan doesn't have to row sweep-oar with a crew. He can row by himself. In the sculls.'

'Look,' she said, turning on him in the office doorway, 'I don't expect you to understand this, but since Nathan's accident I have two rules. I will *not* place my boy in a position of harm. And I will *not* set him unrealistic goals.'

'You don't understand,' said Andy.

'No, Mr Walker, *you* don't understand!' She slammed the door shut.

Andy was silent, anxious and flushed as he stood before the grizzly's den. 'Shit,' he muttered, turning to make his escape.

'How did it go?' the boy asked from the dock, already suspecting the answer by Andy's expression.

'Not good,' he replied. 'Why didn't you tell me she was so tough?'

Nathan shrugged. 'I thought I did.'

'Losing the battle doesn't mean we've lost the war,' Andy said, sitting at the water's edge. 'I need to give it some thought. Maybe you can put in a good word for me at home tonight.'

Nathan sat beside him. 'Oh boy,' he said quietly.

*

Andy was nodding off to *The Sullivans* on his new colour TV when the telephone rang. Yawning, he checked the wall clock and rubbed his eyes, the taste of chilli lingering from dinner.

'Hello.'

'Is that you, Mr Walker?'

'Uh huh,' Andy answered, checking the time again.

'It's Grace Saunders, Nathan's mother.'

'Oh.' He frowned, confused. 'What can I do for you, Grace?'

'I want to apologise for this afternoon. I was out of line.'

Andy fell silent for longer than he felt comfortable. 'Thanks,' he said, 'but there's no need. I understand, really I do.'

'I'm afraid I get a little overprotective with Nathan,' she said. 'It was so easy when he was a baby, but he's growing up so fast. I guess I need to let go a little.'

The conversation made Andy think about his own son. 'Yeah,' he said rubbing his eyes again, 'time gets away, huh?' He carried the phone to the armchair and sat. 'Look, it's okay. You're his mother, and I've got to respect your wishes. To tell you the truth, I think I could have handled things better myself. I had no right ambushing you at work. Nathan's a good kid, Grace. He's passionate about the sport, and I wanted to help him out, that's all.'

'He told me you were at the accident,' she said. 'He told me you stayed with him until help arrived.'

'Anyone would have done the same.'

'Maybe so, but *you* were that anyone and I wanted to thank you.'

'Like I said, he's a great kid.'

'I'd like to know more, Mr Walker. Tell me what you and my son have been up to down in that boatshed? Maybe we can start there.'

Andy smiled. 'Well, okay, but only if you promise to call me Andy from now on.'

*

Grace hung up, surprised by the time when she looked at the clock on the kitchen oven. God, they had talked for over an hour. She tip-toed into her son's bedroom and watched him sleep. It was going to be difficult letting go.

62

Monsters Finding Monsters. That was the newspaper headline in the story about Kyle Tucker's work with the Prisons Department. I couldn't help but recall Toby's saying all those years ago: the real monsters in this world are right out there in the daylight.

TESS Jansen considered the facilities made available to her at the prison farm. Although it was over a two-hour drive from the office, the more casual surrounds lent themselves to her work with Tucker. Again she had her own office to work from, and although not as large as the one at Long Bay, the view across the fields to the mountain made for a more relaxed environment. *But at what cost?*

The positive press had seen her practice grow to the point of taking on a junior partner, leaving her time to work with the Prisons Department, and already there were profiling offers coming through. Yet her ambition still battled the guilt of compromising the ethics she once held dear. She sighed, knowing her thoughts were simply justifying what she had done, somewhere deep down waiting for that first chink in her armour, that weak link in the chain that held these lies together. She was in too deep, her unholy alliance with Tucker sealed until she could secure her place in the field that she felt owed her a future.

Each time she sat waiting for Tucker, Tess thought about how he had manipulated her. How he had manipulated the system itself to achieve his goal. To get his horizon. And a shiver ran up her spine. *Tucker … would he become that weak link?* But here they were, making good progress in the eyes of the board. Yet the question remained: *What else is he capable of manipulating?* She took up a folder from the desk in front of her, the name Rodney Ellis written on it. Inmate Ellis was their first live case, and now, more than ever, Tess needed to know she had Tucker under control.

The office door was mostly glass, so she saw him approaching unescorted from reception.

'Mrs Jansen,' he said with a smile as he opened the door. 'Did we get our first case study as promised?'

She stood to greet him. 'We did, Mr Tucker.' She still couldn't call him Kyle.

'Good.' His expression sobered, his head tilting slightly in curiosity. 'You seem distracted. A little … flat, perhaps.'

She couldn't drop her guard. She needed to keep Tucker at arm's length without alienating him. 'I'm fine,' she lied. 'Keen to get started.'

He reached into his pocket, her eyes fixed on his hand as he pulled the small object out. 'For you,' he said, his open hand palm-up, revealing the gift. 'I made it myself … It's a key ring.' He seemed quite proud of it.

A gift? This was a little too familiar, even for Tucker. Out of character. She took it between her fingers and held it up. Carved from plastic, it was an oversized key with a silver ring through the eyelet. The word *Jansen* was pressed into the head to look like a brand name. The detail was fine, and it was painted to look like weathered metal. 'You've been busy. It looks … good. Thank you.'

He sat opposite her, his expression pleased. 'An old timer's been teaching me to carve models from plastic containers we get from the kitchen. I'm getting okay at it, don't you think?'

She returned to her own chair, placing the key ring beside the folder on the desk. This was the first pastime he'd adopted since his intake, and it didn't fit. Aside from fishing, there were no hobbies in his past.

'The detail is good, but why a key?' she asked.

He looked disappointed. 'I thought it was clever. You know … a key on a key ring. But then I guess it's your nature to read what you can into it.'

Control, she reminded herself, *without alienation*. 'Of course you're right, Mr Tucker. An occupational hazard, I'm afraid.'

'So,' he said, rubbing his hands together. 'Our case study?'

She slid the folder toward him. 'Rodney Ellis,' she said.

He frowned, taking up the folder and opening the files. 'I don't know the name.'

'He arrives in a week. I want you to read his case file first, establish your own profile, and we'll compare notes. If your initial profile matches mine, I'll know we're on the same page; a base line, if you will, to establish a foundation. He's in for armed robbery, but there are some disturbing flags in his history that concern me. If he is a murderer in the making …'

'How did he get to minimum security?'

'Plea bargain.'

'Why not just show me your profile and I'll tell you if I agree?'

'I don't want to set any seeds. It's important that I know for certain that we concur.'

Kyle closed the folder and placed it on the desk before standing and walking over to the window where he stretched his arms and back. 'I'm beginning to doubt your trust in me.'

Tess looked down at the key ring. *No*, she thought. *No, I don't trust you.* She recalled with regret the day she'd felt like his equal, recalled how their mutual reasoning fed their drive to work together. The fact is, she still needed Tucker, but wasn't so sure if he needed her anymore. *Weak links*, she thought.

'Trust is important in the work we're doing here,' she said. 'Against difficult odds, I arranged that horizon you're looking at, Mr Tucker, so I don't feel I should have to justify my own level of commitment. All I ask is for your full attention on the project.'

He turned to face her. 'What are you afraid of?'

She thought about the question, but in the end there was only one honest answer. 'Your betrayal, Mr Tucker.'

63

I've always been drawn to the workmanship in the wooden racing boats. How something so frail can be so strong.

ANDY completed the work on Nathan's boat a month before the season's first regatta. He widened the gunwales to accommodate the boy's callipers and raised the oar gates to carry the blades higher off the water during the recovery. Because of the boat's vintage, it sat wider than the new generation of sculls. Andy knew it would create additional drag for Nathan, but would also assist with stability. The restoration was a long process, but after sanding the blistered finish back to bare timber, he patched the dry rot and mended the seams before finishing it with three coats of marine lacquer. The boat was always beautiful in Andy's eyes, but now it had its dignity restored, a little piece of himself added to its history like the boat builders before him.

'What do you think, Nathan?' Andy asked the day he finished. They both stood back in admiration. 'She's your boat. It's only right *you* name her.'

'There's only one name I can think of,' he said. '*Grace … Lady Grace*. After Mum.'

Andy smiled. '*Lady Grace* she is,' he said.

*

Two days later, Grace walked the length of the boat. It was the first time she'd seen it, resting on canvas slings outside the boatshed. Her hand caressed the gunwales. 'It looks wonderful, boys,' she declared.

Andy and Nathan stepped nervously back to give her room, glancing at each other for mutual support. Grace noticed her name painted on the bow in gold and outlined the G with her fingertips.

'Nice,' she said flicking the sprung membrane over the bow section like a drum. 'Very nice indeed.' She appeared a little concerned. 'But this must have cost a small fortune to restore.'

'Less than you think,' Andy said. 'A labour of love. Anyway, the cost doesn't matter. It's my gift to Nathan. He can look after her from now on.'

'Oh, I will,' Nathan said.

Grace smiled, combing her fingers affectionately through Nathan's hair. 'Yeah, I know.'

Andy stepped forward, handing Grace a bottle of sparkling wine from the Esky at his feet. 'Can't afford champagne,' he said with a shrug. 'This'll have to do I'm afraid.'

'Go ahead, Mum,' added Nathan. 'She needs to be christened … For luck.'

'Well, boys, I'd be honoured.' Standing by the bow, she grasped the neck of the bottle and took a deep breath before raising it high in the air. 'I christen this boat –' she began with pride.

'*No!*' Nathan and Andy cried out in unison, Nathan standing between his mother and the boat to stop the bottle crashing through the thin plywood.

Grace stalled mid speech, arm still raised but relaxed. 'What?' she asked, her expression blank.

'Just tip the grog over the bow,' Nathan said. 'It's not a battleship, Mum.'

Andy took the bottle from her hand and pulled out the cork. The wine fizzed over the rim. 'Here,' he said, handing it back to her.

She winked at Nathan. 'I'm sure this never happened to Queen Victoria.' Clearing her throat she began again. 'I christen this boat, the *Lady Grace*.' She tipped the wine over the bow as ceremoniously as she could. 'May God bless this vessel and all who sail in her.'

Andy laughed as Nathan mockingly saluted the proceedings.

Shaking out the last few drops, Grace said, 'I suppose you boys are itching to get her in the water, huh?'

Nathan beamed up at his mother the way he'd done since he was a small boy.

'Not without your blessing,' Andy said.

'No doubt about it, you boys know how to play me.'

'I'm ready, Mum,' said Nathan.

Grace cupped his cheek, realising she wouldn't be able to for much longer. 'Sweetheart, you were born ready. Of course you have my blessing.'

'Yes!' Nathan cried, lining Andy up for a high five.

They slapped hands. 'Well,' added Andy, 'let's get her on the water, Joey.'

64

For something to begin, we sometimes need something else to end first.

LATER that afternoon, Andy wiped the water off the boat's upturned shell. The low sun glistened on its timbers, Andy content, feeling a familiar sense of place and belonging. Grace and Nathan had left for the day, but Andy liked nothing more than spending time alone in the boatshed. Ringing out the damp cloth, he closed his eyes and breathed in the scent of lacquered timbers, listening to the whispering she-oaks and the river … always the river.

'Haven't you got a home to go to?'

It was Sam.

'Just finishing up,' he said, turning to face him. Something was different. It was in his eyes.

Sam pulled out an unused boat sling to sit on. 'The boy's boat looks fine, Andy. You did a great job.'

Andy threw the damp rag into the bucket at his feet. 'Okay, Sam,' he said pulling out another sling and sitting opposite, 'what's up?'

'That obvious, huh?'

'To me? Yeah.'

Sam looked around the boatshed, his expression fragile and melancholy.

'I was hoping to find you here, Andy. I wanted you to be the first to know: I'm retiring. This is my last year.'

Andy had known this day would come, but was still shocked. 'Sam – why? I mean, this is what you do.'

'It's time, Andy. The early mornings and late afternoons are getting hard on this old body. I don't want to grow to resent it. I don't want to stick around just because I think I should.' He smiled. 'And besides, I won't leave any void behind. My job is yours now, and I feel pretty good about it. You're a good coach, and I'm mighty proud of what you're doing here.'

'But Sam –'

'But nothing,' he said. 'Like I said, I just wanted you to be the first to know.'

'What are you going to do?'

'Travel while I still can. There's a lot of this country I haven't seen.'

'I'm going to miss you.'

Sam stood, his eyes glistening. 'I'll miss you, too. Just remember what I taught you. Don't make me come back here and kick your arse.'

'How can I forget,' Andy said. 'It's the oar in the water, right?'

65

I remember the first time I realised I had feelings for Grace. It was frightening and wonderful at the same time.

IT was eight p.m. when Andy heard the knock. He opened the door to the chirping of crickets and turned on the porch light. 'Grace,' he said, surprised.

'Hi,' she said smiling.

They'd shared something special that day, seeing Nathan rowing in his own boat. Yet now, as Grace stood in his doorway, she looked different. Then he realised, it wasn't about seeing her differently, it was about seeing her clearly for the first time.

'Come in,' he said. He expected to see Nathan behind her, but she was alone.

Handing Andy a bottle of red wine, she stepped inside. 'It's only cheap, but it's very nice,' she said. 'A formal thank you from Nathan and me.'

Andy winced. *Just the thing for a recovering alcoholic,* he thought. 'Great,' he lied and closed the door behind her. 'Come on through.'

'Wow.' She scanned the house's interior. 'I heard about the renovations on this place. It's beautiful.'

'Thanks,' he said. 'It's still cold outside. Why don't you sit by the fire.' Walking through to the kitchen, he called over his shoulder, 'Do you mind drinking alone? I'm not much of a wine man, I'm afraid.' He searched the drawer for a corkscrew, unsure if he still had one.

'Put it away for another time,' she said. 'A coffee will be fine.'

Thank you, he thought, aborting his search. He pushed the bottle to the back of the pantry and placed the kettle over the hotplate before returning to the lounge room, a twinge of nervousness biting at him. Grace was sitting on the rug in front of the fire, the light softening her features and dancing in her eyes, the crackle of burning wood comforting.

'It's kind of weird seeing you away from the club like this.'

'Weird?' she queried.

'Weird in a nice way. You know … different.' He shook his head at his own stupidity, then added, 'I'm not very good at this you know.'

'Relax,' she said with a smile, 'I'm not here to seduce you, just thank you.' Then her expression sobered. 'But –'

'Uh, there's always a *but*,' Andy interrupted.

'Okay,' she confessed, 'there has been something bugging me since this afternoon.'

Andy knew enough to know that when a woman was bugged by something, it only led to questions, and as much as he liked Grace, he wasn't sure if he was ready to answer any personal questions right now.

'So what's bugging you?' he said tentatively.

'Okay.' She paused. 'Tell me to mind my own business if I'm out of line here, but … Well, today, when you were talking to Nathan, you called him Joey, then looked a little embarrassed. I know you don't have a Joey or Joe or Joseph in your squad so …' She studied Andy's expression, ready to pull back if he indicated she'd gone too far.

'Oh, that.' He didn't want to lie, but he was uncertain just how much he needed to tell her. Talk about Joey, and you talk about Dana. Talk about the marriage, and you talk about your less than noble exit from the army. Talk about the badshit, and you talk about Tucker and the Game. Where does it begin, and where does it end?

The kettle whistled in the kitchen.

'Saved by the bell,' he said, standing. 'Coffee wasn't it?'

Grace frowned. 'Oh no, you don't.' She followed him into the kitchen. 'Look, maybe it's none of my business. Maybe I *am* out of line –'

'You're not out of line, Grace,' he interrupted as he made the coffee. 'Joey is my son.'

'So you're married?' Grace asked.

He tapped the spoon on the rim, the last coffee drops falling back into the cup. 'No,' he said, then corrected himself. 'Well, yes, I guess I still am. Her name was … *is* … Dana. She took Joey away during my conscription. Word is England.' He handed Grace her coffee and they walked back to the fire. 'Short version is I haven't seen either of them since. They could be anywhere.'

Grace sipped her drink. 'Have you ever tried to find them?'

Andy sighed. 'Not as hard as I should have,' he confessed. 'I was a mess when I left the army. There was an accident that put me in hospital for months. I guess I didn't feel strong enough when I got out. Didn't want them to see me until I cleaned up my act.'

'Your act?' Grace repeated. 'Is that why we're drinking instant coffee instead of wine?'

Andy raised his eyebrows, realising she already knew the answer. 'I've been sober for more than ten years,' he said.

Grace smiled warmly and took his hand in hers. 'Well done,' she said. 'So tell me what happened once you cleaned up this act of yours?'

'Not a lot, I'm afraid. By the time I felt strong enough to look for them, the trail was stone cold. And to tell you the truth, once I thought it out I got scared. Scared I might push them further away if I ever got too close again. So I stuck it out here in Blackwater in case they returned.' He looked around at the walls in the firelight. 'I found this place and got to work. You know, to keep busy.

'When I rebuilt the cottage, I rebuilt my life at the same time, brick by brick. I rediscovered my place in the world, realising it was right here, in Blackwater. But, Grace, for every nail and tear, I never stopped wondering about my son. Nathan reminds me of him every day.

'I saw the way he watched the other rowers, and knew he wanted to be just like them. Not a big dream by world standards, but it was *his* dream. When I found out about his leg and remembered the bus crash, I recognised another soul denied that dream. Perhaps I'm seeking redemption, Grace, but I only ever wanted to do something to prove life's obstacles can be overcome. I want it for me, Nathan, and any other poor bastard out there who's not prepared to wear the *victim* label. I mean, is that so wrong?'

'No,' Grace said, kissing him softly. 'It's very, very right,' she whispered, pulling away.

The taste of her lips remained, and he couldn't help but remember his first ever kiss from Dana. He hadn't intended to share so much, but in the end it was unstoppable. A natural silence followed. They put on coats, made another coffee, and walked down to the jetty together, smoke from the ironbark burning in the fireplace faint on the night air. Beneath the Milky Way, Andy told Grace the rest, truths that until tonight he had forgotten – or had chosen to forget. About the friends he'd lost, his family and the badshit. Even Kyle Tucker. In the end, the night left him drained, yet strangely liberated. Grace went home around midnight, kissing him again, holding him a little longer.

*

With modifications to his rowing callipers complete, by early 1983 Andy decided Nathan was ready to row with the squad. They called him the Bionic Boy. Exploring a new training technique, Andy began handicapping each crew during the training sessions. Nathan set off first, followed by the other crews in order of their times – slowest first, chased down by the fastest. It kept everyone honest and working hard.

But even at Nathan's best, Andy realised his current times would never win a race over one or two thousand metres. It had to be a short course, but the races were limited. Andy knew Nathan well enough now, knew it wasn't about rowing for rowing's sake anymore. This was about proving his worth.

When the squad was off the water, Andy looked up the new regatta program. Pinned to a wall in the coach's room, he scanned the columns for any short-course races, his finger resting on the Sydney Twilight Regatta entry.

'Perfect!'

It was a five-hundred-metre sprint, a race won at the start. He could work on Nathan's opening strokes, have him settle early and use the reach from his long arms. The sprint was perfect for him. He wrote down the details and walked outside to his Ford, parked on Main Street. Waiting for a break in the traffic, his attention was drawn to a passing white Cadillac. *You don't see too many of them around here.* He peered in through the tinted glass, barely making out the driver's face behind the wheel. Andy laughed. If he didn't know better, he would swear he'd just seen Elvis.

66

Sam called it his 'one perfect trick'. Taking a novice and teaching him how to row. But now I understand – it's so much more.

THE course looked choppier than Andy had anticipated, but all the novice crews in Nathan's race would share the same disadvantage. Yet with his boat's custom rigging, Nathan would row higher off the surface than the others, the technique helping his blades keep clear of the white caps. Maybe he had an advantage. The theory behind training was one thing, but now it was time to apply the new start combination in racing conditions. Andy called these the *critical strokes*. Nathan's times were as good as any novice's over a short course; anything else, the boy would need to dig deep for.

'Here it is,' Andy told him from the Sydney dock. 'Just like in training, okay? Remember, it's a *sprint* regatta. Half a kilometre, that's all. Keep it together and don't stray from our game plan for a second.'

'I know,' Nathan assured him, settling his body into the boat. 'Short, sharp strokes out, increase the rate over the first ten strokes and settle at the halfway mark.' He smiled. 'Just like in training.' Searching the terraces below the Sydney clubhouse, he saw his mother waving. Even at this distance, he could see she was nervous. 'Tell Mum not to worry,' he told Andy, looking at his watch. 'Now push me off before I miss the reporting window.'

Andy paused before nudging the boat out into the bay. 'Listen, no matter what happens out there, you'll remember this day for the rest of your life.'

Nathan readied his oars. 'I know.'

The boat glided away with calm confidence. Andy turned toward Grace, then back to Nathan, already out over the deep water. He walked to the terrace where Grace stood waiting, his leg aching a little, his limp more prominent these days. She took his hand, guiding him up the last step. When their eyes met, Andy cupped her cheeks and kissed her gently.

✳

Nathan was the last oarsman to report in.

'You just made it, son,' said the unimpressed starter over the rim of his clipboard. 'You're in lane two.'

Nathan slipped his boat between the Mosman and Glebe rowers, giving a casual nod to them both. The starter began his usual commands. 'Come forward a touch, Glebe … eeeeeasy. A touch back, Mosman … again … again … eeeeeasy. All crews steady … Are you ready?' Nathan came forward on his slides, his heart racing. *Relax*, he told himself.

'Row!' The starter's pistol went off with a crack.

Nathan stayed level with the two leaders, Sydney on the outer and Mosman sticking beside him, the remaining crews falling back early. With the critical strokes behind him, he concentrated on raising the rating. *One ... Two ... Three*, he counted. *Bring it up! Four ... Five ... Keep control. Six ... Seven ... Eight ...* His legs ached, confirming the power they were generating for him. *Need the rating at thirty-six*, he told himself. *Nine ... Ten ...* There, it was working, Mosman falling back with each stroke, leaving Sydney just half a boat length in front. Nathan wanted to row him down then and there but Andy's plan of attack was to wear them down slowly. He powered past the two-hundred-and-fifty-metre marker. *Halfway!* His lungs cried out for air, his arms ached, yet the Sydney boat kept a small distance ahead, accepting every challenge Nathan laid down.

Just as he felt his own spirit waning at the four-hundred-metre mark, he noticed something in his peripheral vision: the gap was closing, the Sydney rower feeling the pressure. Yet with only a hundred metres left, Nathan worried he might not have the time and distance left to pull in front. He couldn't add any more power to his leg drive; couldn't raise the rating. All he had in reserve was possibly a little more length in each stroke. He reached further forward with each catch, gaining progressively over the seconds remaining. Every muscle hurt, his lungs straining for oxygen. *And so are yours, ya bastard,* he reminded himself of the Sydney oarsman. *This is my race!*

The two boats were now extremely close and only a perfectly timed stroke would seal the finish. Nathan could see the marker over his left shoulder. It was just a matter of timing; a matter of which oarsman placed the last stroke before the line.

The gun went off from the shore the moment the two boats crossed the finish. Nathan stopped rowing immediately, his boat rolling unsteadily beneath him as he collapsed over the oars, the blades skimming the surface as he glided forward. Gaining control, he glanced across at the Sydney rower between painful gulps of air. The oarsman's face showed the same pain, but among it all, out there on the bay, he nodded to Nathan. It was a simple thank you for a race well rowed. Nathan nodded back, still unsure who had won.

He watched as the other boats crossed the line, waiting for the announcement. Distracted, he noticed that the padding on his brace had worn through, the frame rubbing at his flesh – there was blood running down his calf. But he hadn't felt a thing.

Then the loud speaker crackled, and the voice came over the water.

'Blackwater first, Sydney second, and Mosman third. All crews please leave the course …'

Nathan smiled, the way ahead so clear, all the time knowing Andy had been right there beside him.

Full Circle

67

*During a restless night's sleep I woke, a feeling of dread
in the pit of my stomach. There was no reason for it – at
least none I knew of at the time.*

TUCKER lay on his bunk. His cell was never in total darkness, the
hallway light creeping under the door to create a constant twilight.
He stared through the dim light of two a.m. at the carved plastic
mobiles hanging from the ceiling above him. T.J. had taught him
well, the bird of paradise still standing on the shelf by his books.
Wisps of air stirred through the mesh on the opposite wall. Birds
soared high and lions stalked gazelle as rockets pursued orbiting
moons and racing cars drove in endless circles above him.

The tedium of prison was in waking each morning and
knowing exactly what the day held. Every day the same … Except
today. He smiled. Within the hour he would get out of bed, collect
Bones from his cell and leave the farm forever.

I can't grow here, he reminded himself.

The notion of escape set its seed the day he'd arrived on the
prison bus. Being so close to his old hunting grounds injected a
sense of home-ground advantage, the fences and soft-core inmates
too tempting, too easy. He had learnt so much in Long Bay. But he

didn't need an *easy* escape; he needed a *smart* one. An escape that would buy him time and lead the police away from his intended road to freedom.

It was all a matter of keeping things uncomplicated. Gaping holes in fences were simple but stupid, and he couldn't afford stupid. He simply needed to vanish. No signs, no trails, no sirens and searchlights. Merely unlock the doors and walk away in an ordered fashion. And that was the key – literally.

The simplest way to unlock any door is with its key, Kyle decided. He patiently watched the prison keys, studying their clustered perch on the utility belt of each guard. Each set looked the same. The same large key rings made from a loop of twisted wire holding a collection of chrome and tarnished brass keys of various sizes. The prison keys fascinated him, and he noted who carried them and where they were locked away when not swinging from a guard's belt. Studying the keys gave him an insight into how the farm worked: how it lived, breathed and operated.

Given his management background, he was transferred from farm duties to the governor's office as a clerk. He was happy to sort mail, update files and help with the guard's rosters – access to the rosters meant gaining inside knowledge of who worked where and when. Whenever a prison guard took annual leave, his shift was covered with overtime. The absent guard's keys would then remain locked in the governor's office, hanging on a board above his name. As tempting as it was, Kyle knew he couldn't just swipe a set, as they would be promptly missed.

But there was another way. He realised it the first day he saw T.J. carving his birds and animals. He collected plastic containers with T.J. and kept spent blades from his safety razor to carve the shapes, wrapping his fingers in Band-Aids to protect them. Fencing wire was plentiful on the farm, and Kyle shaped it into large hoops to suspend the mobile. Using small pots of paints from the maintenance shed, T.J. taught him how to mix the right colour for the right job. In everyone's eyes it was a harmless pursuit, and Kyle and T.J. gave away finished pieces to other inmates and the guards.

But the keys were different. He made them privately, at night in his cell, carving from memory, counting the keys on a guard's belt as he passed. Three silver, six brass, one of the silver keys quite rusty. Silver paint with a touch of black applied to give them an aged appearance; a brown base with thinned-down orange made others look like tarnished brass.

In time, he fashioned a key ring from his stash of fence wire, inserting each plastic key in place as worn by the guards. He stood back after lockdown the first evening his keys were finished, seeing them hanging over the basin in his cell. 'Perfect,' he whispered. Wrapping them in toilet paper, he made a small incision in the side of his mattress and hid them inside.

Involving Bones was not an easy decision. Kyle was a loner by nature, but things were different on the farm, its solitude becoming an encumbrance. For a successful escape, he needed a contact on the outside. Kyle had no one, but Bones had a sister, Ruby.

'Do you think she'd help us?' Kyle asked Bones one evening in the recreation room.

'Yeah,' he said, shrugging. 'If I asked her, she would.' His eyes never left the television screen.

Bones' sister visited the farm the next weekend. She met Kyle, listened to the basics of the plan, and agreed to help for the love of her brother. Kyle saw the methadone glaze in her eyes and scars from track marks down her arms. He recognised the homemade tattoo of an ace of hearts on her wrist as one made in prison and knew that she wouldn't hesitate to help. 'Shove it up the system,' as she put it.

'Sure,' Kyle responded, 'regardless of the motivation, it's important we maintain the same goal.' He paused, making sure they understood him. 'Freedom,' he clarified.

Ruby looked at her brother and smiled.

'Billy Bones,' Kyle continued, 'I know your writing skills are limited, so I've drafted several letters from you to Ruby.'

Billy appeared puzzled. 'How come?'

'Shortly after our liberation, Ruby will drive to Melbourne, posting each letter several days apart. The letters will be addressed to herself, explaining in detail our intended journey across the desert to Perth, where we'd get work on the next merchant ship to South Africa.'

'I don't get it. I thought we were headed north.'

Kyle had every intention of shielding both Billy Bones and Ruby from any details until the last minute, avoiding any risk of unintentional leaks.

'We are,' he said with a coy smile. 'While Ruby plants the letter trail, you and I will be biding our time under the very noses of the police. When the authorities follow the trail to Perth, we'll proceed north. Given time, new I.D.s will take us all the way to Thailand.

'Now, remember,' Kyle told Ruby. 'No one can know you've gone. Post each letter two or three days apart on the way. I won't date them because the post office will do it on each postmark. It all adds to the picture we're painting for the police. You then drive the ten or so hours home, collect the mail, and hand them over to the police as a sister concerned for her wayward brother.' He paused a moment, staring across the bench into her eyes. 'Is that all perfectly clear?'

Ruby nodded. Kyle slid the envelopes across the bench to her. He was uncomfortable trusting others with something so important, but had little choice.

He patted the back of her hand reassuringly as she took the letters. 'Okay,' he continued, 'we're allowed one phone call each week. Within the month, Billy will call you at eight p.m. prior to lights out, so keep the line free at that time. He won't say anything when you answer, just tap on the receiver three times. That message will indicate we're leaving the next morning at three. The call will be brief, so as not to be traced. That same evening you need to hide a travel bag beneath the town side of Queens Bridge at Blackwater. Do you know it?'

She nodded.

'In the bag,' he continued, 'we need cash, as much as you can spare, and two changes of clothes each. You'd best pack some food and cigarettes too.' Kyle studied Ruby's eyes, searching for any misunderstanding.

'It'll be fine,' she reassured him. Then, looking just as deeply into Kyle's eyes, added, 'Don't judge me on my appearance, Mr Tucker. I'll follow the instructions just like you said. Everything will be fine.' And with that she slipped the envelopes up under her skirt and into her undies. 'All you have to do,' she said, 'is take care of my brother.'

Days later, while working in the office, Kyle noticed that one of the guards was due a week's leave. With blood surging through his veins, he made the key exchange, the weight of the real keys powerful in his pocket. Careful of the clink they made when he walked, he returned to his cell and placed them within his mattress.

On the stroke of eight, Bones called his sister. Kyle went to bed, but couldn't sleep. He lay there hearing every second tick over, inching closer to freedom as he watched the mobiles dance above him. At three a.m. he heard the guard's footsteps echoing down the hall, each lock tested with a handle twist. Kyle felt a wave of trepidation at the rattle of his own handle, but the feeling soon passed, the footsteps disappearing around the corner to B wing. It was like this every night, the last walk-through due at the six a.m. muster. Kyle stood, stretching his arms and yawning before pulling the keys out of the mattress.

68

I found this one in Time *magazine, by Gandhi: 'Violent means will give violent freedom.'*

THE key turned with ease. Stepping out into the hallway, Kyle stood in the empty space, savouring the moment. He glanced back into his cell, his eyes falling on Jansen's folder opened on his chair. *Sorry, Mrs Jansen. You're on your own.* He closed the door, locking it behind him, before walking down to cell fourteen and letting himself in.

'Kyle?' Bones whispered uncertainly.

'Time to go.'

'I had a dream,' he said, words slurred from the sudden awakening. 'I was driving away, in a yellow convertible. Man, it was beautiful.'

'Save it,' hissed Kyle. 'Let's go.'

Keeping to plan, he locked Billy's door as they left. With five minutes remaining before the guard completed his rounds, they slipped into the shadows, walking softly past the vacant guard's room, a small TV on the desk flickering black and white images from *To Kill a Mockingbird.* There was the faint smell of pizza from the grease-spotted carton on the desk. They stole through the kitchen's rear door to the garbage compound. Crouching low, they followed the rows of corn stalks toward the machine shed on the western boundary where they took a spade. Continuing along the fence line, they dug a space in the soft soil, the scent of turned earth filling their nostrils as they crawled under the boundary.

Instinctively, Billy Bones was poised to run toward the sound of the river, but Kyle held his arm, pulling him back.

'What are you doing?' Billy spat. 'Let's get the fuck out of here.'

'No trail,' Kyle reminded him with a short tug. 'Fill in the hole and take the spade. We'll dump it in the river when we get there.'

Bones shook Kyle's hand off his arm. 'Fuck the trails, man,' he said. 'I want to get some distance between me and this place.'

Kyle stared him down. 'And you will,' he said calmly, 'but there's no hurry. Remember, don't stray from the plan. Unnecessary haste will only cause mistakes, and I won't tolerate mistakes, Bones. Do you understand?'

Billy saw something cold in Kyle, something desperate, menacing. 'Take it easy,' he said, drawing a calming breath. 'I just went a little crazy, okay?' Shrugging, he added, 'No trails. I've got it. We'll stick to the plan. Just like you said.'

'Crazy is fine,' said Kyle, 'but *stupid* will get us in trouble.' He had no doubt about enforcing his authority.

They covered the hole behind them before following the fence line north to the riverbank, where Billy tossed the spade into the deep water. Kyle waded into the flowing river, expecting Bones to follow.

'Whoa, whoa,' protested Billy, waving his hands for Kyle to stop. 'What are you doing?'

Kyle looked annoyed. 'Escaping from prison, Billy,' he answered. 'I suggest you follow me.'

'You didn't say we were going *in* the water. You never said that.'

Kyle stood waist deep. 'I said we would take the river downstream to Blackwater, remember?'

'Yeah, I remember, but I didn't think you meant *in* the water.' Bones appeared edgy, his breath shortening. 'I thought we'd walk the bank. You know, just follow the river.'

'You're beginning to disappoint me, Billy Bones. Why don't we just leave signs pointing the way?' He smiled cynically. 'Convicts this way!' But his smile faded. 'For the sake of freedom, Billy, just get in the fucking water. No broken flora, no scent for the dogs, and no fucking footprints. Let's use the resources we have here, which at the moment are strictly limited.'

Billy Bones stepped hesitantly back from the edge. 'Y – You don't understand,' he stammered, 'I can't swim. Not a stroke.' The river compelled him to stare. 'The water scares me, always has.'

Kyle sighed, trying to remain calm when all he really wanted to do was slap Billy into submission. 'You might have mentioned this when we were at the planning stage, Bones.' He paused, aware of every second as he searched for the right words. 'Sometimes we don't have too many choices,' he said finally. 'But if you continue this shit, then we'll both be back inside within days, if not hours.'

'I don't care!'

'Well,' said Kyle, holding back his anger, 'I do.' Frustrated, he waded onto the bank, searching the area for anything to use as buoyancy. Fumbling in the long grass, he found a substantial branch at the foot of a willow tree. Muttering, he dragged it down to the water where it floated beside him. 'There,' he said panting. 'You have to trust your own ability sometimes, Billy Bones. Trust yourself to hold onto the branch. The current will do the rest.'

Bones stood silently, weighing up Kyle's proposal, his eyes glancing from the branch to the black water beyond. He took a breath, and for a moment Kyle felt certain he was about to break into a run, but then slowly, cautiously, he took a step toward the water.

'That a boy,' Kyle said. 'Trust in your ability. Trust in me.'

Bones stepped in up to his waist, clutching at the willow branch. His breathing became shallow, his face a pale moon in the darkness.

'Good,' said Kyle, guiding him into the deeper water.

The two men became shadows on black silk. Although the farm was relatively close to Blackwater, it would take over two hours to drift the ten kilometres to where the Hawksnest wound round to merge with the Salesbury. They floated slowly on the current until a thin strip of dawn's hue rose along the eastern horizon. The promise of light and the river's lack of urgency began to make Kyle feel vulnerable. A plover cried out from its nest beneath the she-oaks. Nerves taut, Bones almost let go of the branch. But in time the faint sound of the sand quarry's crushers and conveyors grew steadily louder. The sound was welcome, they were drawing closer to Blackwater.

*

Bones cried out, a cry of pain. The branch they floated on had stopped, the water surging around them. Bones screamed again, shattering the grey dawn sky, threatening their escape.

'What's wrong?' Kyle hissed.

'My fucking leg,' Billy cried, whimpering, clenching his teeth to stifle another scream. 'Something has my leg.'

They had grown weak from their time in the water. The current was doing its best to tear the willow branch from their grip. As the river surged around them, Bones cried out again.

'Keep it down!' Kyle searched the banks for signs of life, the dawn light making him feel more vulnerable every second. The sun was rising quickly now, the night no longer a place to hide. 'I'll see what you're caught on,' he told him. Keeping a firm hold of the branch, he plunged his head into the water, expecting to find Bones' leg trapped in a submerged tree. The sun filtered through the she-oaks above, allowing enough light to make out the dull yellow shape beneath them. Kyle broke the surface, taking a fresh breath. 'I can't make it out,' he said between gasps.

Bones' eyes were filled with pain and terror. 'I – I can't hang on much longer,' he stammered. 'Kyle, I'm scared.'

'Just keep it quiet, okay.' Kyle smiled as best he could, a gentle gesture of reassurance. But as the sun peeked over the tips of the oaks, the added light made him feel increasingly exposed.

His eyes tearful, Bones reluctantly agreed. 'I'll try,' he said, 'but it hurts.'

'Not for much longer,' Kyle said before slipping beneath the water.

The pale yellow began to take shape with the stronger light as Kyle guided himself along Bones' leg, a stream of blood flowing with the current from the boy's calf. A piece of chrome had speared the leg. Confused, Kyle looked closer. It was a car, more rust than yellow paint, its classic VW shape clear. In a burst of direct light, the sun peeking over the trees, other smaller shapes caught his attention through the clear water. Kyle studied the situation coldly, his breath short, deciding what he had to do as a brief wave of remorse overcame him.

Breaking the surface, he clutched the branch to rest.

'What is it?' Bones asked.

'It's a car wreck.' Suddenly he laughed. 'Imagine that,' he said.

'Can you free my leg?'

Kyle hesitated. 'No,' he said.

Bones understood – and began to scream.

Hooking one arm around the tree branch, Kyle used his free hand to take Billy by the throat and shove his head beneath the water. The sensation of his hand squeezing the boy's throat, the muscles protesting, the surge of control was intoxicating. *The Game*, he thought, *let's play the Game …*

Thrashing his limbs in panic, Billy's leg dislodged itself. Already weak, he fought for air, but it was in vain. Kyle released his grip when he felt Billy's hand relax and slip from the willow. The current took Kyle again, guiding him forward from a whirlpool where Billy disappeared beneath the surface.

Billy Bones' body sank through the rusted roof of the VW. His body moulded into the driver's seat, his head nodding gently in the current, hair trailing behind as if in a breeze. One arm rested over the Bakelite steering wheel while the other propped casually on the open side window frame. Bones found freedom in the yellow convertible of his dreams.

69

I found this scratched into the back of a public toilet door:
'Threaten a man's freedom, and you'll witness the animal
within, as the wolf chews off its own paw to escape the
hunter's trap.' Author unknown.

ITS glass face full of water, Kyle's wristwatch had stopped at four
a.m., not long after he had entered the river. The sun was well
above the horizon, Kyle guessing it was around six when he drifted
into the Two Rivers basin. Abandoning the willow, he swam to the
northern shore, listening, wondering whether he could hear the
prison's muster siren over the sound of the quarry's stone-crusher.
Although suffering the early stages of hypothermia, he remained
hesitant about leaving the water.

He clung close to the shore where a thicket of she-oaks overhung
the riverbank. Not prepared to trust the daylight, he searched the
area for early morning fishermen, listening for voices. Exhausted,
he lay back in the shallow water, his head resting on the grassy
bank.

Eventually he heard it, like a memory, faint and grey in the
distance – morning muster. Kyle opened his eyes to listen to
the siren so far away. Minutes later it rang out again, longer this

time, whispering his name on the breeze, telling the world he had escaped. All at once freedom seemed to close in around him, creating its own walls.

*

The phone rang a little after seven, Tess hearing it as she turned the shower off. Even on Sundays she couldn't sleep in. Her robe clung damp as she walked into the hall to pick up the receiver. She turned her nose up at the mess her husband had left in the kitchen before leaving for golf.

'Mrs Jansen?' She recognised the governor's voice, but didn't much like the urgency in it.

'Yes.' She tightened the front of her robe.

'It's Tucker. He's escaped.'

An uncomfortable silence settled between them. *Jesus Christ,* she thought, *the bastard's done it!* She felt her career slipping through her fingers.

'Governor, I'm sorry. Can I –'

'You can get your arse out here as soon as possible, Jansen. We've begun searching the area, but the police need to ask you for anything that can help with his possible whereabouts.'

'Of course,' she said. 'I'll bring Tucker's files.'

Tess' legs weakened and she sat in the chair by the phone stand.

It was over. She noticed her keys in the bowl by the phone, her attention turning to Kyle's handmade key ring, laughing at her.

'Mrs Jansen? Mrs Jansen, are you there? Mrs Jansen —' She hung up.

*

Kyle couldn't be sure of the time – it felt like mid morning – when he first heard the helicopter. Glancing around his hide, the cover of the she-oaks appeared inadequate as the sound drew closer.

Upstream was a muddy outlet from the quarry, a long brown stream of silt staining the otherwise clear water. Kyle spied the reeds surrounding it and thought of the mud. He searched for any sign of the helicopter before making his move, stumbling through the shallows, tripping several times as muscles cramped from hours in the water. Reaching the wide silt patch, his legs sank as he stumbled face-first into the bog. Pulling free, he dragged himself forward, sliding across the surface into a dense patch of reeds. Desperate and out of breath, he glanced behind him, watching as the river washed over his trail. 'Good,' he whispered in short breaths. 'You were always kind to me.'

The chopper blades beat the air, sounding its arrival. Kyle could feel it drawing closer with every breath as he wriggled into the mud, desperately piling as much over his body as possible until only his face showed. Flying low, the police helicopter paused, hovered over the Hawksnest tributary, its tail wheeling left then right like a dragonfly. At that moment, Kyle took a deep breath and drew his face beneath the mud.

He wondered how long he could hold his breath as the beat of chopper blades vibrated through the water and silt. He remained submerged for as long as he could before breaking the surface for a gasp of air, the lungful accompanied by coughing, the taste of silt filling his mouth. Using the reed stems to pull himself upright, he watched the chopper pass upriver before it disappeared around the bend.

It was time to move. Crawling across the mud flats, he pushed through the reeds into the deeper water and waded toward the far bank. He swam slowly, quietly, studying the ruined shelters and outbuildings of the old picnic grounds on the other side. Sipping river water, he washed the grit from his mouth. Trails of muddy water streamed from his clothes as he made the crossing, washing them clean, lightening the load. It was around noon, half a day's light left, and he didn't want to make the crossing at night. Best to wait out the remaining day on the town side of the river before retrieving Ruby's bag of supplies and cash from beneath Queens Bridge. A sense of achievement overcame him when he reached the other side, confident Ruby would be on her way south by now, the decoy letters soon in the mail. Within two days of hiding under their noses in the river's backwaters, the police would soon leave him to follow the useless trail.

But the feeling of achievement left him as he pulled himself onto land with an exhausted grunt. What would Ruby do when she discovered her brother was no longer with him? He didn't care, he'd be long gone before they found the body.

70

Another winter gone, and at thirty-five I felt every cold day bite hard. It proved to be a winter of change, as Robert J. Hawke became Labor prime minister, toppling the Liberal government responsible for the Whitlam dismissal back in 1975. For Labor diehards it became a year of redemption. For me, too, redemption came calling.

AS 1983 drew to a close, the season's warmth eased the pain in Andy's leg. It was Sunday, and he was glad to be home with those he loved. He breathed the rich, warm air. Grace had dropped Nathan off at the cottage on her way to work and they'd had breakfast together. Andy spent the remainder of the morning mowing, the day washing over him until the helicopter began circling. As the rotor blades cut through the morning, memories of his conscription training vibrated through to his soul, taking him back to the night of the explosion. He went inside, the smell of breakfast's bacon and eggs still in the air, until the machine disappeared upriver.

'You okay?' Nathan asked, his eyes barely leaving the TV.

'Yeah,' Andy lied. 'Just came in for a break.'

Nathan turned his attention from an Elvis movie, his eyes pools of compassion. 'You'll be okay,' Nathan said, his hand patting Andy's knee.

Around noon, Nathan's friend Mike came over to show off his new pocket-knife. Mike was new in town and had joined Andy's novice squad. The boys had struck up a friendship, Nathan with his blonde hair and lean body, Mike a little shorter with dark hair and heavier build. He reminded Andy of Butch.

'Count 'em,' Mike told Nathan, handing him the knife. 'Three blades and five accessories. Go on, count 'em.'

After lunch the boys headed down the lane to the far end of the Pond. Andy watched them go, feeling like his own youth was walking away. Then he smiled and shook his head.

He slipped his grey overalls over his clothes. The Ford had been running lean and cutting out all week, the last time stalling at the highway intersection. He'd come a long way in thirty-five years and had no intention of being taken out by a Kenworth on the highway. With the old girl parked out front, he set up his toolbox and lifted the bonnet before starting the engine. It never much liked a cold start, but when it found the juice, the big V8 came to life, as did a little part of Andy. Large engines were a dying breed, the seventies' energy crisis ensuring car engines would only get smaller. His Ford was a dinosaur, but Andy didn't have the heart to get rid of it.

'We dinosaurs have to stick together,' he whispered, brushing a dead beetle from the grille.

Resting his bad leg on the bumper, Andy rubbed his aching muscles and sighed, sick of the pain. What compelled him to look skyward he couldn't say, but shading his eyes from the sun he noticed the rings.

71

'All things truly wicked start from innocence'. – Ernest Hemingway. When I read this, I cried.

'OLIVIA Newton-John,' said Nathan confidently.

'Nah,' protested Mike with a shake of his head, 'she's too girl-next-door.'

With a chorus of cicadas singing in the background, the two boys left the shade of the she-oaks and walked to the eastern edge of the Pond.

Nathan shrugged off Mike's reply. 'I like the girl-next-door look.'

They kicked at the sand searching for flat stones.

'What about the babes from ABBA?'

Intent on finding the perfectly shaped river stone, they each skipped their selections across the Pond's rippled surface.

'Which one?' Nathan asked.

'The blonde one,' Mike answered, making his latest stone skip seven times in the process.

'Yeah,' Nathan agreed, 'she's hot.' He attempted to beat Mike's seven but counted to three before his stone sank.

'Freda,' said Mike, kicking for more stones. 'The blonde's name is Freda.'

'You sure?' Nathan queried. 'I thought it was Agnetha.'

'Nah, Agnetha's the brunette.'

'I'm telling you, you're wrong,' Nathan said. 'Freda's the brunette.'

Nathan skipped his next stone eight times, almost reaching the opposite bank. 'Hey, did you see that? A new world record.'

'Redhead,' Mike said coldly.

'What?'

'Her hair isn't brunette, it's red.'

'Who?'

'Agnetha's.'

'Which one is that?'

*

Kyle found the sun intoxicating, having spent the last hour drying out in a clearing before returning to the shadows. He was beginning to get hungry and craved a cigarette, wondering whether he could wait until nightfall to retrieve the supplies, wondering if Ruby had even left them.

He felt strangely at ease beneath the grove of trees, blanketed in a canopy of balloon vines and ivy, their branches starved of life and bleached white in the shaded darkness. It was a cool relief from the summer heat, the moss-covered ground soft underfoot, providing refuge until dark. Exhausted, he lay on the soft earth, his eyes blinking toward an uneasy sleep and uneasy dreams.

Then he heard the voices. His eyes flickered open at the sound as he stared through the spears of afternoon light piercing the canopy above him. But even awake, the voices continued, laughing like a memory.

Rolling onto his stomach, he remained low, searching for the laughter's source. Two boys skipped stones by the water's edge, a dark-haired kid wearing shorts and a striped polo shirt, the other lighter-haired boy wearing oversized tracksuit pants and a red T-shirt. Scanning the area, Kyle relaxed when he realised the boys were alone. He watched keenly, deep within the shadows of the tree line, smiling at the sights and sounds of innocents, while the wolf within wanted to feed again, the sensation of his hands around Billy Bones' throat returning, the dampness rising in his palms.

His shoulders dropped. 'No trails,' he whispered. But the thought of the hunt stirred him. It was coming back, surprising him with its momentum, with its force. For all those years in prison he'd controlled the wolf and the Game. Now, he wasn't so sure if it wasn't the wolf that had controlled him all along.

Standing, Kyle crept toward the tree line where the shadows met the daylight, wanting to see the boys more clearly. Moving closer, he noticed that the lighter-haired boy was limping. *Just a little closer*, and Kyle stepped up onto a large river stone to peer over the branch of a fledgling oak. But the stone dislodged under his weight, sending him to the ground where he struck his head. And suddenly he was in daylight. The boys heard the fall and saw him. Kyle's heart turned cold, his eyes narrowed, the wolf too strong to control.

*

The boys could only watch. The man was old, but fast, breaching the daylight with intent, a thin trail of blood staining his streak of grey hair. His tracksuit hung heavy and damp on his frame, the knees torn, revealing grazed pink flesh. He was upon them before they could even draw breath. He shoulder-charged Nathan first, knocking him off his feet before reaching forward in a stumbling action to grab Mike firmly by the throat as they fell to the ground. Wrestling to hold the boy still, Mike's pocket-knife fell into the sand with a dull thud. The old man reached forward, his face grimaced, scooping it up with his free hand.

Too afraid to move, Mike heard the knife blade spring open. It was difficult to breathe in the man's grip, but then slowly, infinitely slowly, the boy could feel the strength in the man's hand failing, the fingers around his neck relaxing. Glancing toward Nathan, he noticed he was clutching his hip and crying. The boys' eyes locked, searching for answers. Without a word, his breathing strained, the old man held the flat of the knife blade against Mike's face. And it was enough – something in the cold steel against his flesh that made Mike strike out. He kicked, harder than he'd ever kicked in his life.

The stranger released his grip on the boy's throat, at the pain in his groin. Mike crawled out of reach, the old man doubled up between him and Nathan, his eyes unblinking, waiting for the pain to subside before attacking again.

'*Run!*' Nathan shouted.

Mike ran, feeling as if the old man was still a pace behind, the cold of the blade still strong. *No*, he thought, pausing to turn back. He saw the knife blade again, this time held against Nathan's throat.

'Stop!' cried the old man. 'Stop, or I'll cut the cripple's throat!'

But how could he go back? How could he not turn and run for help?

His voice growing more intense, the old man cried louder: 'Come back or I swear I'll stick the boy!'

Mike tried to say something to Nathan before turning to run, tried to tell him he'd come back with Andy, but it emerged as a sob. He disappeared into the vines and never looked back.

*

'Fuck!' Kyle spat, watching as the boy disappeared. Then a little quieter: 'This complicates matters.' With his free hand he reached behind his ear, studying the blood on his fingertips.

Holding the boy to his chest, Kyle could feel his sobs. The embrace was empowering, the knife was control; sweet, sweet control. It stirred him, stirred the wolf, but the yearnings had to be suppressed in the interests of self-preservation. Control was slipping through his fingers. Having been seen, he needed to cover his tracks.

Time was against him, the one resource he'd had in abundance was now waning. He studied the boy and decided, for now, the kid was worth more alive than dead.

'Get up,' he ordered.

The boy stifled his crying. 'Wh – where are we going?'

'Shut up and do as I say,' Kyle said. 'The less you know, the better chance you have of staying alive.' He nudged the boy forward. 'Move to the water's edge.'

The kid did as he was told, the uneven ground difficult.

'Get in the water.'

He stepped into the flow, the river stones shifting beneath his weight as Kyle stepped in a pace behind.

'Do you know the picnic grounds?'

The boy nodded. 'Uh huh.'

'Good. Stay in the shallow water and head downstream until we get there.' He nudged him on again. 'If you need inspiration just remember this knife.'

He began to wade downstream, stumbling, the tip of the blade moving closer to his flesh each time.

∗

Mike became disorientated once inside the corridor of balloon vines and she-oaks. He searched frantically for the trail, deciding to thrash his way through the wall to the lane. Too long, he thought with every strained breath. It's taking too long. He kept seeing his knife in the old man's hand, its new blade razor sharp.

The trees and vines soon thinned as the light penetrated the canopy and Mike spied the laneway beyond. He cried out feebly, the tension and anxiety released, escaping his body for the whole world to hear.

'Aaaandy!'

He threw himself at the curtain of vines. For a moment he hung suspended like a marionette, its performance finished. But then he found the strength for another cry for help. This time louder.

'Aaaaaandy!'

Mike twisted himself free, bursting from his restraints before stumbling to his feet. Two hundred metres away, Andy stood beside the blue Ford. Mike ran as fast as he could, fearful it was just a mirage, fearful the heat haze would wash the image away before he could reach him.

A flock of sparrows spiralled from the undergrowth as he stopped, panting, at the gate. 'Andy,' he said between strained breaths. 'It's Nathan … Nathan's in trouble.'

72

*'Nathan's in trouble.' As soon as those words left the boy's
mouth, I knew this was about life and death.*

THE boy coughed on a mouthful of river water as he stumbled
ashore.

'Keep the noise down,' Kyle spat as he dragged the boy
up the bank. Leaving him at his feet, Kyle stood surveying the
area. Derelict weather sheds and collapsed picnic benches were
strewn throughout the abandoned park grounds at Two Rivers;
its crowning glory, the vine-covered rotunda, retained little of its
former dignity. The open area was a sea of long grass, bending
in waves with each gust of wind, the rotunda a sanctuary in the
centre, its wrought-iron dome exposing its once fine lattice walls
entwined with vine.

'There,' Kyle said, pointing to the sanctuary. He prodded the
boy with his foot. 'Get up.'

The kid struggled to his feet.

Portions of the rotunda's floorboards had been pulled up to
feed midnight party fires, the holes filled with empty beer cans and
smashed bottles. Graffiti scrawled both obscenities and wisdom,
but one caught Kyle's attention: *Freedom is its own prison.*

'Perhaps,' Kyle whispered, thinking of the road ahead.

That's when he heard the hissing, low at first, building to a growl. His attention was drawn to the portion of removed floorboards where a large white cat, its fur matted and stained, stood at its opening. Two others in the same condition, one grey, the other ginger, crept out from the darkness to stand sentinel either side of the older one, their eyes fixed on Kyle. The rotunda belonged to them.

Unnerved, Kyle waved the blade. 'Go on. Get outta here, ya ferals!'

But their eyes remained fixed, wide and menacing. Then he saw why, as a procession of kittens marched out from behind them, the ginger cat guiding them away.

The boy sat hunched away from the narrow opening, watching the blade in the old man's fist.

*

Andy's heart turned cold when he saw the droplets of blood in the sand by the river's edge. Shotgun in hand, he followed the trail to where it disappeared into the water. He'd bought the gun to control the growing number of foxes in the area, and now suddenly he was back in uniform, a soldier again.

'Nathan,' he whispered with a broken voice.

The distant wail of the prison siren fell silent, or perhaps the breeze had simply turned and carried the sound away. Either way, it was a relief. He searched desperately for clues, anything to determine which direction they'd taken: upriver or down? His stomach had turned in knots since Mike had told him what had happened. He wanted to convince himself that everything would be okay, but there were just too many circumstances suggesting otherwise. The low-flying helicopter; the prison siren; the old man in greens. And Nathan – gone.

All his life, Andy had sensed time's unforgiving presence, and right now, it was against him. More importantly, it was against Nathan. He peered skyward; the unusual rings around the sun had vanished. If the stranger was an escaped prisoner he'd be looking for cover. And if he'd travelled down the Hawksnest he would have seen the derelict buildings in the abandoned picnic grounds.

He turned back through the underbrush toward the park.

On the picnic grounds' outskirts he lay low in the shaded cover of the trees. A wave of panic swept over him as he realised he couldn't remember what Nathan was wearing that day. Then he saw a rosebush struggling for life amongst the vines, saw the single rose bloom and remembered: *Red*. Nathan was wearing a red T-shirt when he arrived this morning. Then something moved amid the tangle of iron and scrub, a flash of that blessed red, a shadow moving inside the rotunda before a strange procession of cats made their way across the grasslands.

Andy heard the police sirens drawing closer. *Good boy, Mike,* he thought.

Kyle ceased pacing when he heard the siren.

'Fuck!'

Nathan sank back against the wall of vines, covering his face to hide the fear. But the look in the old man's eyes … The boy knew he was a killer.

The old man began pacing again, his thumb testing the knife blade, dark eyes searching the shadows like a cornered animal. Now and then he would look down at Nathan. 'That siren changes everything,' he said.

Choking back tears, Nathan took the chance to speak. 'You could run away, mister,' he said in a wavering voice. 'I'll only slow you down.'

'What?' asked the old man, surprised at the boy's pluck.

Nathan repeated himself, this time more assuredly. 'You could run away before they get here. I won't tell anyone, mister.'

The man began to laugh, but then stopped when the police siren cut out beyond the trees. His eyes narrowed.

'Come on,' he said.

'Where are we going?'

'To set you free,' he said. 'Relax. I know you won't tell.' He then tried to smile. 'Our little secret,' he told Nathan.

*

While the pacing and talking was going on inside the rotunda, Andy crawled through the knee-high grass toward them. Peering through the broken lattice, he tried to make out the old man's features, but his back was to him. He focused on his voice, but recognised nothing, just the glint of the knife. The police siren had ceased, and Andy wondered if they had any idea where to start searching. Mike would have told them about what happened at the Pond, but that was downriver.

Then he heard the man tell Nathan they were leaving. He watched as they stepped into the afternoon light; watched as they headed toward the river, his eyes fixed on the knife.

Andy stalked to the front of the rotunda, the hiss of the grass husks on the wind disguising his footfalls. Then, his way clear, he charged.

*

Kyle sensed the presence of another from behind seconds before the butt of a gun smashed his hand holding the knife. He knew his hand was broken from the searing pain. He cried out as he fell and the ground met the palm of his broken hand; he clenched his teeth against the agony as he fumbled for the fallen knife in the grass ahead of him. But he froze when he felt the twin barrels of the shotgun cold against the back of his neck.

'Relax,' said the man holding the weapon. Although the voice faltered, Kyle had a sense of sureness. The barrel pressed firmer into his flesh. His face itched from the grass seeds, the pain in his broken hand intensifying.

'Go home, Nathan,' the voice said, adding, 'when you get there tell the police where we are.' And the boy was gone.

Kyle spat an ant from his lips, groaning at the rush of pain from his hand. 'I think you broke it,' he said. 'I think you broke my fucking hand!'

There came a distinct *click-click* as the weapon was cocked. 'You're lucky I didn't shoot you.'

'I wish you fucking had.' Kyle eased his damaged hand from beneath him, hissing at the pain as he slowly rolled onto his back.

'Just take it easy there. It's not too late to take that shot.' The man took a pace away, the gun trained steadily at Kyle's face.

As soon as he stared into his captor's face, an inkling of recognition drifted through his consciousness. He thought he saw someone he knew ... or once knew. A boy – Kyle's thoughts were momentarily distracted by the gun's movement, a brief pause of silence following as he stared at the face of the man standing over him. Their eyes met, the recognition was mutual. The face behind the shotgun grew red with sudden anger. And the prospect of dying became very real as Kyle watched his finger tighten at the trigger.

'It's you.'

Kyle drew on his battered memory to place a name to the face behind the gun. He considered the eyes carefully and still nothing came to mind. 'What the fuck?' he said, trying his best to mask the growing fear, his eyes returning nervously to the taut finger over the trigger.

Despite the rage, the man's voice remained strangely calm. 'You don't know me, do you? You don't remember.'

Kyle moaned at the discomfort in his hand and the fear rising in his heart. He knew, at this moment, that it was important to recognise him, but he couldn't.

'Let's stop with the guessing games shall we? I don't know you, I don't know that kid, I don't know a fucking soul anymore.'

He drew a breath, about to say more, when it happened, that spark of recognition seeping in like water into sandstone. He began to look beyond the hard weathered face, and remembered a boy. Another wolf cub who'd found his way into Kyle's den. He remembered grooming the boy. Remembered *Night-Mare*, and – and – the Game. The boy had been special. He remembered buying this boy a book about astronomy.

'Wait a minute,' Kyle said. 'Andy Walker,' he said calmly. 'Stargazer.'

73

This was a spray-painted tag on the side of a passing coal train. It read, REDEMPTION. One word, meaningless to anyone who hasn't coveted it, but to me, it was a train I'd been riding all of my life.

THE memories washed over Andy in a tide of anger and rage. Aware of his finger tightening around the trigger, he recalled all those long nights as a boy fantasising a thousand ways to murder Kyle.

'Get up,' Andy said.

'What are you doing?'

'I'll shoot you where you lie if you don't get the fuck up.' Andy's cold stare reinforced his words.

'Take it easy,' Kyle said, teeth clenched, wincing again as he stood. He staggered at first, spitting out the remaining grass seeds.

'We're just gonna take a walk,' Andy said, his finger relaxing on the trigger now that he had control. 'I'm taking you back.'

Kyle expelled a little air, not quite a sigh, more like a laugh. He shook his head. 'Sorry, but I can't do that.'

'You don't have a choice,' Andy reminded him.

Anger began to surface in Kyle's eyes, the silver streak of grey hair falling across his forehead. 'That's where you're wrong,' he said, 'that's where you're *so fucking* wrong!' He raised his arms, gesturing wildly at the surrounding area. 'Do you think I'll do as you say because you're holding a gun at me?' He shook his head. 'Then you don't know me. You don't know what scares me. You have no fucking idea what fear is, Stargazer. Fear isn't staring down the barrel of your gun, it's the prospect of living the rest of my life behind bars.' He smiled tauntingly. 'Right now I've got a shitload of choices!'

As Kyle staggered forward, Andy raised the barrel to his face. But Kyle laughed. 'Go ahead,' he said. 'I'll pull the fucking trigger myself before I lose my freedom.' He wiped the sweat from his eyes. 'How's this for a choice,' he said calmly, 'I'm going to walk away.' He searched Andy's eyes for a response, then said, 'You have your own choices,' his gaze falling to the gun before he turned toward the river and walked.

'Don't,' Andy said. Then louder, 'I said *don't*!' He spat bile from his throat. 'You can't honestly believe I'll let you walk away like that. Not after the hell you've put me through. Don't you understand? This is it! This is what it's all been leading to. This moment! This time, you sick fuck!'

Kyle stopped to face Andy across the grasslands, a smirk curling his lips. More than anything, Andy needed to wipe that smile from the Earth forever.

'Whatever you are now, I helped make you,' Kyle said, standing his ground, eyes unblinking. 'We have many fathers in life, I was but one of them, you fool. Yeah, I shaped a piece of you, just like I did with others before and after you. Just as *my* father shaped me in his own fucking image, so don't talk to me of your hell.' He glanced over his shoulder at the river. 'I have my own hell to contend with.'

'Don't try to justify what you did to me. To the others. You had no right.'

Kyle stepped forward, treading like a wolf's pad on twigs, stopping as Andy brought the gunstock to his shoulder. 'Had no right to what?' he said in a quiet voice. 'To care for you? Buy you things and look after you? What happened on this river back then took just a few minutes of your life. So fucking what? Your father treated you like shit. Did I? Your mother was a fucking drunk. Was I? No! I treated you and the others like adults for the first time in your miserable fucking lives. I treated you all like friends ... And all ... *all* I asked for in return ... All I ever wanted was –'

'*What?*' Andy cried. 'Tell me, after all these years. Give me something to make sense of it all.'

'I wanted my fucking youth back! Without the fear! I wanted to see it from my father's eyes. I wanted to see what he saw!'

'You tricked me, just like you did the others. You had no right to do that!' The gun shuddered in his hands.

'I earned the fucking right, okay? Praying that my own father would pass out when he came home in the middle of the night; praying my bedroom door would stay closed. So don't talk to me of your *hell* over a few lousy minutes.'

Shaking his head, Kyle began to chuckle, then laugh, then, throwing his head back, he howled. Andy frowned, his fingers numb around the weapon in his hands. *So easy*, he thought, *to pull the trigger before the police arrive.* 'Knock it off,' he murmured.

'Who's afraid of the big bad wolf, Andy?' Kyle pointed at him and laughed again. 'You are, Stargazer!'

'You're no wolf.'

'Oh, but I am. I never wanted to run with the wolves, but what chance did I have? When I realised the power I could hold over those weaker than me, when I realised the thrill of the hunt, felt the blood in my veins. It all seemed so natural. My father's actions taught me to *take* the things I wanted.'

He bowed his head. Turning slowly, he walked toward the water's edge, toward the river that had played such a prominent role in both their lives. 'Do what you want,' Kyle told him. 'It's over.'

'Come back,' Andy mouthed, each word escaping as nothing more than a silent breath. Then louder: 'Come back here!'

'Fuck you,' Kyle mumbled.

You don't face your demons just to let them walk away, was the one thing running through Andy's mind – the rest was instinct. He aimed the gun at Kyle's right thigh, the weapon braced firmly into his shoulder. 'Stop or I'll shoot,' he said clearly, his finger tightening around the trigger.

'Then shoot,' Kyle muttered as he walked on.

Andy fired off one of the barrels, the weapon kicking harder than he remembered as the buckshot found its mark. As Andy stepped back with the recoil, Kyle spun with the impact of the shot, grabbing his leg as he collapsed. He howled as blood ran down his leg.

Cautiously, the barrel aimed squarely at Kyle's chest, Andy stepped closer. 'I'm not letting you back into this world. You don't belong here, do you hear me? You're a monster!' *The real monsters in this world are right out there in the daylight.* He remembered Toby's words. 'I won't be responsible for another stolen youth, another murdered childhood. I'd rather kill you now.'

Kyle's cries soon became an unsettling laugh. 'So kill me,' he spat. 'You want to save the world from the wolf, then *fucking kill me!*'

Then Andy understood. He heard it in his plea, saw it in his eyes. The man wanted to die.

Shaking his head, Andy lowered the gun, pity masking his face. He glanced at the shotgun in his hand, then at Kyle's bleeding leg. 'How far do you think you can run in that condition?' He took a last look at Kyle and turned away. He was going home, to find the police. Kyle was right – it was over.

'Don't you walk away,' Kyle cried. 'Don't you do this to me. Come back here and finish it!' He stumbled forward, tripping on something in the long grass. His hands searched for the obstruction, finding a brick-sized river stone. He lifted it to his chest, standing unsteadily, raising the stone above his head as he staggered forward and lunged. The stone crashed into Andy's back, causing him to stumble and fall, dropping the gun.

Kyle's momentum carried him on, falling beside the shotgun. He gathered it up, fumbling the butt to his shoulder as he rolled to a sitting position, facing Andy. The barrel wavered in his weak grasp, his swollen finger gripping the trigger, his leg aching from the wound.

Andy sat opposite, arching his back, grimacing from the pain. 'You've got one cartridge left,' he said, straining. 'Why don't you do us all a favour.'

Kyle laughed, his eyes glazed. 'Do you think I can't do it? Is that it, huh? Do you think I can't finish it myself?' Kyle crouched on his knees, placing the barrel firmly beneath his chin, eyes fixed on Andy. 'I'll show you courage! Do you hear me? I'll show you fucking courage!'

Andy could feel blood trickling down his back, soaking into the fabric of his overalls. 'So do it,' he said, standing. He had no fight left, and suspected neither did Kyle. If he was going to shoot Andy, he would have done it when he grabbed the gun. 'You don't matter anymore.' He turned and limped across the open field.

*

Kyle, his body trembling, felt his finger on the remaining cocked trigger. He imagined the powder igniting in a flash behind the lead shot in the cartridge; imagined his jaw separating from his skull in a storm of crimson rain. Closing his eyes tightly he whispered, 'Daddy,' before pulling the trigger. Kyle heard the hammer strike the breach. He grimaced, waiting for the pain before escaping his torment forever, but it eluded him. The cartridge was faulty.

What was left? Kyle wept. His body ached while his soul cried out for release. His leg, full of buckshot, began to go numb. He was losing blood fast. One of the pellets had pierced the artery behind his knee. Using the useless gun as a crutch, he stood, his legs unsteady beneath his weight as he continued toward the riverbank. *Escape*, he thought. *Take the river downstream ... Leave no trail ...* Kyle staggered by the water's edge and his reflection stared back at him. He expected to see himself as he was twenty years ago. Clean back then. Confident and brash, but today, even through the tears, he looked more like his father. Kyle howled, throwing the shotgun into the water, the splash shattering his father's reflection. The water was so clear at the bend, he could see stems of dead men's fingers reaching up from the depths to touch the surface.

Then he saw the boy.

Steadying himself against a small tree, Kyle stared at the face in the water. A boy, familiar, appeared amid the forest of weed, his face smiling up at him, wisps of dark hair drifting across his innocent features with the current. Then he recognised him from an old photograph in the steamer chest. *It's me.* A small hand drifted toward him, beckoning him to follow. He returned the smile. The child understood, he could tell. Kneeling by the edge, Kyle held his good hand out, desperate to feel the touch of his youth, but the image appeared disappointed that Kyle wouldn't follow. Hesitantly, the child drifted back, deeper into the curtain of weed.

'No!' Kyle whimpered, overreaching in an attempt to clutch the hand. 'No,' he repeated, before falling into the water.

Instinctively he held his breath, his eyes open, searching for the boy. Then glancing below, deep into the mass of weeds, he saw them ... all of them. *The secrets left at the bottom of the river.* They drifted up to meet him, arms extended in welcome. They held his hands and caressed his damaged body. Then he became aware of the constricting pain in his lungs. Although weak, he reached for the surface, but something held him back. The boys wouldn't let him go, not now – they'd waited so long. They were all around him, frenzied, pulling at him. At first he struggled, caught between delusion and reality, unaware if it was the river weed or the children holding him back. As he drew water into his lungs, Kyle realised it didn't matter anymore, the shroud of unconsciousness drawing slowly down around him. *Freedom is its own prison.*

So he relaxed, understanding everything, accepting everything, as the spectres took him in their arms, another secret for the river to conceal.

Epilogue

Now, I am complete.

WITH the last greys of winter gone, the riverlands created a fresh palette of colour, destiny's brush dipped and poised to paint. Grace and Nathan moved into the cottage with Andy. With Kyle's confrontation behind him, it was as if life permitted him to start anew, and he decided it had become his own springtime.

Grace gave him the journal in 1985. 'You need to get it out of your head,' she told him, 'and down on paper where it can stay.'

When New Year's Eve of 1989 arrived, he couldn't help but remember the same day thirty years earlier, the music of Hank Williams, the smoke of the bonfires. Now, alone in the lounge room, he closed his eyes and leant back in his favourite chair, wondering if he'd ever really been ready for life's changes. He tried to remember what it was like to be eleven again.

Andy stepped out onto the back veranda overlooking the Pond, the smell of honeysuckle drifting in. He wished Nathan was home. But he was at university in Victoria, staying back there for his holiday job. Andy sighed, then cocked his head at the sound of the knock on the front door. His spirit lifted for a moment, thinking it might be Nathan coming home to surprise them. *Wouldn't that be just like the boy.*

'I'll get it,' Grace called from the kitchen, her footsteps sounding off the floorboards as she walked through the house.

Andy's attention was caught by a mullet jumping for mosquitoes out on the Pond.

'Andy?' Grace called from the doorway.

He turned. 'Yeah?' Then he saw the expression on her face.

She paused, frowning. 'There's … There's someone here to see you.' A tear formed in the corner of her eye. 'Andy, he … he –' But the words seemed to smother her.

Andy stepped past, gently stroking her cheek. 'Take it easy,' he said.

A man in his early twenties stood on the other side of the flyscreen. He was well kempt, although pale for this time of year, and dressed in heavy clothes. A hire car was parked by the gate, its motor running. A young woman sat in the front, turned to the back seat to coo at a baby in a capsule. The woman glanced his way and smiled before the child stole her attention again. Andy looked back at the young man. All three appeared tired, travel weary.

There was an awkward silence between them until Grace stood behind Andy, her demeanour changed, softened.

'Sorry,' the young man said gesturing toward Grace. 'I didn't mean to upset anyone.' He had a broad British accent.

'It's okay,' Andy said, still unsure of what was going on.

'Are you Andrew Walker, sir?'

Andy glanced at Grace, her smile widening, her hand covering her mouth. He turned back to the man on his front veranda. 'That's right,' he finally answered.

The man paused to draw a breath. 'Sir, my name is Joseph Walker. Mum said you'd know me better as Joey.'

Acknowledgments

People can be in your life forever, but contribute nothing to it. And others can drift briefly through and leave so much ...

THIS is one of my favourite quotes from the novel, and I believe it captures the spirit of *Blackwater Moon* ardently. It's often said that a novelist should write what they know, which is why this book began many years ago, before my first published novel *The Crossing*, in fact, as a loosely connected series of stories based in part on events in my own life, or of those close to me. Blackwater's geography, although purely fictitious, has its genesis in the NSW riverlands of the Penrith, Richmond and Windsor areas during the 1960s and 70s of my youth. It was during those long summer days on the river and its floodplains, that many of these stories and characters were born, so here I'd like to acknowledge just a few of the people who briefly touched my life and left so much.

To my high school English teacher, Mr Earp (*Wyatt Earp we called him – though never to his face, because the cane was still widely used back then*). He was the first person in my troubled youth who pointed out, in his own exacting way, that I was good at something … writing stories. And that simple affirmation was the beginning of something wonderful.

In my early rowing days, it was my first coach, Peter Walker, who coined the phrase, "It's the oar in the water that counts," an expression paid homage to in these pages. Once I truly understood its meaning, it became a course I've followed ever since, although not without getting wet from time to time.

And to the Rosier family; I will never forget your kindness for taking that leather-clad biker in from the cold all those years ago, and showing him the true meaning of family. Your generosity and love remains with me always.

To the late Raymond Birks, a fellow cavalry man, who served gallantly in WWII and who, many years later, taught this humble lance corporal the true meaning of *esprit de corp*. If a man has many fathers, then you were indeed one of mine.

In part, I owe my successful career in the printing industry to Lindsay Hannan, and the Hannan family, for employing me all those years ago and offering me the opportunities, guidance and knowledge to succeed in the business. Lindsay was always interested in my writing ventures, and generous with the time I needed to pursue them. And for that, I will forever be grateful.

And always – *always* – to my family, for they are my prize, my reward, at the end of a long, hard race, on waters that weren't always clear.

But no book is written alone, and I owe the success of *Blackwater Moon* to many, particularly my publishers, Alison Green and

John Green of *Pantera Press* who saw the merit in this book long before I did. To my wonderful editor, Kylie Mason, who helped me discern the forest for the trees. Gratitude also to my publicist, Trudy Johnston, of Vim & Zest Communications for giving me a voice and making it heard out there in the marketplace. To Jeanette Krass, for her guidance on the psychology aspects of the story when it was obvious I had bitten off more than I could chew. And to Sergeant Matt Thomson, friend and neighbour, for clarifying the duties and mindset of a small-town cop. Thanks also to Luke Causby at Blue Cork Design for the cover art – you nailed it again, man.

I once posed the philosophical question: *If an author wrote a book, and nobody read it, did an author write a book?* So to you, dear reader, I am eternally grateful.

BMR 2012

LET'S READ

When you picked up this book, you let yourself into another world. For many kids, this joy may never be possible. Some kids are left behind their peers even before reaching school because they come from disadvantaged families where books are not enjoyed.

Let's Read is a national initiative that helps pre-school kids in regional, rural and metro communities across Australia, to have fun reading with their parents. Research has shown that, reading with young children is an important activity to develop a child's future literacy skills. As poor literacy skills are associated with lower education, earnings, health and social outcomes; teaching kids from socially and economically disadvantaged families to read is a vital step towards breaking the cycle of disadvantage.

Simply buying this book will help us support these kids. Want to do more? Make a personal donation to *Let's Read*. Visit: www.PanteraPress.com/donate

1 in 4 Aussie kids start school without the building blocks for literacy*

Over 20,000 students don't meet the national minimum reading standards*

The proportion of Indigenous students achieving this standard is significantly lower*

Alicia's Story
Let's Read Parent, Qld

"I attend an Indigenous playgroup in Nambour which a *Let's Read* trainer comes to regularly. She uses puppets to bring her reading to life and the kids love it. I have four children aged seven and under. *Let's Read* has encouraged me to read with the family at home, as well as at the play group. We've started reading together every night. It's a lot of fun and really opened my eyes to the point where I am now reading to my seven-month-old, which I wouldn't have done before. It's also helped my two-year-old with talking. Getting him to sit down is hard but he knows when it's reading time and now he wants to listen along with the other kids."

CENTRE FOR
Community
Child Health

THE SMITH FAMILY

everyone's family

Let's Read was developed by the Centre for Community Child Health. Let's Read is being implemented across Australia in partnership with The Smith Family.

*Australian Institute of Health and Welfare AIHW(1), 2008.

PRAISE FOR B. MICHAEL RADBURN

"… *a riveting tale of deception and desperation; superb suspense … An impressive Australian thriller, full of anxious anticipation and simply tingling with tension. One for the dark, cold winter nights ahead!*" – **ABC RADIO**

"… *a novel guaranteed to send shivers down spines.*"
– **SUNDAY TASMANIAN**

"*Plenty of suspense in this thriller …*"
– **WISH MAGAZINE, THE AUSTRALIAN**

"… *felt a bit frightened and found my heart pounding at the 'jumpy bits'.*" – **GLOSS**

"… *gripping throughout...fast pace and three-dimensional characters gave it a momentum that held my attention until the end... delivers the thrills that it promises.*"
– **GOODREADING MAGAZINE**

"… *undoubtedly poignant … the result is really quite moving … Radburn has written a most unusual book … the emotional journey of this man, combined with the wonderful sense of place that is built around him … one of those books to step outside your comfort zone with …*" – **AUST CRIME**

"… *a superior summer read.*" – **BOOKSELLER + PUBLISHER**

"*Riveting! Bristles with menacing suspense and believably secretive characters … Radburn has the stuff, and will enthrall you with this tale of nightmares, loss, grief and redemption.*" – **AHWA**

B. Michael Radburn

B. Michael Radburn lives with his family in the beautiful Southern Highlands of NSW. Although he works for a large printing group, in his spare time Radburn enjoys farming his small property and taking road trips on his Harley Davidson. Aside, of course, from writing, he possesses a deep passion for music and treasures the time he spends with his guitar, banjo and harmonica.

Radburn has been writing successfully for many years, having published more than 80 short stores, articles and reviews in Australia and overseas.

Through the late '80s he was Publishing Editor of the *Australian Horror & Fantasy Magazine* and founder of *Dark Press Publications*.

Radburn has won several Melbourne University Literary Awards and more recently was short-listed for the Henry Lawson Festival Awards.

His first novel, *The Crossing*, was published in 2011. *Blackwater Moon* is his second novel.